THE WORK[illegible] ALMANAC

'A STORY OF SHREWSBURY'

Kate McLanachan

DEDICATION

For my wonderful family, especially sons Adam & Toby, niece Jasmine, Mum Julie, & husband Pete. Also, my 'best friend' Lisa, who read it & always had faith in me.

'Among other public buildings in a certain town, which for many reasons it will be prudent to refrain from mentioning, and to which I will assign no fictitious name, there is one anciently common to most towns, great or small: to wit, a workhouse'

A quotation from *Oliver Twist* (Chapter 1) by Charles Dickens.

CHAPTERS

ACKNOWLEDGMENTS

So many people to mention, not least my friends and family who have supported me throughout my writing of this debut novel.

Thank you to my friend Lorraine Fletcher of 'For the love of Shrewsbury' on Facebook, who designed my front cover and Etsy's 'ArtbyLadyViktoria,' for allowing me to use her print as an overlay.

A huge thank you to my friend Kaine Pritchett who edited the book for me when I realized there were errors beyond my technical abilities.

Thank you to all the authors of books on Shrewsbury and especially Peter Higginbotham's books and web pages on Workhouses. Much research was done via the good old internet, where I explored life in the early asylums, Witchcraft and the history of mental health.

Please let me know if there are any typos or errors by email.

Katemclanachan.author@gmail.com

If you enjoy reading my book, would you kindly consider reviewing it on Amazon?

I look forward to connecting with my readers on my website which I am developing now.

Printed in the United Kingdom

For more information, or to book an event, contact:

katemclanachan.author@gmial.com

Book and cover design by Lorraine Fletcher, 'ArtbyLadyViktoria' & put together by author.

First Edition: October 2022

1

REFLECTIONS

They could see her every move and read her thoughts. Sometimes they even inserted violent video recordings inside her brain and they always talked about her in a hateful way. It just confirmed everything she already knew about herself, but it was relentless and repeated torture, however much deserved.

Her mother seemed to know and had told her it was time for her 'uninvited guests' to leave. She had made it very clear she could not carry on if she lost the last member of her family. Getting rid of such things had been her mother's life's work but Jasmine knew this was different, as it was really happening. She had heard her mother talking on the phone saying the assessment tomorrow could 'go either way,' as the mind was not an exact science and it depended on how she presented at the time.

Jasmine knew 'assessment' was really a pretext for her own trial and sentencing and kept seeing images of the judge wearing a black cap. 'You'll be hung by the neck until you die,' the voices whispered.

Jacquie felt powerless as she watched her daughter sat perched on the edge of the bed, locked in her own distorted world, restless and focused only on her own mental anguish. Her breathing was rapid and noisy, but even to an untrained eye she was clearly hallucinating. Her secret given away by the strange grimace of her lips and darting movement of her eyes, listening only to the voices in her head.

Observing helplessly and covertly from the landing, her only surviving child a young woman now, the age she had been when she had birthed her. It seemed like yesterday that Jasmine was confidently waving them goodbye with a beaming smile, after they had safely deposited her at the halls of her new university. A bright future lay ahead unlike for her brother Joe, who had taken so many wrong turnings. Jasmine was taking a degree in History having loved the subject since first studying it at school.

With a seven-year study plan starting at sixth form, she intended to be a history lecturer, 'a professor,' no less, confident and motivated enough to have achieved it, had the tragedy not occurred. Fleeting memories returned of phone calls from Jasmine in the first two years at university. Her reassuring laughter, reports of good grades, tales of new close friendships and even her first love. Although her choice had come as a surprise to them. All nice, reassuring and fairly normal before the worst year of their lives. This was her first-born child, regressed like an infant, dependent and helpless but unreachable as she responded only to an invisible world of unseen stimuli.

One hand on her mouth to stop the silent scream of despair, Jacquie suddenly became aware of the tension in every muscle of her own body and the overwhelming exhaustion, from waking frequently in panic and cold sweat, to check on her troubled daughter.

Each day was like a living nightmare, re-visited each time Jacquie opened her eyes in the morning and tried to push away the knowledge that it was all reality and not the preferred bad dream. Night after night, with her own disturbed sleep she was falling apart with very little strength left. Helpless witness to her last child disintegrating before her eyes.

Initially, the family shared a contained grief, but soon they inevitably entered very different stages of bereavement, leaving them less able to reach out to each other. Unable to see beyond their own internal conflicts without the sense of safety and security they used to have. At make-or-break point, the family unit shattered and her husband Mark went his own way, leaving two broken women with a previously close mother and daughter relationship, unable to connect.

Some of Jacquie's old colleagues would be attending today, for her daughter's Mental Health Act Assessment, although after last time, they would make sure the team they sent had never actually worked with her. This time they would surely see how bad things had become and admit Jasmine for compulsory treatment she hoped, exasperated. It would be the second home visit for a formal assessment in two weeks.

Only last time, Jacquie had stared open-mouthed in disbelief as Jasmine had fooled them all that she was 'okay.' Jasmine had managed to conceal her paranoid delusions, explain bizarre behaviours and justify actions that were minor, but disconcertingly odd. She even put her disheveled, unkempt appearance down to the guilt of what had happened to her brother; but told them she was going to have a long soak in the bath, accept something to eat and had agreed to re-start her medication. This never happened of course and things inevitably became much worse.

It had not helped that Mark now estranged from her, had abruptly and dismissively, 'up and left,' after the decision to not detain their daughter had been made. Insinuating, that whilst he knew his daughter wasn't fine, if 'they,' the 'professionals' thought she was ok; then there was nothing more he could do. She assumed he was probably embarrassed by her response to their decision, which started with attempts to make them see sense, from pleading with them, to shouting in despair before finally making a loud, threatening demand that they should 'leave the premises immediately.'

Mark was also clearly angry, but had not considered her feelings and had left Jacquie alone in turmoil with an unresolved, worsening situation. She alone, was left with the magnitude of managing their daughter without the help of professional care that she so clearly needed. With the family unit in pieces, he had deserted two women, one spiritually fragmented and the other barely coping, functioning on automatic pilot.

On the last assessment Jasmine had not mentioned to the doctors her obsession and fear of 'a portal,' appearing in her bedroom mirror, and how this led to her being pulled through to another era. At first, she had described in some detail the horrors of this occurrence to her mother. Of late though, she had become increasingly guarded and paranoid about speaking of her 'experiences,' except in practically inaudible whispers, believing that mentioning it, led to the vortex reopening.

A sure sign in Jacquie's mind of a florid, mental health problem, but she doubted herself at times lately. During her career her responses and interventions had come naturally to her, but this time she was personally and emotionally involved, not observing a patient with her 'nurse's hat' on. She was now standing in the shoes of her patient's families, ever present as a mother, who barely recognised her own daughter. She had decided not to mention 'the mirror,' today during the assessment, it sounded too bizarre somehow and hadn't helped last time.

Jacquie knew from studying the ancient art and science 'Feng Shui,' that you should not ideally place mirrors in the bedroom, because they are supposed to reflect restless energy. Rebounding light and magnifying movement, they could create strange illusions, which could be the cause of Jasmine's interrupted sleep. The mirror in Jasmine's bedroom which faced her bed needed to go, as it seemed to stir up and disturb the atmosphere in her bedroom, and she wondered now if it was capable of worse.

Jasmine had a large collection of stuffed and ornamental owls in her bedroom. Since the accident, Jacquie had recently found a black bin liner in the corner, with her daughter's beloved owls shoved inside, two china ones broken. There had been so many, the room looked bare without them, but Jacquie had been surprised at Jasmine's immediate response when she asked why.

'The owl van killed Joe,' she had stated in a matter-of-fact way.

Jacquie remembered having to sit down quickly, as hearing words like, 'killed' in the same sentence as 'Joe,' still struck her like a lightning bolt. She thought of the owl's association with lightning because it 'brightens the night.' Placing owl effigies in each corner of the home was said to protect it against lightning. If the Owl was also a symbol of 'too much Yang,' the bright, masculine, active energy, it had certainly been taken from her son, as she remembered viewing his lifeless, wax-like body at the morgue.

She shuddered as her mind drifted back to the mirror. Jasmine had inherited the antique gilt mirror that had belonged to Jacquie's mother, having always admired it. Although Jacquie had remembered it well as a child, hung over the fireplace and recognised it originally from her own grandmother's house, she had always found it somewhat creepy and shied away from it. As a child Jacquie had noticed that if she came too close to the mirror, some unseen energy seemed to push her away like a repelling force. Although she did posses a vague, very faint memory of being pulled towards it once, like a magnet. Something she never mentioned to her mother putting it down to imagination. But as she had walked through her childhood home and more recently her daughter's bedroom and passed that old mirror, Jacquie had sensed eyes watching and following her.

She mostly dismissed this as a remnant of her own childhood fantasy and figured the tiny engraved owls with their large eyes around the frame, no doubt gave one the impression of being watched. But there was something else she could not bring to the surface, despite trying for many decades. It lurked in her own distant memory and disturbed her deeply.

If only she could remember? All she knew was it involved the mirror. Her mind was wandering now, questioning if these could be portal glimpses? Doorways in time opening to other dimensions through an antique mirror. An unseen vortex of energy, allowing Jasmine to travel from one point in time to another, connecting two places through time and space, by passing through the portal.

Jacquie wondered if there was a family connection, having completed the family tree, with her daughter around nine years ago. At that time, she had hoped Jasmine would one day follow in the long line of psychiatric nurses and before that, asylum attendants in her family, working to help people with mental health problems. As with the strong matriarchal line, including her own grandmother and as far back as her great-grandmother several times removed

All this before her daughter became mentally unwell, but not the first in the family. There were at least three distant relatives on her mother's side, including briefly her own mother Ellen-Grace, who had endured the confinement and treatments of yester year's mental health provision.

It had been the reason she had taken such an interest, seeing her mum enter the 'Big House,' the local Psychiatric Hospital, with what she now knew was diagnosed as endogenous depression. She had learned that her mother had been given 'ECT' or Electric Shock Therapy, but always recalled her coming home, back to her normal self again. In her research, Jacquie had even uncovered a very sad, well documented account of one poor, young woman, after discovering the death certificate of a young female ancestor with the same family middle name of Grace. Just as her own daughter Jasmine-Grace and Jacquie's mother Ellen-Grace, which had been given to nearly every generation of the girls in the family for at least 250 years, according to the genogram.

She had not shared details of the young woman's fate with Jasmine, as she had only found this out after her daughter had started to develop mental health problems and lose touch with reality herself. But she knew Jasmine had taken the genogram out to examine it alone recently, during some lucid moment, but had made no comment. Jacquie, her own grandmother and great-great grandmother before her, all psychiatric nurses, or attendants; but every other generation appeared to be somehow 'cursed by madness.' Jacquie's fascination with the history of mental illness, made her realise how far psychiatry had come since her ancestors were attendants to the so called 'lunatics,' as they were sadly known as back in the day.

An era when people were viewed as 'insane,' possessed by the devil or demons or even demented. When treatment was more like punishment, with wide use of restraint, or even chaining, or their blood was 'let out.' They were administered untested concoctions and sometimes had electric eels applied to their skulls. Many treated like so called 'Witches,' had been in the past, another fascination of Jacquie's.

Jacquie recalled how Jasmine's nightmares had started around aged six, when they had first moved into the house and mirrors had covered the whole door of a double fitted wardrobe in her bedroom. They had coincidentally changed them to pine fitted ones, and the bad dreams had stopped. And then several years later after her mother's death, the large inherited mirror facing the bed arrived. Jasmine had begged her mother to hang it in her room. Looking back, since her son's premature death, Jacquie had noticed Jasmine had covered the mirror with a pretty scarf at times, but not decoratively, it was sometimes completely covered. And on two occasions, Jacquie had walked past the bedroom and stopped in her tracks, as her eye caught sight of some unusual wording on the mirror, scrawled in tiny unrecognizable writing in fluorescent pen. She was able to decipher one which read like a bible verse.

'My prayer is not that you take them out of the world but that you protect them from the evil one.'

Shocked and disturbed to read it, as her daughter had never previously expressed any religious beliefs, she found an opportunity to gently challenge her several days later, but Jasmine appeared startled at the question and Jacquie could not make sense of her strange, yet evasive reply.

Back to the present, Jacquie was almost willing Jasmine's 'insane laughter,' to restart. The senseless sound that had kept her awake last night, penetrated her own mind and left her eyes stinging with tiredness and etched a deep worry frown. All her hopes were pinned on the mental health team observing the signs of Jasmine's deteriorating state of mind, which appeared to be close to the point of no return if left untreated. Jacquie was confident she could explain to them what was happening to Jasmine, but knew she was being labelled as an 'anxious mother,' and treated like it was all 'too close to home,' for her.

They would all be aware of the family tragedy and consider Jacquie unduly fearful of losing a second child, which was almost 'expected,' after the family's devastating loss. Jasmine had always blamed herself for some strange reason, but could never say why or be persuaded otherwise. This was despite the court convicting a man who would spend only a few years sat comfortably in jail, whilst her family lived through a life sentence, eaten up with guilt and hatred, wishing he was rotting in hell for all eternity.

Jacquie felt like she was not being taken seriously, despite her training, professional experience and knowledge of her own daughter. She wondered, looking back on her dealings with the relatives of her patients, if she had ever been guilty of dismissing their views and if this was 'Karma,' coming to get her. One thing was certain, this time she couldn't walk away at the end of a shift as she could at work, as Mark always did.

It had become impossible when she returned to work, after Joe's death, to deal with people who were there because they said they wanted to die, but clearly didn't. She could cope with the clinically depressed patients, and those with psychosis, but not the ones who seemed to manipulatively 'play the system.' Patients who had learned to know exactly what to say, to gain compulsory admission and take up all of her time, chasing non-suicidal self-injury and writing endless incident forms. Whilst less demanding patients with severe and enduring mental health problems, often seemed to get side-lined.

But finally, Jacquie practically lost her job, ordered to go home and see her GP and then summoned to attend Occupational Health, after she had not held back from saying what she thought about one such manipulative patient. To her, this woman was like 'queen bee,' seeming to get away with ruling the roost and running amok on the ward. The sad thing was, she had previously been able to empathise and help patients like this, always aware of the usual underlying, life destroying trauma, often caused by systematic abuse, severe bullying, or horrific life events.

She also, found herself in a situation where a patient on the ward called Jake, had to call another member of staff to her aid, as she had sat shaking her head, saying 'No Joe,' tears rolling down her cheeks, when he had bravely disclosed, he wanted to end his life. Later, making the difficult application for early retirement on medical grounds, she began to feel an inadequate failure, depressed that her long career, more a vocation, had ended in this sorry way. And now having lost her son, her husband, her career, with her dreams and retirement plans left in tatters, she was also seemingly losing her daughter.

Moving her hand up from her mouth to rub her tired eyes, the location of the sudden noise was confusing at first, was it a knock at the door? Had they arrived? Or was it coming from Jasmine's room? And then as she opened her eyes the mystery was resolved. The door opposite had been slammed open, no longer a crack through which she could safely observe her daughter's misery, however helpless it made her feel.

Filling the doorway, despite her slender frame, her daughter now stood, catatonic, staring ahead as if she was a mannequin in a shop window. Her appearance reminded Jacquie of a wax figure from the Chamber of Horrors at Madame Tussauds. Although motionless, there was something about her presence making Jacquie uncertain about passing her, so close to the top of the stairs. There was something menacing about her appearance that did not look like her daughter.

Last week, Jasmine had lowered her head and ran at her; making a low-pitched animal-like noise, that had turned into a piercing scream as she made physical contact. They had both landed on the floor, Jasmine then sobbing, her body notably relaxing as she felt the warmth of her mother, albeit winded below her. Jacquie had dared to embrace her daughter, feeling the brief release of tension before Jasmine stiffened, a stranger again, pulling away abruptly and staring at her mother accusingly, paranoia setting back in.

The next sound was clearly the front door opening, it was always left on the latch now to allow help to get into the house. There was always the chance that Jasmine would abscond in a psychotic state, but her mother knew that if she was picked up by the Police, on a Section 136, and assessed in a place of safety, there would be a glimmer of hope that she would be admitted to a more secure environment and made to have treatment. The potential risks within the house, were now deemed to outweigh the dangers on the outside.

Her estranged husband Mark, was walking slowly, almost soundlessly upstairs. He would be able to see Jasmine from the bottom, standing motionless and she wondered if he could also sense the tension in the atmosphere, that was so palpable, you could almost cut it with a knife. He spotted Jacqui, his wife of twenty-five years, locking wide eyes briefly, before both fixed their gaze back on their poor child again. But not a child now, their daughter was an adult at twenty-five years old, but vulnerable and helplessly unable to recognise or meet her own needs.

Always a 'daddy's girl,' Jasmine made no response when he made a gentle, reassuring remark that his wife couldn't quite hear, but she didn't miss the sadness in his eyes, as he recognised his daughter was also lost to him, at least temporarily. She couldn't accept this was a permanent state, not her last surviving child, but realised she had a long journey ahead. With Jasmine having no insight, her recovery would have to be forced upon her at first, which although necessary, felt like failure and punitive, with a betrayal of her trust.

Mark motioned for Jacquie to come towards him across the landing, indicating that he would ensure her safe passage down the stairs. It felt like a great comfort and relief, as she had never felt so alone as of late, and although she resented Mark for what she deemed his 'weakness,' and inability to cope with Jasmine much of the time; he was the only person who could come close to truly understanding and feeling the pain that must be so like her own.

Jacquie had angrily shown him her bruises last week, after Jasmine had launched herself and landed on her, as his expression had implied 'surely it wasn't that bad.' He had closed his eyes and silently gasped when he saw the seriousness of his estranged wife's situation, but could still seemingly block out 'their predicament,' by being mostly absent. Feeling her heart beating faster, Jacquie eased herself past the three-foot square of carpet outside Jasmine's room and down the stairs, imagining the sprint of her daughter launching herself at her and the animalistic noises, but thankfully it did not come this time. Her own levels of anxiety were through the roof. Jacquie had known Catatonic states like this to go on for hours, it was common to block a doorway too, but this was her own daughter, unreachable, unpredictable and unrecognisable though she was.

Jasmine appeared almost rigid, as if in a stupor, her bizarre posturing, making her look unreal. Jacquie knew if her daughter remained like this, she was at risk of dehydration, exhaustion, and accidental self-injury. Catatonia was most commonly associated with mood disorders, making Jacquie wonder if Jasmine had a schizoaffective disorder.

Putting the kettle on came next, once a family ritual that symbolised and encompassed calm and resolve and a bit of normality. Jacquie watched Mark fill it up to the max; he made some comment about the number of cups needed for this meeting.

‘Five,’ she said, her voice cracking and barely audible, having not uttered a word for hours, but she was now preparing herself for the Mental Health Act Assessment at 11.00 am. She knew there would be a minimum of three health and social care professionals, herself and Mark. And Jasmine-Grace of course, but her daughter would either drop the cup or ignore it in her present state.

It was 10.50 am now, her mind and body longed to shut down for a few hours, to hand over the reins and full weight of responsibility to Jasmine’s father, but he had come too late for her to take a short break and she hadn’t even had a quick shower.

2

CERTIFIED INSANE

Mark answered the door to the team of mental health professionals, scratching his head. He felt like a visitor himself, having not lived here for the last six months. Jacquie was so angry with him, she rarely allowed him to even enter the house, unless there was a crisis with Jasmine, which was becoming more frequent and then he was criticised for not being there immediately. With the locks changed, his post was now forwarded to his sister's house and if he requested anything, she left it in the shed in a bin bag.

It was he who had suggested the front door be left unlocked after the incident last week and it had surprised him that Jacquie had nodded in agreement. He wanted to keep her safe and get help for his daughter more than anything, but the bereavement and subsequent court case had destroyed their relationship, and he knew he would never live in this house again. He had turned to the arms of another woman, a drunken one-night stand that meant nothing, but he had blown away twenty-seven years of marriage and any hope of an amicable reconciliation or cordial contact.

All visitors politely refused tea, the two doctors and social worker seemed slightly nervous and behaved in a very formal and serious manner. As Jacquie entered the room, the tension rose and Mark realised it was definitely her they were wary of. It was clearly due to her outburst last time and the awkwardness of having worked for the same hospital trust. There was an uncomfortable silence as they all took a pew in the sitting room, the stairs looming above where his dear Jasmine, the purpose of their gathering stood hovering in the doorway, an unrecognisable shadow of her former self.

The loud rap of the door knocker and a combination of deep and hushed voices had brought Jasmine back to a glimmer of reality for a few minutes. There were few visitors to the house these days, the last time the atmosphere had felt like this, the Police had been knocking on the door with news that would destroy her family forever and permanently fragment her soul. Her mind started to drift back to the night the Police solemnly entered their front room, filling the space with the cold air they brought in and the uneasy silence, only broken once they insisted her parents were seated. There followed a tale of horror and a response of hysteria from her mother.

She had also watched back then from the top of the stairs, as her mother fell to her knees, accompanied by a heart wrenching sob, while her father shook his head rapidly in disbelief, eyes wide. The news delivered back then was that her brother had been killed in a 'hit-and-run' accident, his short life extinguished by a man in a white van who hadn't even stopped. He had been walking home in the dark, streetlights turned off by the council to save money after Jasmine had forgotten she had promised to pick him up. She had wanted to confess to her parents straight away; it just wasn't the right time. It got harder over the week to broach the subject, and then it was too late, so never happened.

As usual, visions played of the horror that accompanied these memories, the pictures she had formed in her head, having heard the evidence in court as it unfolded, growing in detail over the weeks that followed. Even when she didn't attend court herself, it was all her parents talked, cried, and shouted about. She quietly brooded over the fact that it was all her fault. Lastly, in court, when she glanced down at the face of the alleged perpetrator and saw an owl perched next to him, she couldn't understand how her mother could blatantly deny it was there and treated her like she was seeing things, hushing her too.

What was an owl doing in court? The man had read her thoughts, stared up at her, smirked and mouthed sinisterly, 'You're next.' Her response was to scream, then kick and fight, until they carried her out of the courtroom; eventually taken away by ambulance, restrained and sedated.

She had slept for hours and awoken calmer, but nothing ever felt the same in her mind again. It was as if something had exploded in her head, opening a doorway to let unwelcome accusers in. It was like a second court case with a panel of jurors now present to judge her. Worse still, her parents had shocked her by saying the perceived spoken threat to her had also never happened. Maybe they were lying to protect her, but she couldn't trust anyone now, or allow them to read her thoughts, or to insert lies that were not her own into her head. They were trying to block her mind, so she couldn't think or speak, whilst both broadcasting and withdrawing her thoughts, which had to be kept top secret.

Her response in court had led to four months in the local Shelton Psychiatric Hospital, her mother too distressed and exhausted to insist on her being transferred farther afield, away from the place she had worked for nearly thirty years. The place where many of Jasmine's care providers were family friends, who had been to parties and BBQs hosted by her mother at her home. Jasmine's 'sentence,' to be sectioned to the 'Big House,' was only fourteen months shorter than the murderer in the 'white owl van,' as the family and media had christened him among other names.

The 'voices' told her this was her deserved punishment and she believed them. Jasmine would listen intently trying to work out who the voices were, sometimes there were two or more persons, a male and two females, talking about her in a disparaging way as if she wasn't there. Always making derogatory remarks, accusatory in nature. Unable to escape them, she sensed them as separate from herself and yet intrusive and out of her control. If she didn't listen, she knew something bad would happen to her surviving family members. They threatened her with that all the time.

There were voices downstairs now, but also in her room, whispering to her the gory details of her brother's death, inserting pictures in her head, naming her as the one to blame. The trial had been mentally and physically exhausting but it had never ended for her, with a jury of malevolent, faceless persecutors who lived in her head, attacking her mind with insults, ridicule and abuse.

She was breathing heavily now, self-preservation trying to kick in but tinged with an underlying despair, as she knew they were only speaking the truth, not lies like her parents. There was very little let-up to this unbearable torment. Unable to resist or question them, as they knew her intimately, all her strengths and weaknesses, secret fears, guilt, and shame. All the things she loved and cared about and because they knew her so well, they attacked her in places where they knew she was most sensitive, where they could do the most damage.

Trying to put a face to them, to diffuse their power, she only saw birds with sharp talons, short, curved beaks, hooked at the tip for gripping and tearing their prey, and large eyes, moving independently, not missing a movement, which was why she now stood motionless. The owls were pinning her to the spot.

She could hear the odd word floating up from downstairs, mostly from her mother who seemed to be making a point by saying things like 'psychotic,' and 'catatonic,' but the responding voices were deeper and unintelligible, misinterpreted in her mind as saying, 'she's evil and deserves to die too.'

Her father, who's loud, baritone voice seemed to penetrate her skull, could be heard to describe her 'obsession with a door in the mirror,' but she homed in on her mother, whose shrill response was to dismiss his comment, almost belittling him. 'Oh, mum!' she wailed, inside her fragmenting mind, 'the mirror is my main problem.' She turned her upper body inwards, to face her bedroom and then glanced sideways at the large oval mirror, drawn to the magnetic energy.

And then, it started again, as if mention of it made it re-appear, her vision became blurred and she felt lightheaded and closed her eyes tightly. She knew when she opened them there would be whirling colours and she would see flashing lights, zigzagging patterns and shimmering stars like her old ocular migraines, but a hundred times more intense. Then an opening would appear in her mirror, followed by a strange force pulling her through and however scary she found this world and tempting another was, she had already experienced it and did not wish to go back. Another dimension, like a wormhole or time tunnel stretching over centuries into the past.

Suddenly, as if coming to her senses, Jasmine leapt up, scrambling over her bed to the window and fumbled with a key she had hidden from her mother to open it. Oblivious to the clattering noise she was making as she fought loudly for what she thought was her life. She was nearly out of the first-floor window when the officer caught her left leg and pulled her back in. Hearing the commotion, the Special Constable who had agreed to be at hand at the time of the assessment, had been true to his word and raced up the stairs on hearing alarmed, raised voices.

And then, more people were crowding her, nonsensical voices all around, invading both her physical space and also mentally inside her head. There were many hands preventing her from thrashing around, before she felt the sharp prick of a needle accompanied by an enforced sleepy feeling. Eyes fluttering open to a bright light only to close heavily as if forced by extreme drowsiness, she became aware of the motion of a vehicle and sound of the engine. It was then she became aware her own restricted movements, but felt too weak to even try to free herself.

'We're nearly there Jasmine,' said a uniformed, female voice reassuringly, but with no committal as to where the destination might be. She recognised the interior now as an Ambulance and found herself laughing almost manically, 'committal' was appropriate, her freedom lost again and her destination was obvious as she knew the 'Big

House,' would be waiting for her again. But what era and which house? She then blacked out, unable to remain awake.

3

STRETCHNECK

Seconds before her eyes opened again, the putrid smell hit her nostrils making her retch, her head automatically lifting and then hitting back down on the hard surface that felt dank and coarse. There was a strange dingy light in the room and unfamiliar noises. As her vision came into focus, she gasped in horror just before the bile rose in her throat. Looking away, her mind working overtime trying to comprehend the scene in front of her, she soon became aware of her own restricted movement.

Turning slightly, her face was now exposed to the full blast of cold air and a bright light shaft from a narrow, unglazed opening in the wall. The ventilation only partly reducing the build-up of the disagreeable effluvia's peculiar to all madhouses. Where had that thought come from? It was a sentence she had quoted in her essay from a report on Bethlem Asylum by Dr Latham in August 1815. She must be dreaming.

But it was all vaguely familiar, she had been somewhere similar before where she was also incarcerated in appalling conditions, but somehow found her way out. She closed her eyes tightly, willing it all to go away but it remained.

As her eyes adjusted to the shadows in the semi-darkness, she caught sight of a wall of dirty, ragged looking people before her, bound with ropes and chains. There were women and older children, who seemed to be continuously coughing or moaning. Others like her lay confined in straitjackets on the floor. The rough surface below her appeared to be straw, but unlike cattle who defecate away from the place where they lie, these poor, helpless creatures lay close to their own excrement.

Her whole body was aching, blood pooling at the elbows, where swelling was starting to occur. Her hands were numb from lack of circulation, and she was experiencing excruciating, shooting pains in her upper arms and shoulders, her bones and muscle stiff. Beside her, one woman was thrashing around in her straitjacket, but Jasmine could see it was an ineffective method of attempting to move and an impossible way to free herself. The small room housed about ten females, the chains on those across the wall allowed them merely to stand or sit on a fixed bench. Rough, sack like clothes loosely covered the near or complete nakedness of each woman. She looked down and noticed her own sparse, ragged attire, and suddenly felt exposed, dirty and itchy. Was she in prison?

Distressed at these frightening sights and smells, coupled with her memories of previously studying this Georgian era, Jasmine began to sob. A soft, reassuring voice suddenly interrupted her self-pity and blinking through tears that clouded her vision; she looked across at the dirty, but smiling face of a young woman of a similar age. She wondered if this was a nightmare or perhaps, she was an involuntary 'extra,' in a freakish film set. Jasmine could hear the girl singing, her vocabulary strange, an old English dialect, but she recognized the rhyme.

'Georgie Porgie pudding and pie, kissed the girls and made them cry, when the boys came out to play, Georgie Porgie ran away.'

It was comforting in one respect, as it was childlike and familiar and Jasmine's mind floated back to an O level History lesson about the relationship between nursery rhymes and actual historical events. George Villiers; Duke of Buckingham (1592-1628) was the bisexual lover of James 1. He was said to have had affairs with many of the ladies at court, as well as the wives and daughters of powerful nobles. He 'kissed the girls and made them cry,' but managed to avoid prosecution or retaliation. 'When the boys came out to play, Georgie Porgie ran away.' He was an abusive coward really. Jasmine wondered what she and these poor souls had done to be imprisoned here.

It occurred to her that her supposed crime, punishment and fate were unknown and, in these times, human rights and proper legal defense were not even recognised. This realisation led to panic that consumed her. Fighting to breathe, she hyperventilated and her chest tightened. Anxiety was a familiar unpleasant feeling, but the techniques she knew so well to control it, seemed distant and inaccessible in this alien environment. Seeing her reaction, the girl stopped singing abruptly and Jasmine calmed slightly at the concerned look on her face. Her voice was kind and reassuring.

'They be coming for us later this day; a reprieve has been granted for thee and me.'

As if someone was waiting in the shadows for her to utter these welcome words, two bulky male figures appeared in the doorway and she was wordlessly hoisted to her feet, a string yanked behind her releasing her arms and the girl's chain restraint, quickly unfastened. They were pushed to walk slightly ahead of their gaolers with a tight, pinching grip on their arms. She was filled with terror at the thought of the unknown, but relieved to be moving out of the filthy area she had been housed. Jasmine had to focus on the word 'reprieve,' right now, as opposed to some of the alternatives, she was anxiously pushing away from her mind.

Moving through a candle lit corridor, in the poor, hazy light, Jasmine cast her eyes on many other unfortunate men and women, locked up in cells like sheep pens that they passed. Some naked and chained and lying on straw. In a wing with just men, to her right, there were several unfortunates, chained close to the wall by the right arm as well as by the right leg. The distressing scene was like that of dog meat farm in China. Jasmine was astounded at the bestial treatment of these people and the thuggish nature of the gaolers. One man housed in a separate area and lying on a mattress, arose naked from his bed, and deliberately and quietly walked a few paces from his cell door along the gallery. He was instantly seized by his keepers, thrown onto his bed, and leg-locked, without enquiry or observation (bizarrely, an enactment of a paragraph she had read in Wakefield, 1814).

Two men cried out and moved around restlessly like caged animals in one cell they passed. Their swollen faces, oozing puss with skin hanging, bloody and red. The smell was not unlike bacon coming from their burnt flesh, their skin smoking and clearly causing them to suffer excruciating pain. She remembered a morbid curiosity she had had with reading about 'branding,' in her history lectures. Branding on the cheek, chest, or thumb, was a barbarous custom of an age gone by, inflicted on persons convicted of even petty crimes. Raw physical pain with lifelong disgrace was considered a powerful deterrent. It appeared that the two men had both sides of their faces recently branded with hot irons and were perhaps still there to face further punishment.

She spotted another man through an archway, a metal ring fastened around his neck attached to bars on his shoulders. He had limited movement with both arms held close to his sides with a waist bar and connecting chains inserted into the wall. This was just like a picture she had seen in a book of a man who had been incarcerated, encaged and chained like this for more than twelve years (Wakefield, 1814). It was strange that her most difficult reading, in her studies of Crime and Punishment in eighteenth and nineteenth century Britain was in plain sight. Whilst she would never forget the words on the pages of Edward Wakefield's findings of conditions in prisons and madhouses of this era, it was as if his reflections had become her own reality.

Nothing seemed real to Jasmine, even the pains in her muscles and joints and the tight grasp on her arm by the attendant were only noticeable when she focused on them. The candles in the iron wall sconces seemed to go out behind them as they passed through and the strips of daylight flashed fleetingly, through the small barred window openings.

Jasmine and the other female, still attired in loosened restraints, were finally brought out into the open where the full daylight stung their eyes. Taken over to a rickety cart pulled by two horses, Jasmine was hauled into the back with the girl, where two older women half lay, one in a skeletally weak condition looking close to death.

The girl with Jasmine seemed to know one of the women and tried to cover her shaking body, whispering to Jasmine that a bad-tempered attendant had punched her in the face and hosed her down with freezing water earlier in the cell. The other woman, her body covered in scabs and her knuckles red raw, was quietly crying and repeating that her mother had been 'accused,' as a witch and condemned to death.

'We're off to the new Big House,' the girl nodded eagerly at Jasmine, appearing quite sure of herself, despite no word from the men. Jasmine stared at the girl's smiling face, she had few teeth and most left were black or rotten, but she was kind and friendly and this made Jasmine feel less alone. The Big House Jasmine wondered? This was too early an era for Shelton Asylum surely?

Without any communication, other than a slap on the flank of the horse on the right, the cart pulled away, through vaguely familiar, cobbled streets. Strangely, for the first time in longer than she could remember, Jasmine could only hear her own frightened thoughts and despite her confusion and anxiety at the situation she found herself in, her head was clearer. Sensing that she was keen to talk and not so strange to this world, Jasmine began to ask the girl questions, as she appeared to hold information as to what was happening and maybe of their fate. Her name was Emily, and she was twenty-five years old like Jasmine, although in some ways she looked much older close up, as though life had treated her harshly. She laughed when Jasmine asked what year it was but had a caring nature, as immediately took back her mocking and announced it was 1734. Jasmine took a sharp intake of breath and shut her eyes tightly, still convinced she had been here before and just needed to find her way home again.

Although the streets looked very different, there were many recognisable Tudor buildings of the medieval town of Shrewsbury that she originated from. They looked odd against the dilapidated dwellings and hovels crammed alongside, long since demolished in her time, replaced by the brutalist architectural style of the 1960s. Tall, narrow buildings blocked the light, giving a gloomy feeling to the streets.

The highways were bumpy, rutted, and full of potholes in this Georgian landscape, the oxen and horses struggling to gain a foothold in places. She could see chickens, and pigs housed in pens and some hens loose, pecking at the side of the road. Traffic was sparse, and she could only see horse pulled carts and traps and the odd stagecoach on the main route between London and Holyhead on their way to Ireland. This was definitely Shrewsbury, but not as she knew it, far from her friends and family. She would only find ancestors here if she was lucky, who would still be strangers to her. But something was ringing a distant bell in her head and she had a strong sense she was here for a reason.

Passing many coaching Inns with archways into the stable yard behind, every other building appeared to be a hostelry. There was a stark contrast between the stagecoaches with their steel spring suspension that reached the great speed of twelve miles an hour and rickety old carts, such as was the one she travelled in. She spied women on the streets, dressed in shawls, capes and cloaks, the men in either frock coats with wigs and cocked tricorne hats or the poorer chaps in shabbier coats wearing caps and breeches. Groups of children played at the roadside with marbles, hoops, and dogs. She noticed the young boys wore knee high breeches and cloth caps and the girls' long dresses, with bonnets like their mothers, but most of the clothing, was well worn, grimy and poorly fitted and few had footwear.

Along the way they passed street-side butchers and fish vendors who tossed innards and unwanted flesh into street gutters. She looked up to see a toothless old woman whose shrill cry of 'Gardyloo,' sounded seconds before she threw dirty water and slops from her tenement window into the open drains in the streets below, just missing them. Others at street level poured effluent and refuse into them. They passed public wells where people queued chatting, but far too close to them were dung heaps, another deadly route of infection.

She knew contaminated water had spread cholera and this was how public water sources became polluted. The past was in front of her like a film set, but frighteningly real. Evidence all around her of a world from another time, where mistakes had yet to be learnt, before diseases like Cholera would be eradicated. She placed her hand over her mouth. Strangely, she could barely detect the smells, but she remembered what she knew about Cholera. It caused profuse and violent stomach cramps, vomiting and diarrhoea, with dehydration so rapid and severe, the blood thickened, and the skin became deathlike and blue and death was within hours.

Keeping low as ordered for some time, she raised her head again very slightly to see over the side of the cart, as the sound of an angry, jeering crowd grew louder and she realised they were now passing Shrewsbury Market Square. High above the people, stood a fixture of two parallel posts with a beam across the top with holes, where the heads and arms of two unfortunates protruded.

Today, onlookers partaking in their punishment, were either laughing and mocking or venting their anger. Rotten fruit, stones and animal dung were thrown at full might at the accused, one even slung a dead cat. Judging by their dress, despite the distance from the track, she could see there was a male and female in what looked like giant stocks. As the cart moved closer, she could see the man was dressed in knee breeches and stockings, a long waistcoat, his hat long gone. The woman was attired in a 'sack back' dress worn over a hoop petticoat with a whale bone bodice and cotton bonnet. It was difficult to distinguish which marks were the blood from their injuries and which were the splatters of rotten food and worse dripping off them.

'It's only the Stretchneck,' said Emily, as if talking about a daily performance or spectacle, which it indeed was; being the most popular form of punishment and entertainment that drew crowds at that time. She had read in her studies that some felons were flogged at the same time or even hanged on the Pillory. Jasmine remembered her teachings on local history at university. Dead people were sometimes displayed there, like Henry Percy who died on Shrewsbury's Battlefield in 1403 and was initially buried by his nephew with honours. Rumours soon spread that he was not dead, so in response, King Henry IV had him disinterred. His body was salted and impaled on a spear between two millstones, in the marketplace pillory.

Both the felons were now looking like they were struggling to stay conscious and at risk of dying at the hands of the rabble. Although too far away to read, she could see both had their crimes displayed around their neck, the male's cocked head indicated he might have an ear nailed to the post. She remembered criminals were expected to remove the nail themselves at the end if they could, if not; the bloody ear would be left behind on the pillory. Sometimes it was not intended that they should even survive their ordeal. With the public humiliation and moral degradation from which they would never recover. A lasting, visible stigma.

What of those taken 'from pillar to post?' An expression still used now but with a sinister connotation, 'from pillory to whipping post.' Jasmine could see the post close by, two people were leaning on it taking in the show in front of them as if it was a Maypole, its ropes hanging down. The brutality with which these two persons were exposed to on the pillory by the mob, was offset by their supporters, who appeared to include several ruffians, who undertook to drive off the assailing crowd. The mob was malevolent, and the luckless wretches appeared in danger of being killed out-right by missiles.

Repugnance not apparently morally felt by the crowd; whose mission was to grievously injure. It was like watching a documentary in her history class at college. Even some of her observations and thoughts were like the narrative that accompanies these re-enactments. The kind of film where you shudder, feeling relieved you were not around in these times.

Jasmine was pulled down under the sacking by Emily. 'Don't be letting yourself be seen, they'll turn on us just as quick.' She smiled as she spoke as if it was an adventure and she wasn't afraid at all. 'Look lie low, we can see through the cracks in the side at the bottom,' she urged, beckoning Jasmine.

'What have they done?' Jasmine asked as if her companion was the oracle of all knowledge. She seemed to like being asked and began to explain how it could be anything and they were unlucky to get caught. Jasmine wondered if their crime or accusation could have been witchcraft, but probably a century too late. But then the sobbing, shaking woman in the cart had mentioned her mother had been accused of such sorcery. More likely, theft, violence, adultery, fire setting, or the attempted rape of children or attempted murder.

Or even, for a woman of that time, guilty of being a 'nagging, gossiping or scalding wife'. Or maybe a prostitute who had entered the trade after serving in bawdy and disorderly houses. Or the 'crime,' could have been attempted sodomy. The early homosexuals who were caught or accused, were often afforded the fatal punishments by the mobs. She trembled at the thought.

This punishment seemed too severe for hoarding, speculation, dishonest shop keeping, cheating at cards, pretended fortune-telling, and all other minor forms of confidence-trickery. It was a crime if caught keeping an unruly and disorderly house, short measuring or serving out of date or watered-down ale, and all could be punished this way, but surely never this brutally? A butcher or fish wife trying to make a bit extra on the side by cheating customers might find themselves in the stocks but this was vicious.

Suddenly, a woman's piercing scream rose from a window above, as a large turnip hurled from the crowd, shattered the pane from where she watched the scene below. Blood gushed through her fingers as she held up her hands, but the shard of glass appeared embedded in her face. Jasmine dived into the relative safety of the cart, under the musty cover, her heart thumping in her chest and her eyes widening, as she uttered the dreaded question that suddenly entered her head. 'Where exactly are we being taken?'

4

GUMBOLSTOL

'THE DUCKING STOOL'

As the sound of the crowds grew more distant Emily, eager to reassure Jasmine replied that she thought they'd be safe later, but... 'I think, we may be in for a ducking firstly.' Emily shivered, and Jasmine froze in fear. It all felt surreal and yet her senses were telling her everything before her was most certainly happening.

The irony was that she had been unable to distinguish what was real for weeks; hearing voices, believing her thoughts were being broadcast to the world and convinced that others were plotting to harm her. Her severely impaired thinking and odd behaviours had been difficult to hide, and her family had called in help that made her even more scared. She had been unable to filter sensory stimuli and had enhanced perceptions of sights, sounds, and smells around her, but this was like a scene from her black and white history books she had poured over, only in colour.

Her bachelor's degree in eighteenth and nineteenth century British Studies, had taken her off on lengthy reading tangents due to her interest in everything from this era. All before she stopped functioning at university and later woke up in this cruel, distant world, even though it seemed so familiar.

One new pastime had been learning about her ancestry and studying her genealogy, which she had then become obsessed with. It had taken her way back, into the branches of her own family tree and extended her interest into the past way of life. Jasmine had researched back even earlier, where she had learned of the barbaric accusations and punishments afforded to her great grandparents several times removed and also learned that her mother was not the first in the family to 'attend to,' the mentally ill, with an interest in herbal remedies and a child who went 'mad.'

'In for a ducking' Emily had said, Jasmine had read all about the Gumbolstol or the 'Ducking Stool.' The female to be ducked, had her hands and feet tied to the chair. Her weight would pull the chair under water. The Gumbal Man pulled down on the other end to lift her out of the water before lowering her back in. Punishment of this kind attracted hordes of people and was often used exclusively on women, as said to be 'too embarrassing for men.' It was given to so-called nagging, scalding or gossiping wives and before that, women accused of Witchcraft. The one used in Shrewsbury had been known as 'Ducking-Stool Marsh,' she wondered if it was still here. She was disorientated in time and although she recognised numerous landmarks, her hometown was now a very scary place.

She also knew all about the practice of submerging 'accused witches', who were usually poor, elderly healing women, who underwent trial by water in the 'swimming test.' After being flung into the water, with thumbs tied to opposite big toes, the ecclesiastical authorities would proclaim her innocent if she drowned, but the floaters would be hoisted out of the river and taken to the highest point of the town walls and 'roasted for witchcraft' or hanged to death. What year had Emily said it was? Surely the persecution of accused 'witches' was all but over by the 18th Century?

Emily seemed confident that if they were 'ducked,' they would reach safety following this, and the other two women in the cart with them seemed almost relaxed now, either resigned to their fate or as though they feared nothing.

'For what are we accused?' Jasmine asked Emily, noticing that her own formatting of sentences sounded strangely 'olde English.' As late as 1730, at Frome, a poor old woman, suspected of being a witch was thrown into a pool and drowned by twenty of her neighbours, in the presence of two hundred persons, who made no attempt to save her life.

Her studies had shown her an accused Witch was publicly stripped of clothing and all body hair shaved, to look for hidden 'Witches marks.' Pins were driven into scars, calluses, and thickened areas of skin to look for them. These could be just moles, scars, birthmarks, skin tags, supernumerary nipples and natural blemishes. If anything was found it was said to be 'undeniable proof of a Witch.' If the accused was found to have nothing, pins were simply driven into her body until an insensitive area was found.

The Witchfinder General used a 3-inch-long spike, to prod women and then retracted the spike into the spring-loaded handle so the unfortunate woman never felt any pain and could be condemned.

Jasmine would never forget seeing a heart carved on a wall in the marketplace at Kings Lynn, which was supposed to mark the spot where a condemned Witch, was burnt at the stake and her heart leapt from the flames striking the wall. Gun powder had been put around her neck, which led to explosive body parts and a greater public spectacle. Jasmine had wondered if the woman had been 'lucky,' and the executioner had pulled a cord around her neck before the flames licked

She knew so called 'cunning women,' who healed the sick preparing potions and medicine, were left alone until someone died and were then accused of deliberate foul play, making a pact with the devil and sorcery. There was little opposition in these God-fearing times and mass delusion and hysteria was easily triggered. Jasmine was aware that her own strange views and disorganized speech, thinking and behaviour related to her illness could be easily misconstrued in these times and was grateful it was 'quiet,' right now. Insight came easier when her head was clearer, beliefs were fairly normal and the only voice she heard now was her own.

'It's just to clean us up a bit, before we go in, we're the lucky ones!'

Emily proclaimed.

Jasmine could hardly remember the question; her thoughts were racing and jumping, tangentially from one to the next, making her lose track of time and switch between random thoughts and memories.

Perhaps she wasn't as well as she thought, but it was a big leap even recognising this after no insight for so long. Homing in on the word 'lucky,' Jasmine looked around her in the cart at the other three women, two of them 'crone-like', snaggle-toothed, sunken cheeked and one having a hairy lip, the epitome of the accused 'witches' and Emily, a young woman like her, but from two centuries before. Still encased in the grubby, but loose straitjacket, an itchy blanket only half covering her aching, thin body, she wondered what 'unlucky' would look like if this was the better option.

The strangest thing was on one level, she could stop and think with more clarity and for the first time in a long time, Jasmine knew what was real, and this most definitely was. It had been her fear to be drawn into the portal again, but she now felt if she had been before, it meant she could find her way home again, so this experience was not permanent.

As they approached the water's edge, she realised that they were now in what was known as the Quarry Park. A formidable, but recognisable building towered in front of them, although it all looked quite different in the starry night. Wondering for a second how it had suddenly become dark, she took a deep breath and shivered in the cooler, night air. The banks of the river then came into view and appearing from the hut he sheltered in, the boat keeper assisted to manhandle them onto the ferry, although there was something about his kind eyes that made her feel less afraid and they began the short journey across the river, using a fixed line of rope.

So, this was their destination. Before Shropshire & Wenlock Borough Lunatic Asylum that became Shelton Hospital was constructed, the local mentally ill population were sent to the Kingsland Workhouse, now Shrewsbury School. As Jasmine looked up it appeared exactly the same from the outside, bar the clock tower, only added when it became a public school.

The Workhouse was a spacious and handsome structure of brick commanding an elevated position over the River Severn, which flowed immediately beneath it. Beyond it lay the town, directly surrounded by gentlemen's houses partly hidden by the leafage of the Quarry. The high turrets of the castle and the church spires could be seen poking up.

'What year is it?' Jasmine spoke quickly. '1784!' Laughed Emily,

'You keep asking that and they'll think you're an idiot if they hear and then we're done for.'

That wasn't the year Emily had said before. It fitted though somehow, with the Workhouse in front of her and what she was about to experience, which for some strange reason she could almost foresee. Another date had entered her head. 'Shrewsbury House of Industry' had opened in December 1784, with the intention that poor relief should be self-financing. Entry was gained by ferry, followed by a steep walk up the bank. The house and other buildings surrounded by twenty acres of land.

She must watch what she was saying, Emily was correct and an 'idiot,' in these times had a different meaning and response to today, only today was now and yet now was the past. Also, a 'lunatic,' might utter things too random for others to understand and she didn't want to be labelled that either, not with such connotations and stigma attached, which made those of her own time seem like nothing in comparison. Despite being forcibly taken across the river, her fears of the ducking stool were diminished. Emily meant they were going to receive a bath. Time had moved on fifty years if she remembered rightly from the year Emily had first given her, 1734. This did make her question how this could be real, but she was definitely physically experiencing it, all her senses on fire.

Her previous hallucinations were gone and her mind and clearer now. They were a distortion of the senses, a misinterpretation of a true sensation, exploiting her assumptions about the physical world. She'd had hallucinations of sight, smell and sound, but with this feeling of Déjà Vu; perhaps this was just chronoceptive, the subjective experience of time. It was also like a dream. A succession of images, ideas, emotions, and sensations occurring involuntarily in her mind. What was happening was certainly outside of her control, surreal and bizarre with a connection to her unconscious mind, the subject matter very close to her recent studies in so many ways.

Checking to see if she was dreaming, she pinched herself hard but only cried 'Ouch,' and didn't wake up, although wondered if she would be any freer where she came from right now. Where she would be on waking in her other world was unknown. Maybe on a ward again in the local Shelton psychiatric hospital, or still in the Ambulance where she had last closed her eyes. At least here, her mind was oddly much more lucid. Her inner torment was at bay and the only whisperings she heard now, were clearly spoken and appeared to be heard by others too.

Jasmine shivered as the cold air seemed to penetrate her bones and she realised her straitjacket was no longer there, as if it had just dissolved away. Just like the lights going out behind her when she left the old gaol, as if they only existed as she experienced them. The smock she wore was different to the old sewn blanket she had been draped in. She and Emily walked ahead as instructed, but the two older, infirm women, were wheeled up the steep bank and she heard their custodians complain and utter loudly about what 'cost and little use,' these two 'imbeciles' would be.

For a second, she stopped and thought about making a run for it, but decided she had to go along with it quietly for now and stay strong, so that she could find the gateway home. Away from this cruel and barbaric time that she did not belong to, but which was somehow more healing for her mind. Until she could find the portal from the eighteenth century to the twenty-first, maybe through a mirror, as had occurred before in her bedroom at home.

It was going dark and wintry and she knew she would not last a minute outside of the walls of this house right now.

5

THE HOUSE OF INDUSTRY

On arrival, there was no introduction or welcome. They were ushered like sheep into a reception area with a hard-wooden bench fixed to the wall. One by one they were taken, Emily first, who looked back at Jasmine and winked, with only slight concern etched briefly on her face. One door had a sign on saying, 'Shrewsbury Pest House,' a former plague house, or fever shed, used for persons afflicted with communicable diseases such as tuberculosis. Jasmine hoped she would not be taken through that door.

When taken moments later, there was no sign of Emily, and Jasmine was not bathed but stripped down and scrubbed in the cold room. Treated mercilessly, like she was an inanimate object by the two women, the strong smell of disinfectant made her cough and burned her skin slightly. The nurse and apothecary then medically inspected her, 'to ensure you are free of any putrid or infectious distemper.' This was the only time they addressed her personally, as they lifted and dropped her limbs and bodily parts and roughly inspected her intimate areas, to check for infestation and disease. It was total humiliation and she shivered, forcing back the urge to cry or retaliate as her ordeal continued. They then talked about her as if she wasn't there after that.

'Not found any vermin, creeping and crawling on her skin,' one said, seemingly surprised.

'Nor rickets yet,' said the other knocking her knees, observing no swelling or bow leggedness.

Her clothing was tied in a bundle, 'they'll be fumigated with Sulphur,' she was told none too kindly. Seeing her swallow hard and blink back tears, the other woman added they would be cleaned and stored and returned to her when she left. They seemed surprised she had no personal possessions and eyed her suspiciously, checking her pockets twice wearing gloves.

'Well, she's from the gaol and set to go to the asylum ward, so she won't have anything,' answered the other after a long pause.

'Can't have been there long without no vermin,' said the other.

'I am here!' Jasmine said loudly with frustration.

They stopped briefly, as if surprised she could speak, only to then scowl at her and roughly dry her with a dirty, torn, damp towel. Issued next with the house uniform, a petticoat, a faded gingham dress to be worn underneath a calico shift, day cap, worsted stockings and woven slippers that 'roughly fitted.' The emphasis obviously on coarse materials that were hard wearing rather than on comfort and fitting was immediately apparent. They looked massive and although clean, well worn by other unfortunates.

'Just for now, until you sew your own to your fitting.' Uttered one of the women as they left her to dress.

'I keep forgetting she's a loony,' laughed the unkindest woman as they shut the door.

'Nah she'll not be doing a lot!'

They were mocking her. Dressing quickly, fuelled by anger and cold, she was ready to say something as she stomped out of the room, but she was instead met by a kindly young woman, who introduced herself as 'Nurse Victoria.'

'Well, I'm not a proper nurse yet, but I will be,' she stated, nodding enthusiastically, 'I'm a pauper nurse who is like on an apprenticeship and one day I'll be like Beth.'

Not knowing who Beth was, or where Emily was right now, Jasmine was led down a corridor and up some stairs, told only they were heading for the annexe called the 'Lunacy block', where there were two wards for men and women. Along the way, they passed other segregated areas, which Victoria proudly explained were the new separate blocks for boys and girls under fourteen. 'Babes under two get to stay with their mothers unless they're orphans, and then we've got the nursery. Everyone wants to work there with Nadia, she's so kind.'

Jasmine found herself smiling at Victoria's enthusiasm and could see she enjoyed doing the grand tour and showing off her knowledge. She pointed out the different areas designated for the able-bodied men and women from age fourteen to sixty, then one for the over sixties.

'The aged and impotent,' she said memorizing the unfortunate title. Lastly, they took a sharp turn to the left, down the corridor that led to the annexe that held the infirmary and the lunacy block.

'For the insane, imbeciles and idiots,' she announced but stopped suddenly, turning slightly red, with embarrassment. 'Are you sure you're not down to come and work here?' Jasmine had to think on her feet quickly.

'Yes, I'm here like you to help.' Jasmine was sure she could pull this off. In the real world, she had been on her way to Shelton Hospital, to a mental health ward, similar to the lunacy ward here, but it would be barbaric here in comparison in this day and age. She wondered if she had imagined the first part of her journey here, after waking up in a Georgian prison and finding fifty years had gone by on the short route to this house. Oddly though, she still felt mentally stable here and came across as 'normal,' to Victoria, so it was to her advantage that it was assumed it was a mistake, that she was on the list as a patient or inmate here.

'Oh good!' enthused Emily, 'We'll probably be working opposite shifts, but we can be friends.' She stopped, wide eyed, touching

Jasmine's arm gently, 'I've just thought, you're the last one through today and I'm off until tonight after this, so I'll show you around everywhere!'

They turned a corner and headed back downstairs, where there were more corridors and long rooms, which Victoria said included the dining hall, workrooms, kitchen and laundry. There were also private rooms. Victoria said she could only show her one, but cautiously listened at the door and then looked both ways, making Jasmine doubt if she was really allowed in there. They peeked through the doorway at the elaborate décor and grandfather clock, so unlike the rest of the sparse house so far. It was here apparently, that the board of directors met to select the inmates from the parish applicants.

The grand dining hall was next, where all the paupers ate and supped, in a long room 115 feet by 20. Victoria showed her how they were classed at separate tables, men, women, boys, and girls.

'There's a bell rung for breakfast, dinner and supper, but we eat mostly on the ward as the lunatics don't ever leave the ward.' Jasmine was shocked, but Victoria didn't seem to notice.

'Its prayers first thing and last,' she said rolling her eyes, 'even we have to go when we're not on shift or we do it on the ward with those inmates that can.'

There was a brew house on site and beer was available each day, as a safe alternative to water. As they approached, the strong smell of the hops permeating the air made Jasmine heave slightly. If only she could close her eyes and wake up at home, having a milky coffee with her mum on the overstuffed sofa in the snug. Victoria was talking incessantly, and Jasmine found herself switching off and dipping in and out of listening, feeling weak and tired. She heard her say that those who did heavy labour, like in the laundry, or bone crushing, or stone breaking were rationed extra beer. Victoria stated she was disappointed that nursing wasn't considered physical enough when they had to do lots of 'lugging.' Washing, scrubbing, and cleaning were counted as heavy work but not work on the wards.

Jasmine remembered her studies had shown, that the liberal supply of alcohol had all changed in a short space of time, with the Temperance Movement. Their cause crusaded against the 'evils of drink,' where alcohol abuse was blamed as 'the root cause of much of the squalor and distress experienced by the poor.'

The workrooms were next, where Victoria said the long-standing paupers in the house were employed, and given work in the woollen manufactory and taught scribbling, carding, spinning, and weaving. Many were making the uniform of the institution. Men's tasks were varied, but the least skilled workers or vagrants, spent the day crushing bones for fertiliser and breaking stones. There was a shoe making workshop where even children, presumably over fourteen, sat working arduously in front of their craft. Some would be apprenticed out.

There was so much information and Jasmine was starting to feel strange again, her head was fuzzy, her mouth dry and her limbs ached, but she had to go along with this if she were to be accepted as 'staff,' rather than patient.

'Can we get a drink please Victoria,' she butted in as Victoria was whisking her off again to see the chapel. 'Yes of course,' she said apologetically, as you do with any guest you've forgotten to offer a beverage to.

'I know, I'll take you to the kitchen to meet some real nice folks,' and with that, she followed Victoria who turned at some speed to embark down more corridors and stairs.

The kitchen was huge and had several female paupers preparing vegetables and stirring big pots. But Victoria took her through to the back, where there was a smaller garden kitchen; and a striking looking couple sat talking, their very presence instantly captivating. The man stood and smiled at her directly and the woman pushed back her chair and brushed down her long skirts laughing.

'We had a feeling there would be a new visitor here today,' she said her eyes shining.

Joseph introduced himself first, he was handsome and towered over her but despite his strong presence, he had a kind, gentle persona. He shook her hand and introduced Helen, a charismatic woman, who smiled kindly and pulled out another chair for her to sit down. Victoria set about making tea and Jasmine wondered how to introduce herself. She didn't even know what she was doing here or why. She knew she had travelled back in time before, and it was a brief, but bad experience and her memories now were extremely hazy. She remembered trying to climb out of her bedroom window at home, because the pull from the mirror was getting stronger.

She had seen an owl peering through from the other side, its huge face, with large eyes locked in its skull, summoning her and following her movements like she was prey. To her now, an owl was a harbinger of death. Nothing was the same since her brother's hit and run, by the man with the hand painted owl on his van. She had put her lifelong collection of owl ornaments and soft toys in a black bin bag and almost thrown it into the wheelie bin, as the association with death was so strong.

The last thing she had remembered was lying in the Ambulance on the way to Shelton Hospital, or the 'Big House,' as she called it, but she could never have known her journey would end in this big house! This was Shrewsbury School in her lifetime, but before that the Workhouse as she well knew, both then and seemingly again now.

She suddenly became overwhelmed at the kindness and acceptance of these new people and with her mind so confused, she found herself sniffing back tears, but was unable to stop the big tear globules falling from her eyes. Helen immediately comforted her, and hot tea and scones were bought to the table. They all sat down, leaning towards her, Helen's arm around her still.

'I'm Jasmine, I was sent here as a mental patient from the prison, I don't know why, but I'm ok now and if I stay, I want to work here and help. But I'm not from this century.'

Whether they heard her right, it was unclear, but they quickly reassured her that everything would be fine, Victoria would look after her and she was welcome down here anytime. She nodded and smiled, deciding to not go on about being an unwitting time traveller. She wasn't even sure if the concept existed in this era and if they had misheard her, at least they wouldn't think she was mad. Nobody had believed her back home and look where that had gotten her.

The conversation moved on to how to survive here and how it was not all that bad. Helen and Joseph were married, she was in charge of the kitchen garden and grew herbs and healing plants and Joseph was the head vegetable gardener, who was over a group of pauper helpers. There was also a farm she was told; she would meet the workers and be shown the animals in due course. They all immediately clicked, there was no-one interested in prying into her past, just talk about the here and now, and how they could help each other. Jasmine's natural interest in horticulture and healing herbs was quickly noticed and they pressed Victoria to get Beth to send Jasmine down, when she could be spared. Jasmine felt relaxed here and hoped that if she had to stay here for any length of time, she could come down often to the kitchen.

Seeing how tired she was, Victoria said she would take her straight to the dorm and collect her at 6 o'clock tomorrow to meet Beth and Elsie on the Lunacy Ward. Before she left the warm comfort of the kitchen, Jasmine felt a surge of panic return and stuttered.

'I was brought here with Emily and I don't know where she's gone.'

She did not fail to miss their deep frowns and exchange of concerned glances, Joseph spoke first, 'Worry not, we'll search for her and aim to reunite you, we did not know she had returned.'

They know her though, Jasmine thought, relieved that she needn't feel entirely responsible for losing her. She knew somehow, she would be safer in this world if she was alongside her new friends. Until she found her way home.

With that, Jasmine reluctantly left with Victoria. Joseph clasped her hand in his warmly and Helen hugged her tightly. She felt herself blushing at the slightly prolonged embrace followed by Helen pulling back to face her, her wide smile lighting her eyes, causing them to crinkle at the corners. Jasmine was in awe of her and it was if they were drawn to each other, which felt awkward with Joseph stood there. It was probably her imagination though, everything was confusing.

On the way to the women's dorm, Victoria confided in Jasmine, perhaps more than she should have at this early stage of knowing her. Joseph and Helen, she said, were really siblings, who had changed their names and disguised their relationship as one of a married couple, to protect themselves and avoid detection. They were from a family of accused 'Witches,' who's not so distant ancestors, had been tried and hung as 'bad cunning women.' As descendants with 'the gift,' they remained potentially vulnerable targets.

'I'm telling you because I think they know you have it too.'

'Me!' Jasmine exclaimed, surprised at this revelation, that if true, she was unaware of. She thought of her enjoyment of gardening as coming from her father but did share an interest in natural remedies and healing with her mother and grandmother come to think of it. It made her smile though to think of them as brother and sister. She shook off her risqué thoughts and attempted to ignore the fluttering feeling in her stomach, as she focused on her pretty dire, but not quite so bad situation ahead.

The women's block had bunks, presumably to fit more in. She would be working days and nights sometimes Victoria informed her, so as we're opposite shifts, we might have to share at first.

'At least we ain't got no vermin and we get the chance of extra washes under Beth's watch too!' she chuckled.

Any trepidation about sharing, quickly dispelled when she saw the state of some of the other beds. Although all perfectly made as were the regulations, some were dirty and cluttered with cheap, but probably priceless possessions from previous, shattered lives. Victoria's was clean and tidy, although right now she could have slept on a clothesline. She thought briefly of her reading about the 'Two penny hangover,' where destitute men spent nights hanging over ropes which were strung across rooms for them to sleep on. Cheaper than a bed.

There was no-one else in the dorm, the able-bodied females still working no doubt. Victoria had four scones wrapped up in her apron pocket and handed Jasmine two of them. She had seen Helen give her them and presumed they were for Victoria and Beth. Jasmine had devoured one with jam down in the kitchen earlier and her mouth watered at the thought of more.

'That's your supper, better than the slops in the dining hall anyway. Keep your head down and sleep soundly until tomorrow,' she urged, 'I'll go straight to tell Beth and we'll sort you out a helper badge, so you don't get questioned about being here as a loon,' she laughed. If only she knew thought Jasmine, cringing slightly at the word 'loon,' but by now she was under the cover, her eyes closing. Perhaps when she opened them again, she would be in the other 'big house,' but as she fell asleep the only face she saw was Helen's, smiling.

6

RAT RACE

Jasmine woke up to the sound of a noisy, clanging bell, her eyes opening wide and her brain scrambling to register where she was. She had slept right through, but as she moved, she became aware of the coarse, chaff filled mattress and pillow with grain husks and straw poking through and the rough coverlet. Despite assurances from Victoria the night before, it seemed to move and twitch, making her skin itch. Her heart sank, as she took in her surroundings and started to recall the day before, but also skipped a beat when she remembered her brief encounter with Helen and the feelings it evoked.

As she focused on her mind, she realised she remained free of any tormenting 'voices,' or persecutory thoughts. She was symptom free of her illness somehow in this place and had some insight at last.

She wondered how she had fallen into such a deep sleep last night, after devouring the scones once Victoria had left. She hadn't even heard the others come to bed and now the dorm was full, each narrow bed accommodating one or more females and bustling with women and children getting ready. She hoped she would see Helen and Joseph again soon and that Emily would reappear. It was Victoria she yearned to see right now though.

Looking around, she became aware of the Nightingale style dormitory, with pairs of opposing high windows allowing a through draught, the beds situated between them. She noticed the sour odour of inadequate sanitary facilities, just two, situated at the top and bottom ends of the room. The dorm was now full of woman stirring, some quietly pulling on their daywear and others more animated, interacting and even laughing with each other. Sleepy babies and young children under two, were lifted out of beds shared with their mothers and older sisters. One tiny baby was tucked into the top of her mother's red dress, still attached to the breast as the woman tidied around her small bed area.

An unmarried mother, in these times, made to wear the 'uniform of shame.' The practice of which, would soon be condemned if she remembered her history. She could see the paper, produced by the PLC in 1839 entitled, 'Ignominious Dress for Unchaste Women in Workhouses.' Jasmine had studied this at length, pouring over her books well into the night, her subject disturbingly fascinating and compulsive reading was now seemingly a reality.

Sleeping fully clothed, she noticed she had perspired slightly, although the air was damp and cold as she tentatively pushed back the covers. Sitting up and placing her feet on the floor a smiling face peered over from the top bunk, but the expression quickly changed.

'You're aren't Victoria!' a loud shrill voice, belonging to a freckled face girl exclaimed.

'Where is she then?' asked another walking over, and then a silence descended across half of the room, as many eyes turned to examine her. She need not have worried though, loud footsteps approached, and a familiar voice was heard.

'No, I'm Victoria and Princess Victoria, if you please,' her new pauper nurse friend declared laughing, saving Jasmine this time from providing an explanation.

There was tittering all around, before the women drifted out of the dorm, the majority by the main entrance. Jasmine noticed other doors that should have been fire escapes were now unlocked; the women who had queued behind now descended the stairs. Victoria explained there were some inmates going down to help prepare breakfast, others to clean, but many would have to go to Morning Prayers before eating and then go to their work rooms.

'Where are we going?' Jasmine asked anxiously.

'To meet Beth,' Victoria answered succinctly, with a wide smile as she brushed her skirts down. Jasmine followed her new friend, 'Is there any sign of Emily?' Jasmine asked as other memories from the day before resurfaced.

Victoria turned around quickly, placing her hand gently across Jasmine's mouth. 'Hush, the walls have ears,' she whispered. 'We're still looking for her.'

This did not sound too hopeful to Jasmine; how could she have simply vanished when they had both entered together for the same purpose? Moreover, if they had both been destined for the lunacy ward, why wasn't Emily there, why was it a hushed secret, and how could she have vanished? Victoria repeatedly yawned loudly and apologised for not talking much but said she had not stopped all night on her shift. As they walked along the corridor in silence, Jasmine noticed the candles on the walls going out behind them, one by one as they passed, just like in the prison.

'What's up?' Victoria asked puzzled, noticing Jasmine lagging behind and staring at the walls. 'It's just...' she stopped and turned, they were all lit again now, flickering gently.

'Nothing.' She continued despondently, perhaps she did belong as a 'lunatic,' rather than helper on the ward. However, the craziest thing was the fact that she was here at all in this woebegone era.

As they approached the Lunacy Wards, she felt her anxiety levels creep up. She needn't have worried about meeting Beth though; there was an instant warmth and compassion about the woman, who welcomed Jasmine like an old friend.

'We've got you out of morning chapel anyhow,' smiled the small, raven-haired woman. Beth did not ask for any explanation regarding the mix up, if there ever was one. A helper's brooch was pinned to her apron strap and a breakfast consisting of a pint of tea with bread and butter put before her, releasing hunger pangs that she had not been aware of.

It was strange she was so famished and relished the food, despite knowing what was supplied in workhouses was second rate and meant to serve as a deterrent to residing here for too long. Victoria had mentioned a bakery on site and the bread tasted fresh and satisfied her hunger. Her thirst appeared unquenchable and she surprised herself by gulping the tea down only pausing for breath once. Beth chuckled and proceeded to show Jasmine the dorms and day areas, occupied by the many patients in their care.

Jasmine quickly learned that the 'insane,' received the enhanced diet also given to the aged and infirm. The food rations given to the indoor staff, were much more generous than that of the paupers, but she was told bitterly by Beth, that the Master and Matron received six times the amount of food of a pauper.

The dormitories were at least 120-foot-long, like the workers dorms, but the lunacy ward beds were far too close, some touching each other. Beth pointed out the many physically sick cases, the bedridden patients, who could not be moved due to their combination of disease and aggression. They had only one nurse and a pauper helper to tend to them, as well as everyone else. Ventilation was poor and there was a foul air, drawn from the water closets, onto the ward at each end. The bowl washed straight into a fetid cesspool below, and Jasmine heaved at the smell, aware of this century's lack of knowledge on the spread of microbes and germs causing deadly disease. She did not have the nursing skills or experience of her mother Jacquie, but she wondered if she might be able to help educate people here, if only on basic hygiene and sanitation.

With her twenty-first century knowledge to offer, it would surely give her some credibility here and in turn improve conditions. That was if she didn't succumb to Typhoid, Cholera, or any other malignant fevers herself. A quote she had previously read jumped out at her, as she viewed the communal areas of the ward.

'The gutters, privies and airing-courts were dirty and offensive, the drainage deficient, the walls damp and the clothing and bedding filthy and inadequate.' (1831 Report to the Guardians of the Poor of Shrewsbury).

Jasmine wondered if this may have contributed to the outbreak of Asiatic cholera in patients in the Kingsland Asylum in the 1849-50 epidemic, she remembered reading not long after the Asylum part was closed.

One physically sick patient Norman, was reduced to a most distressing condition, the disorder of another Jake, so offensive, Jasmine could not remain near him without a handkerchief pressed against her mouth and nose. Yet there were other sick patients lying close to these poor souls and those labelled 'highly disagreeable cases,' were not separated from the more physically healthy others.

They lay in iron bedsteads, with straw mattresses, chaff pillows, rough blankets and one sheet that proved difficult to keep clean with so few facilities. Beth explained regretfully that clean bed sheets were only provided once a month, or oftener if essential and a change of personal linen once a week. 'They need draw sheets,' Jasmine volunteered automatically. She had seen her grandmother use one in hospital that could be quickly whipped out and changed if soiled. Beth looked perplexed after listening to how it could be achieved but agreed they could possibly try it with two of the 'worst culprits.'

Of course, draw sheets from modern times were disposable, with absorbent layers, almost like disposable nappy material, something well over a century off invention, but she knew they could put something together to improve patient comfort. She needed her mum Jacquie, a 'proper nurse,' from the future, whose ideas and methods really would open the eyes of her predecessors.

Separated into male and female, unlike the last ward Jasmine had been sectioned to, and that was in the twenty-first century, was at least something. She had hated the male patients being so close in her living space when she was acutely ill in hospital, but could see the benefits of a mix in recreation and therapy groups. She had been part of a service users' group, petitioning to end mixed wards, until she relapsed again and crept back into a world where she would only allow the 'voices,' in.

In the male day room, up to ten men were walking around aimlessly, many oblivious to their surroundings and some semi-naked. The room was confined and too small. She knew that before the nineteenth century, with no medication, wards like these served to isolate the mentally ill and socially ostracize them from society, rather than cure them or improve their health.

Beth said, 'It's better now we have a night attendant, there had been problems with wardens absent from duty and at one time and drunkenness prevailed.' Nurse Beth however, appeared wise and showed genuine kindness, reminding Jasmine very much of the matriarchs in her own family.

Each Lunacy ward had sections for cleanly patients and for paupers of 'dirty habits,' as well as a seclusion room, an attendant's room, and a day area with a table and benches fixed against the wall. It was very bare and poorly lit. Jasmine was told she would be sleeping in the able bodied, working female pauper's dorm, but would attend the lunatic ward as part of her work. She and Victoria would be on opposite shifts of days and nights, and would need to share a bed at first, otherwise Beth said, 'questions would be asked.' It seemed Beth had been expecting her arrival as a 'pauper lunatic,' rather than a 'pauper helper,' and luckily, Victoria had convinced her otherwise.

Jasmine felt compelled to ask Beth about Emily, quietly this time, after Victoria's warning about 'the walls having ears.' Again, as with Helen and Joseph, there was an immediate recognition, but a deep sadness.

'I heard last night.' Beth knew her too! 'We will find her,' said Beth despondently, looking down, but then she raised her chin and smiled, 'I promise.'

It would take time, but Jasmine was sure she could help Beth make changes to improve things. But as she walked back to her dorm, exhausted at the end of her first day, she wondered why she was accepting all of this, even making future plans, as opposed to saving her energy to find a way home. She should search for a portal, it must be a mirror she thought, the same way she was sure she had once entered other time zones from home. Her memory of this was so fuzzy though. It was as if now was real and the past was imagined.

Over time, Jasmine learned from Beth that Shrewsbury House of Industry held a license to operate a lunatic asylum within the Workhouse complex in 1821 and obtained a license to run a private asylum in the East Wing in 1835. Numbers had steadily increased, although the ratio of staff to inmates in the Workhouse and the Asylum continued to be low.

Victoria had told Jasmine all about her dreams to work at Kingsland Villa, the private asylum situated on one side of the path running down to the river. Furnished to high standards for the comfort of the upper classes of local society, it was apparently very different from the conditions afforded to the pauper lunatics. Designed for the 'treatment and management of insane persons,' patients in this house received high quality care, comfort, and seclusion, 'suitable to their situation and rank in life.' Beth told Jasmine that Victoria had, 'not a hope in hell,' as they all had their own private medical attendants and servants and she would not stand a chance herself even as a trained nurse. Rosemount was a privately-run school on the one side of the path, again, apparently quite different from the Workhouse classrooms.

Jasmine asked Beth about Shrewsbury's Shelton Psychiatric Hospital, which would be a new purpose-built county asylum around this time. She laughed at Beth's curious expression and remembered it was originally called 'Shropshire & Montgomery County Asylum,' and wouldn't be built until 1845. She must have said this aloud as Beth's eyes widened.

She would try to explain. 'One day in the near future, there will be laws passed to legally provide Asylum for the so-called 'lunatics,' and they'll be removed from within the workhouses and go to special hospitals called county asylums.'

She recalled this confidently, the idea being to provide them with more a sufficient and dedicated care system but remembered that those labelled 'harmless and incurable idiots' remained in the workhouse when asylums came about. Beth did not seem shocked, 'There's already places like that in the big cities like Bedlam in London.'

Jasmine responded, 'Yes, but in the future, it will be called the Bethlem Royal Hospital and the word 'bedlam,' meaning uproar and confusion, is derived from the hospital's prior nickname. Although the hospital became a modern psychiatric facility, historically it was representative of the worst excesses of asylums in the era of lunacy reform.'

Beth appeared flabbergasted and sat down to steady herself. 'You're obviously educated, but know stuff that is not possible,' she said shaking her head, but looking slightly shocked. Jasmine's face dropped, but Beth smiled.

'This is not madness you are portraying, but could be seen as witchcraft, so we will speak no more of it... not for now anyhow,' she added, shaking her head but smiling and Jasmine realised she was intrigued and would want to know more, but not just not at this time.

‘It can wait.’ Jasmine said smiling.

7

REFORMS

The eighteenth and nineteenth century descriptions used for patients and labels for conditions were fortunately archaic in Jasmine's experience of life on the psychiatric wards. Although Shelton Hospital where she had been a patient had its days numbered. Strange she was trapped in a time warp where the magnificent Shelton building, with its Nightingale dormitories hadn't even been built yet.

Methods of managing aggression that appeared to stem more from distress, were heart-breaking to hear and she decided this was the first area she would try to influence change. She was told that before Beth came, the treatment of one suicidal lunatic inmate, was to beat him around the toes and head with a stick, the only way they could control the 'poor creature.' Those paupers unable to look after themselves, due to frailty from age or disability, were known as the 'impotent poor.' They had their own ward, where couples were permitted to stay together and had extra flocked beds, but although many had dementia, some individuals were wrongly placed on the lunacy ward.

Jasmine was introduced to derogatory classifications like 'natural fools' or 'idiots,' for patients considered to have lifelong mental impairment. Other descriptions she heard included 'the feckless and idle,' the 'feeble minded,' the 'incurables,' and the 'moral imbeciles.' This horrified her, as they were people who had learning disabilities. She discovered the 'moral imbeciles,' also included people such as prostitutes, mothers of illegitimate children and criminals.

It was upsetting to find that unmarried mothers were segregated, from 'those paupers that were the real objects of compassion.' There were even adverts put in papers, offering a 10-shilling reward to apprehend men who had abandoned their families, to make them return and support them. Strange that the 'red-light district,' symbolised areas where prostitutes worked over centuries and had worldwide connotations, but here, many unmarried mothers were humiliated by being made to wear red dresses and prostitutes ironically wore yellow.

The dayroom was gloomy and cheerless, in great want of whitewashing, with one small fireplace and hot water pipes that ran close to the ceiling. Enclosed by high walls, with iron sashes on the windows that looked out onto endless, dead walls. One window looked out onto the airing court, where more high walls gave no view from below, only a feeling of imprisonment and claustrophobia.

There was strong emphasis placed on Christian ideals. Day room walls scribed with words like, 'God is Good, God is Truth, God is Holy,' as well as the Lord's Prayer and Ten Commandments. The other signs predominately placed on the walls were the regulations governing conduct. There were 'Rules and Orders to be observed' and 'Punishments for the Misbehaviour of the Paupers.' All the surroundings appeared geared to reform and control the inmates.

Every day would start with a bell that rang at half past five, followed by morning chapel for the majority and breakfast. Work for most was 6 o'clock in the morning to 6 at night Monday to Saturday, but Jasmine did some night shifts and day shifts that ran into nights. Prayers were also said in the evening in the chapel, with 'Divine Service,' twice every Sunday. Only the necessary housework and cooking were done on the day of rest, but as Beth joked, 'there's no rest for the wicked,' and nursing had little let-up, without the calming drugs of the future.

She began to relish the short periods of free time, where you could go out of the grounds on a Sunday using earned privileges. Although it was a scary old world out there. More so, because although she recognized it as her hometown, it was most definitely not the same era.

Bed was always by 8 o'clock, but most were ready to drop after the daily grind.

The regime was strict, it was ordered that the larder, kitchen, and other offices, together with the utensils and furniture thereof, 'be kept sweet, clean and decent.' Tables and dorms were cleaned directly after use and windows thrown open to air the house, but most doors were kept locked, the keys taken by porters to the Master at 8 o'clock.

Jasmine soon became a fully-fledged member of this institutionalised existence, but with a clear mind. She reminded herself daily that this was not entirely real and she did not belong here or intend to remain, but kept in mind that she must be here for a reason. So, she endeavoured to make good, to see if she could somehow earn her way home. But despite a clearer head, she still blamed herself for her brother Joe's death.

Strange things continued to occur daily, but due to her past trauma and psychosis, she had become accustomed to 'intrusions,' which she now accepted were hallucinations, delusions, and flashbacks, but recognised these were different. The lights going off behind her continued, and sometimes, as she left a room, everything went quiet, as if it only existed whilst she was in there. But if she left and stood still, with her back to the silent room and then turned around to look upon the scene, activities resumed as normal as if they had never halted, making her shake it off a sensory phenomenon. If she was back at home, she would get her ears checked out, but God knows what the treatment here would be for that, probably leeches!

None of this routine and order was the case for poor Emily. After a few more days of asking around and being given blank stares or told to let it go, Jasmine discovered the Workhouse Master had Emily assigned as his 'personal pauper maid.' It was impossible to get close to her to see if she was well and Beth's counterpart Elsie, was on duty when Jasmine found out. She merely shook her head sadly and stated that others before Emily were, 'more than just maids to him.'

Jasmine made numerous failed attempts to sneak down to the back kitchen to talk to Helen and Joseph. Beth had disappeared for a while around this time and Jasmine was desperate to talk to her.

Life was so harsh, that only the truly destitute would apply to the Workhouse, unless ordered by the courts or rounded up and taken there. Although this was a deterrent to the able-bodied poor, it offered better food, free medical care, and education for children, more than that available to many outside of the workhouse. Those who used tobacco were allowed 2oz a week.

The whole idea being to reduce the 'immorality and social evils emanating from indolence,' and to encourage the poor into a 'habit of labour.' You could only get poor relief by being admitted as an inmate and 'farming the poor,' was a description of how inmates were provided with work and the Workhouse made money from any income generated.

Three simple meals, often bread and broth with occasional meat and cheese were served on long, segregated tables in the dining room. Over time, Jasmine experienced a more varied menu, especially on a Sunday, with butcher's meat, garden stuff, hasty pudding with butter and treacle sauce, or stewed meat with potatoes, yeast dumplings and Pease pudding.

From the onset, due to working shifts, she had to eat in the main hall on some days to receive her meals. It was so regimented, strict and unwelcoming. She had pushed some food aside at first, but seeing it forced down the throat of another inmate and the hunger she quickly experienced, she soon tucked in, taking more when it was available. She was a vegetarian but hadn't told anyone here yet, finding she had to put it aside at times, even though she had an intense dislike for meat, more so than her decision being on moral grounds. There was a shortage of food and times were tougher than anything she had ever experienced. Jasmine was relieved she wasn't put to work in the kitchens, where she heard some of the produce like chickens and rabbits, initially entered, living, and breathing, and the first job was to kill, pluck and skin them. But then at least if she were there, she would see more of Helen and Joseph.

The dietary regulations were pinned up on the walls, for all to see, with daily variations. Today was Saturday and the pauper inmates checked the sheet as they passed hungrily, before they took a pew at the long tables.

'The quantity allowed for breakfast, is either a pint of broth or milk-porridge to each adult; and to the children in proportion.'

'For dinner, the grown-up persons shall have six ounces of solid meat after boiling, a trencher full of potatoes or greens, and a pint of beer, by order of the Workhouse Medical Officer.'

'Working children shall have each three ounces of solid meat, with roots or greens and drink water.'

'At supper, the adults are allowed a pint of broth or soup, and six ounces of bread; and the children in proportion.'

Other suppers consisted of a trencher full of potatoes mashed with milk, and a pint of beer. The steward and matron attended all meals, to see that the meat was properly distributed. Jasmine noticed paupers often asked for their bread to be weighed and scales were provided to do so. She guessed that as with anywhere where there are restrictions and rations, corruption and dishonesty were rife.

Eating in the main dining hall, Jasmine did get the opportunity to meet other inmates doing different jobs. Long standing paupers in the house, were employed chiefly in the woollen manufactory and taught scribbling, cording, spinning, and weaving. There was a bump-room with 22 spinning wheels and an equal number of reels. Women's work also involved cooking, full days in the laundry or scrubbing and cleaning.

Men's tasks were such as shoe maker, tailor, farm labourer, gardener and porters. On the casual wards, or as punishment for broken rules, pauper men and vagrants were subjected to hard labour, crushing bones for fertiliser and breaking stones for roads. The female casuals picked oakum to earn their board and lodging, tediously picking out fibres strand by strand, from old rope for ship building.

Water was still pumped by hand by the paupers from the river. Jasmine helped with this sometimes, mostly volunteering to get her bearings on the landscape and look for hope of finding home. Even as a pauper helper, no-one admitted to the Workhouse, could leave the site without permission. Sometimes she would look up at the building from outside, knowing it still stood, centuries later and that her own home, although not yet built, was not far from it, but this Victorian Shrewsbury was so different.

Beth was now back, much to the relief of Jasmine. The only cause of concern from Beth, who treated her well, was when Jasmine spoke of things that had not yet happened, which gave rise to a fear that she was 'underlying mad.' But for Beth, there was something special and mystical about Jasmine and what intrigued her and the attendants most, was Jasmine's future knowledge of preventative measures, that did seem to reduce the fast spread of disease, mainly through simple cleanliness.

It was obvious really, but Jasmine had emphasised strongly that infections were contracted and spread via poor living conditions and bad hygiene. The use of vinegar was introduced by Jasmine, its use also helping to sanitise and mask the terrible odours. Beth knew Jasmine was different and over time, the truth would unfold, as there was no real trace of where this young woman had come from and her connection with Emily was uncanny. But Beth kept very quiet about Emily, Jasmine had her secrets and for now, for the protection of Emily, so did she.

Beth's nurse training had coincided with steps to improve conditions since the mental illness of King George III. An important change in the case of admission of lunatic patients, was that it became necessary for two doctors to sign the admission form of a new patient, after thoroughly examining them. However, this was still often done haphazardly by a medical examiner who appeared more interested in scribbling his name and getting away as fast as possible with his fee.

On Jasmine's arrival at the institution, she was supposed to have been examined, classified, and placed in one of the workhouse wards, but written records did not appear to have been kept of that process. This was a bonus to them as she was a hard worker and although a little strange, clearly not mad or bad. They would rescue Emily but it had to be soon, before too much damage was done.

Society was not yet looking that hard into complaints regarding the absence of legal safeguards for patients, lack of qualified staff, inadequate medical treatment, prevalence of restraint, improper diet, filth, lack of space and amusements, and lack of proper records. Jasmine could only play a minute part in change, but considered what had helped her as a former patient. She knew 'talking therapies,' would have no benefit with many patients who were off the scale with their mental health. She remembered herself, how she was unreachable at her most floridly psychotic. But not all here were this sick and she demonstrated skills of reaching out to those with intractable depressions and acute anxiety, with good effect. The list of 'reasons for admission,' was something she had read in awe as a history student from her own time, but was now seeing it as a reality.

The book of admissions at the Workhouse had under the heading of 'Lunacy Patients Admission Registers,' the conditions and details about the pauper patients. There were even people confined for novel reading. There were men like Craig, John, and Philip on the lunacy ward, originally admitted with complaints of, 'self-abuse, greediness and laziness,' who were now so institutionalised, recovery seemed unachievable. The whole environment was dehumanizing and the inmates spent their time pacing mindlessly, rocking back and forth, or standing motionless and there was an absence of all attempts at improving social and life skills.

A young woman named Carina, wore a 'strong dress,' a form of canvas shift that could not be torn by distressed patients, who self-harmed. Locked up along with many other women suffering from post-natal depression or 'puerperal insanity,' after giving birth, their babies long since removed but possibly never forgotten. Who knew the inner torment and self-blame their minds had created?

Older women like Kathryn, were here due to 'melancholia,' associated with the menopause and treated with leeches to the pubis. The male doctors of the day saw 'hysteria,' from the Latin for womb everywhere; almost any form of behaviour, such as excited chattering with other women, could be diagnosed as 'hysteria.' Calomel, really Mercury, was used to treat hysteria, but like most of the medicines prescribed for mental illness, it was highly toxic. Antimony, a toxic chemical that would later be used in fire retardants, was dispensed to keep patients in a state of nausea, making acts of violence less likely. It was an early example of the 'chemical cosh,' or controlling behaviour through sedation.

Male Victorian physicians took a keen interest in women's sexuality, believing 'hypersexuality' or 'NYMPHOMANIA,' to be a dangerous trait in female patients and led to hysteria. Many ordinary women carried smelling salts, as it was believed through the teachings of Hippocrates; when emotions were aroused, she was likely to 'swoon,' and the 'wandering womb' was said to dislike the ammonia vapours and would go back to its proper place, letting her recover herself.

Jasmine was witness to the so called 'treatment,' of some of the worst cases found in the workhouse asylum, that included genital massage given by shower bath to douche, or cold applications applied to the regions of the uterus. The strangest thing Jasmine heard from the mouth of a women called Sally who had experienced 'hysteria,' which

Beth nodded to be true, was the 'medical masturbation,' they had received from their doctors prior to admission. Jasmine had read in her studies about the electromechanical vibrator invented in the 1880's but was quite shocked to hear about the earlier prescribed 'digital manipulation,' administered by hand from a doctor.'

Administered to the point of 'twitching, pleasure and the release of abundant sperm,' known then as achieving 'hysterical paroxysms,' or what was now known as being brought to female orgasm, with female ejaculation. Although this was thought to temporarily relieve the symptoms of hysteria, she wondered if the vibrator was invented after doctors complained of cramped fingers and the high numbers of patients queuing up for another dose of this enjoyable treatment, as 'wifely conjugal duty,' of the times, was often only a perfunctory performance.

She saw those like Jane, whose manic behaviour was deemed due to cerebral congestion, were assumed to have blood in need of cooling and thinning. This was done with leeches applied to the temples, followed by cold showers for overheated and overstimulated brains and cold lotions to the shaven scalp.

One day, the doctor and Elsie, Beth's counterpart, subjected Jane to a 15-minute cold shower. She had shivered uncontrollably, her jaw chattering violently, her legs unable to support her weight and her pulse was, 'small, slow and contracted.' She collapsed, losing consciousness and on waking it was pronounced, 'reason had returned.'

The shower bath was cold and sometimes used as a punishment or to quieten excited patients. There was one warm bath, but no set times to use it, so Jasmine fought to bring in a rota to provide more frequent warm bathing, to reduce disease and improve the morale of the patients. Beth was already calming patients with her mysterious whispers and herbal tinctures and teas, which had a relaxing affect on the whole ward.

The biggest change though, made with Beth's help, was that Jasmine actually managed to get the medical officers to change their poor practice as regards supplying medicines. They previously left no instructions, directions, or labels on medicine bottles and pill boxes, not even the name of the intended patient. Without this, the inmates had previously helped themselves at night, swallowing unknown pills and nothing was locked away.

As the doctors were often arrogant, supercilious men, not used to being told what to do by nurses, let alone women, matters were put to them in the age-old way, making them feel like it was their idea. The same way woman had always gotten men to do what they wanted through the ages until 'equality,' came about. Although Jasmine recognised that equal opportunities were something that even in the millennium years, were a long way from being achieved.

The Lunacy ward was supposed to have a doctor visit once or twice a week, who then reported to the keeper the condition of the house and state of health of the patients. In reality, they paid lip service to this. Mentally ill patients were thought to have a 'spiritual problem,' and thus no real medical help could be given to those in need. The view of the Lunacy Commissioners was that workhouse care should be restricted to those insane persons who had no prospect of cure. On the lunacy ward, physical conditions were often masked by 'madness,' and got missed. Any treatment offered was still experimental, often causing more harm and distress than good.

Luckily, Beth used the doctor's inadequacies to her own advantage, to get what she needed for her patients. Also, she only had to look at them at times, which to Jasmine appeared to make the Apothecaries stop in their tracks, backtracking any decisions that Beth did not agree with. Although salaried, doctors had to provide any medicines from their own pocket. Grateful to be relieved of their examination duties, two of them followed Beth's advice, trusting her, and relieved at the way she kept their expenses lower. Beth needed just enough to grow the herbs and tinctures required to calm and soothe her patients. When she asked for medicinal alcohol, which she tricked the doctor in to believing was the main reason they were calmer, she then sold most of it on, using the money for her plants. Some was also used for Jasmine's suggestions of materials needed for those incontinence drawer sheets, also to start an early form of, 'occupational therapy,' to provide purposeful activity.

Only Dr Moody commented, he had come from Ludlow and was intrigued by the set-up Beth and Jasmine had in place and referred to the difference between the two shifts. Elsie's methods were quite distinct from Beth's and it was noticed that her shift had far more incidents and invasive treatments. Victoria didn't really know any different, as she mostly worked with Elsie, but when she talked to Jasmine, she admitted feeling uncomfortable at times with her methods.

This compliment made to the board of governors, regarding Sister Beth's shift, only made the establishment more suspicious about her practice and real intentions, something Jasmine's mother Jacquie had talked of encountering in her nursing career. Where those in high up places were only interested in corporate, conformist behaviour in-line with out of touch policies.

It was always sad, but often a happy release, when the older senile paupers, particularly on the Lunacy Wards and Infirmary, died there and were buried in unconsecrated ground by the death house. Jasmine noticed the compassion and care Beth gave to these men and women in their final hours and she had Helen bring some powerful tinctures that quickly stopped their woeful cries putting them into a gentle slumber until their passing. Jasmine had observed Beth speaking to them, in whispers that she had a strong feeling were not Christian prayers, but appeared to have a powerful, reassuring affect.

Divine service was read and performed for the benefit and consolation of any sick Christian patients, but Jasmine noticed Beth only requested the chaplain if it was the patient's wishes. Jasmine had helped prepare several bodies of the incurable dead. Grave digging was fortunately not a task for the nurses, but she had struggled with an attendant down the back stairs carrying a heavy corpse on a few occasions, their bodies wrapped tightly in sheets. There to be, 'prisoned in a workhouse coffin and moulder in a pauper's grave,' she thought quoting Charlotte Bronte from her novel of these same times, Jane Eyre.

Jasmine managed to get a few newspapers and books to provide some distraction and occupation, but few patients were able to read, so she persuaded her friends from the woollen and sewing rooms to provide some materials. This went down quite well and lifted spirits in some paupers no end. It was quickly observed that Jasmine could obviously read well and she began to introduce the reading out loud of novels and interesting news items to the patients and not just the Bible readings they were exposed to.

This appeared to have a profound effect, bringing calm, distraction and obvious pleasure to many, who asked for more of these activities. Some, unable to sit still, paced around the room as she read. Pete, an elderly man never made eye contact and did not speak other than his constant, but quiet, tuneless hum, as he walked in anticlockwise circles around the room. Thus, making Jasmine believe he was not listening, but she noticed once when she paused, he would stop all movement and noise, freezing like a statue, until she began again. Jasmine loved books and storytelling but after a time, she could not resist capturing them with imaginary tales, which of course were really facts about the future.

Her stories about rockets that travel to the moon and planets in outer space and planes, cars, and submarines gained the attention of her audience including her helpers, who were mesmerised. Mary always appeared to stare into space, but the curious glimmer behind her wide eyes told another story. Stanley liked her stories about the telephone and radio and how the Personal Computer came about and what you can do on the internet. She told them she came from the future through a time machine and what it was like in 2006. Jasmine never mentioned the death of her brother Joe or her own illness though, but she raised their hopes with advice on how to recover, things that helped her from her own hospital admission.

The biggest obstacle to reform was a lack of staffing, so everything she introduced had to be done in groups, or at least with one eye on everyone else. This had its challenges as the patient's social interactions had been limited. She did manage to persuade some of the older able-bodied women to attend in the evening to teach lace making and knitting on a one to one. The helpers had initially met these requests with negative pre-conceived ideas, which gradually turned into curiosity, to eventually something they volunteered regularly for, seeing the difference it made and the satisfaction they got back in return.

Barriers started to be broken down and the stigma and idea of 'them and us,' eroded slightly. For the male patients, who wouldn't consider needle work and were often too shaky for shoe making, Jasmine introduced basic art, in the form of simple sketching and although she had gathered some picture books for the purpose of copying, she was astounded at their detail and talent in free style drawings. Colourful memories depicted in illustrations from the patient's lives, before the bleak, dead walls of the institution.

Music was easier than she thought to introduce, and with the help of Victoria and Marie, this moved on to dancing. Initially, they made small movements, from foot tapping to head nodding, to shaking homemade maracas, then on to twirling around to sing-a-longs. Jasmine could not resist teaching them her favourite song of 2005 '(Is This the Way To) Amarillo,' by Tony Christie, the version she knew featuring comedian Peter Kay. She associated the tune with the good recovery made following her discharge from Shelton Psychiatric

Hospital, when she had started to put the blame for Joe's death behind her. Her old University friends had descended on her, and she had agreed to a rare social night allowing herself to be with them and they ended up watching Children in Need. Not like the old days of shopping, pubs and clubs, but a start. They had laughed, cried, and bonded again, over cheap vodka mixes, on the sofa at her mother's house and here, she saw the pauper inmates make similar connections, as they allowed themselves to laugh and have fun, releasing pent up energy in a safe, positive way.

Fortunately, Victoria took the lead the following week and introduced the patients to songs and dances of their day, after Beth had stood wide eyed at the door, with mouth agape, at the Peter Kay dance that accompanied the Amarillo song, although the patients seemed to like it.

Jasmine was not permitted to mix the sexes as the master would not allow it. The only reason they had female carer's was due to a lack of resources. It wouldn't be long though, according to the time-line of Jasmines studies that mixed dances in the hall of the new insane asylums would be all the rage.

Jasmine only had a few items she had acquired since her arrival, most precious to her was the novel Jane Eyre by Charlotte Bronte (who lived 1816-1855), whose work she had loved two centuries later, yet in this world, she was waking up to the same sunrise as the writer and the famous Bronte sisters. Charlotte had lived the longest out of all her siblings, yet died herself in childbirth at only thirty-nine. These times were not known for longevity and life expectancy was a worry at times, especially when she was now a pauper helper-nurse, attending to patients with deadly diseases like Smallpox, Typhus, Influenza, Cholera and Tuberculosis, that had been wiped out in Jasmine's future lifetime.

She had discovered Bronte's well-thumbed book in the day room, the cover worn, but newer at that time than her re-published 1954 copy at home, she had found in her favourite Candle Lane book shop in Shrewsbury. The book brought some comfort and familiarity to her, coping with the new era she now found herself locked in. Jasmine would rarely lie awake for long, despite her own inner torment, glimpsing a return at quiet times.

She worried about Emily and thought about her escape plan constantly but could somehow never find the portal. There were no mirrors to be found anywhere in the workhouse. Her head ached, from daily exposure to noisy wards, as did her limbs and muscles, from the continuous grind, of heavy physical chores. At times, she couldn't stop thinking about Emily, listening to the gossip of a scandal in the Workhouse. Could the Master really have her in his clutches? Another female pauper, Sarah, previously alleged the Master to be her unborn baby's father. The enquiry led to the Directors labelling her a 'dissolute, drunken character,' accusing her of repeatedly allowing a male pauper to sleep with her and said the Master was entirely innocent.

The recommended change to stop this from happening again, was to end the system of management which could give rise to such complaints. Jasmine knew she had to free Emily and herself, if she could only win their complete trust, Beth, Helen and Joseph were key to it happening.

8

THE SPIKE

One morning, a stern looking woman wearing a pauper helper's badge from the casual ward, woke Jasmine, by shaking her shoulder. 'Get up, you're with us for a while,' she said not giving her a chance to respond as she turned to walk away.

Jasmine had a strong feeling of trepidation and was wary about following this woman without Beth knowing where she was going. Catching her up, she decided to approach her assertively, 'There must be some mistake? We need to inform Beth and check with her.' Badly prepared for the woman's response, she cried out as her hat was yanked down, hair falling loose from the day cap. Her head was then pulled back up, with a demonic like force, until their eyes were level and face to face, and she could feel the woman's fishy breath on her face.

'There's no question about this, I'm telling you where you're going Miss.' she spat out the words, venomously and roughly pushed Jasmine in front of her. 'Keep moving, I'll tell you when to turn off.'

Jasmine's mind was in turmoil, although she suspected that her asking questions about Emily had something to do with it. She had been warned the Workhouse Mistress had been making enquiries about her and advised to keep her head down. Moving along the corridor her legs shaking, she was instructed when to turn right, then to go down the steep stairs, and along a covered passageway to a separate block with an intrepid looking sign, 'CASUAL WARD.'

It appeared she was now to work over at the ward known locally as the 'dosshouse,' or the 'Spike.' This was always full of the 'the houseless poor,' mostly men and a few women, regarded as the 'lowest of the low.'

She pushed her hair back under her cap, aware she looked more like a dishevelled vagrant herself right now. On arrival, she met the paid worker in charge, known as 'Tramp Major,' who looked and sounded like a stereotypical Sergeant Major. He ruled with an iron rod, alongside a porter Mr Biggs, on the door, who reminded Jasmine of a modern-day bouncer, minus the charm. 'You'll address me as Mrs Lewis and we're on the female side,' snapped the woman. 'But as we ain't got any ladies, we see to the men on arrival.'

She followed the woman into the dormitory to checkout the men who shuffled through carrying their well-worn bedding, most contorted with hacking, phlegmy coughs, as their lungs met with the drop in temperature. The room had dull drab walls, with plaster rotting with age. All ventilation holes within reach had been stuffed with straw or rags by the men, as keeping warm to allow for sleep, seemed preferable to the foul-smelling effluvia. At night, there appeared to have been no privacy or dignity afforded them, only a few screens appeared to divide the draughty area.

Bedding in the form of rags and thin rugs were handed back, to be stacked and used again for the guests that night. The well used toilet was a bucket. Crouched over in the darkness during the night, it was dripping down the sides, and full to the brim with strong smelling, frothy urine. And then she saw the reason for her being brought in, as the woman nodded sharply at the bucket and ordered her to, 'fetch it out and empty it into the earth closet, in that out-building at the front.'

Jasmine heaved and covering her mouth and rolling up her sleeve, reluctantly obeyed. Holding it as far away from her body as she could, only made it heavier and some sloshed out just missing her. 'And you can come back and scrub that up, what you just spilt, on your hands and knees!' Mrs Lewis yelled. The walk to the closet was quite far and she thought about bolting down to the river or back towards the kitchen or Beth's ward. Something stopped her though, and she attended to the tasks assigned to her, whilst switching her senses off somehow.

Without even a drink or breakfast offered and Morning Prayer ignored, she was set more work to do. Deemed idle and disorderly, the pauper tramps had to work at 6 o'clock for four hours, in exchange for the one night's board and lodging they'd just had. If they refused to do so, they would be stopped from leaving, the authorities sent for and they'd be given one month's hard labour in prison.

All were compliant this morning, with seemingly only food on their minds, no doubt to warm them up she thought shivering. Jasmine was put next to serve breakfast, which was thin gruel, gone sour, as left overnight and re-boiled, with a stale wedge of bread and a pint of bitter, sugarless cocoa, slopped out into a tin billy.

Work for the day was promptly read out by order of command from the Tramp Major. Men had to break at least two hundredweight of stone that would then be sold as smaller pieces for roadmaking, in exchange for supper last night and bed and breakfast.

She was relieved there was no bone crushing today, the pounding of old bones for use as fertilizer. Her future studies had taught her it was eventually banned after a group of vagrants were found fighting over scraps of rotting meat left on some bones in the Andover Workhouse. It seemed some would eat anything; their brains were so starved, and bodies malnourished.

The things she could tell these people if she could only get them to believe she was from the future. Maybe one day she would be like Alexandria Alexis, who claimed to have travelled from 2025 and took New York society by storm in 1898, only to completely disappear on New Year's Eve one year later. Some had thought she was insane, others fawned over her. Jasmine hoped she had made it home and she would follow suit. But then, she remembered it had all supposedly been a hoax to entertain people. Alexandria was in fact Grace

Rawlinson, an English actress who had performed two seasons on Broadway, before returning home by ship. It was ironic that Jasmine's middle name was Grace, and she was supposedly 'insane,' and yet seemingly a real time traveller.

The casual wards also attracted hawkers, peddlers, drifters, and 'itinerant labour,' passing through town in search of work. Local lodging houses were often full, with rooms sleeping over twelve men at a time, so with 'no room at the inn,' and no money, they would descend upon the Workhouse.

There was always a steady movement of vagrants and vagabonds queuing at night, who would come to devour the meagre supper and take shelter from the cold or wet night in return for set work. Tramps were admitted at the mercy of the porter who guarded the door of the casual ward. Allocation of a bed for the night, was his decision, but if turned away, and found sleeping rough or 'panhandling,' as they called begging in these times, they could be prosecuted and receive two weeks hard labour. Viewed as wasteful, drunken, idle and debauched, separated from the decent and orderly destitute. Given rancid food, housed like animals in inferior dormitories and work rooms exposed to the elements.

Any women entering the casual ward, had to pick oakum; teasing out the fibres from old ropes with a large metal nail called a 'spike.' Jasmine thought this must be the origin of the workhouse casual wards' nickname. It was sold on to shipbuilders apparently, for mixing with tar to seal the lining of wooden vessels, hence the expression, 'money for old rope.'

When it came to dishing up the supper to the next arrivals, Jasmine was told to put some by for herself first, as she would miss dinner served in the main hall. The food on offer was bread and 'skilly,' a thin oatmeal soup. The bread was puffy and full of holes, but none of the men complained, even though it clearly did not weigh the regulation amount.

Their eyes lit up as another dish described as 'a real treat,' for them, was wheeled through in a trough, piled high with leftovers from hospital scraps. It had the appearance of slop, already contaminated by the hands and bodily fluids of the sick, with their contagious diseases. It consisted of stale bread, chunks of grease, animal fat, burnt skin, bones, and vegetable peelings.

Ravenously plunging their own dirty hands through the layers, they scrambled for the swill, eating like pigs, ploughing in deep, mixing it up, spitting back bones and jabbing each other aside. A pecking order was established, the 'top dog,' getting the lion share. Never sure when their next meal would come, they rolled up leftovers in dirty hankies that they then stuffed into pockets.

'Want some?' asked the female attendant as she eyed Jasmine with cruel contempt. Jasmine looked away, curbing the anger that had begun to well up inside her, making her want to grab this horrible woman by the hair and shove her smug, cruel face in the trough. Instead, she busied herself with a broom, making little impact on the grimy, rubbish strewn floor.

After eating, the men moved to a day room, one wall she noticed heavily decorated with religious texts and large printed sets of rules, threatening dire penalties to any 'casual,' who misconducted himself. They didn't stand a chance, with the strict regime in the Spike and the nature of the law outside the gates, they were very limited in choice in how they conducted their lives. If they were found wandering, sleeping rough, begging, or selling, with no means to self-support and unable to give a good account of themselves, they could be rounded up, 'to suffer such corporal and other punishment that the directors shall inflict.' At other times, when desperate with starvation and frost bite, there wasn't always shelter to be had, even here.

Conditions were such that the inmate's time here was so dire; they would only return if truly desperate and with their next meal never quite secure, it was all many could think of. Their transient lifestyles meant they frequented many different Workhouses over their lives and many would deliberately head for particular areas, which housed the better ones. They left the Spike, having literally 'earned their crust,' but still destitute and penniless. If they were to come by a penny or two, the Salvation Army and some lodging houses had facilities available, moderately better than the streets.

She remembered watching a documentary at university where the dire choices were described. A 'penny sit-up,' provided food and shelter, seated on a bench for the night, but you were not allowed to lie down or sleep. The 'two-penny hangover,' permitted the men to sit in rows on benches and lean their heads over a rope, strung across the room, where they could attempt to sleep. She remembered her own grandma saying, 'I'm so tired I could sleep on a clothes line,' and thought this was where the expression derived from.

A man known as a 'valet,' would break their slumber, at 5 o'clock in the morning, by cutting the rope. It was four whole pennies if you wished to lie down flat on your back to sleep, your bunk being a coffin shaped box made of wood, all measuring a standard 5'7' long, and lined with straw with a tarpaulin cover. She recalled seeing an old photo in a history book of a gloomy room in London, with rows of 300 bunks crammed together. The sleeping men resembling corpses awaiting internment following a major cholera epidemic or identification after a fatal disaster.

That evening, Jasmine's was tasked to oversee baths for the men in the Disinfecting Room, where new arrivals went. She soon discovered for these poor folks, the vermin really did creep and crawl on their skin. The two large baths were side by side, and they began the laborious job of filling them with boiled water carried in heavy kettles and then added buckets cold river water. Many new admissions were bathed in the same lukewarm bath, before it was changed. By the end, after a trail of despondent men had passed through, the water looked like weak mutton soup. Drying themselves with threadbare towels, already soaked from the repeated use of other men, her task was to take their clothes, tie them in a bundle and give them a nightshirt. Clothes were fumigated with Sulphur and a bed was allocated, already crawling with another guest's lice and bed bugs.

Trying desperately to show respect and treat the men with dignity was not so easy, when the intolerable sensory assault mounted by these unfortunates hit her full on. Dried grime and fresh sweat mixed with urine and solid excrement produced a toxic haze that hung over them. Their every movement wafted the added aroma of tobacco, rubbish, dirty roads, open drains, and unwashed clothes. Not eating regularly, meant their bodies were in a constant state of ketosis, that led to an even stronger smell of urine and bad breath, the latter not helped by zero dental care.

'Look at me!' one man said cheerfully after the soaking had removed several layers of black grime and uncovered an unfamiliar white skin, albeit covered in scratches and sores. Jasmine laughed with him, but the woman who addressed herself as Mrs Lewis scowled at her.

After the night porter returned with another two kettles of boiled water, the next man queuing to be bathed, stepped back, a look of terror on his face at the hot steam rising from the murky water. He stated he'd never had a bath before and trembled as he dipped his toes in and quickly lifted his foot out.

'It's ok I promise,' Jasmine reassured him kindly and noticed his mouth slowly curl upwards into a brave smile.

Standing on one leg, Mrs Lewis took advantage of his unstable position and grabbing him by the ear and a handful of hair, she forced him in, dunking him and holding him down, head under the water for a few seconds as he struggled in panic, arms flailing helplessly. As he resurfaced, gasping for air, the man spluttered and sobbed, his whole new experience of a bath now a trauma he would never likely overcome.

As he clambered out, a broken man, Jasmine wanted to shout at this evil woman, punch her, or throw her in the water and hold her down. But she would bite her lip and bide her time. Until she found a way home, she would try to make a difference here, she owed it to these people.

'You've got a lot to learn my dear.' Mrs Lewis said, spitting out the words and foaming at the mouth with anger, as she flung a wet towel at the poor man. Jasmine just smiled which seemed to unnerve the woman, whose whole demeanour changed, until she saw the real reason, as the woman's eyes appeared wide and fixed on something behind Jasmine. She slowly turned around, half expecting the Master, to see who was stood behind her.

'I've come to take Jasmine back where she is needed with me.' It was Beth speaking and Helen beside her. Reinforcements had arrived for Jasmine and she could see there would be no arguing, as Mrs Lewis muttered something in agreement that she could be excused, trying desperately to avoid eye contact with the two women. Jasmine was ecstatic, but Beth and Helen quietly bid her to follow them and walk away, keeping a low profile, back to the main building. 'Go with Helen for sustenance and join me shortly.' Beth whispered, taking the stairs without a backward glance, to the Lunacy Ward.

Once in the back kitchen, Jasmine found herself encapsulated in the warmth of the cosy surroundings, which made her feel safe and comforted once again. Seconds later, Joseph frantically came through the back-door exclaiming, 'Oh thank God!' his expression one of relief at seeing Jasmine but also Helen's safe return. They hugged, and Helen gestured for Jasmine to join them, enfolding her in their embrace.

'And Beth?' he questioned, 'Yes fine, back upstairs.' Helen said briefly. Realising her 'rescue' from the Spike, had not been without danger or as easy as it had appeared, Jasmine waited until the ritual of making a pot of tea and cutting thick slices of honey bread had pacified them all enough to speak.

'How did you make her release me?' Jasmine said directly to Helen, remembering the fear in the evil Mrs Lewis's eyes. Her new friends locked eyes as if making some unspoken agreement and Helen turned to face Jasmine, taking her hand in her own.

'We used a spell.' She smiled. Jasmine beamed, she believed her and was full of intrigue, and sure she would be a part of all this soon.

9

RULES & RIGHT-ANGLED TRIANGLES

For a brief time, Jasmine's life returned to normal, whatever 'normal' was these days. She found her job on 'Luna Ward,' as opposed to Lunacy as they now referred to it, hard work but immensely rewarding. Beth was very receptive to trying many of the new techniques Jasmine suggested, which were based on what she had seen as a patient herself and the subtle changes had good effects. Without the added, future tranquillisers though, some patients were often too disturbed to reach at all and Beth focused her efforts here on promoting calm, offering dignity and respecting their needs, this not being as well achieved on Elsie's shift.

Beth swore by a tincture of tranquilising herbs and with Helen's help, they produced a lemon balm fermented in alcohol. Lavender sprigs were inserted in pillows and a small number of hops in chamomile herbal tea had a relaxing effect. At times, when things started to get dangerously scary, after a patient became very disturbed and lost control, Jasmine noticed Beth would whisper something that she then seemed to repeat over and over, at the same time making small circular movements with her hands.

Not long after this, the patient, who could not have heard her and was usually facing away, would stop, turn to look briefly at Beth and resume calm and collected behaviour. Although Beth was very open, she dismissed this when Jasmine asked saying, 'I was praying.' But Jasmine knew Beth was definitely not religious and wondered just how much like Helen and Joseph she actually was. Jasmine pined for her mother, and often thought about how much a modern-day nurse would be able to show Beth if she was here, she missed her so much, her heart ached at times. She pondered whether her family ever wondered where she was or if time had time stood still. Would she always be stuck here? Trapped in a time loop that kept moving without the population changing or aging.

As if this wasn't strange enough, odd things continued to happen alongside, the strangest phenomenon still being the silence and darkness that descended behind her when she walked away, say from a room. Yet upon glancing backwards, everything continued as normal. It was as if this world only really existed whilst she was directly present or looking upon it.

Payment of one-sixth part of their week's work was made to all, except in cases of misconduct. Money was withheld and punishments administered to inmates who profanely cursed or swore, who appeared to be 'in liquor,' who were 'refractory or disobedient,' those who 'pretend sickness,' in a bid to excuse or avoid working, those who 'destroyed or spoiled materials or implements,' or acted in a 'lewd, immoral, or disorderly behaviour' (Report by Eden 1797 survey of the poor in England). Rules were aimed at 'promoting honesty, sobriety, diligence, cleanliness and decency.' Punishments ranged from loss of 1/6 of wages, to solitary confinement in the refractory or 'dungeon' as known, the stocks, the 'brank's bridle,' to corporal punishment.

Out in the yard in the airing courts, conversation was often made in whispers, in case 'the walls had ears,' and was often centred on complaints about the harshness of workhouse life. Talk covered the poor quality, meagre amounts of food, the cruel and oppressive rules and ill treatment by some attendants. Downcast faces, moping around, their heads filled with wretched memories, reflections of sad times, lost opportunities, loss of freedom and the break-up of the family home. On Sabbath day, many paupers would spend free time lounging on benches or lay out on the floor in the hall or yard in the summer, on the 'sunny side,' by the high wall.

There was compulsory Divine Service in the morning and after supper, where Preachers descended upon the inmates. There was no escape from their moral advice, often proclaimed in a pompously, self-righteous way, with no real help or understanding.

Other than the religious manuscripts left by the do-gooders, tatty novels with missing pages, an occasional copy of the local Chronicle and a bible were the only reading materials available to the many paupers. She quickly learned many were illiterate and had no opportunity of changing this.

After St. Chad's Church had collapsed in 1788, following attempts to expand the crypt which compromised the structural integrity of the tower above; it was rebuilt just four years later as a large neo-classical round church in a new location close to the Quarry Park. The circular design, was a clerical error made in minuting the meeting, where the planning decision was made for a rectangular 'Gothic edifice.'

Parishes complained about the cost of subsidising the workhouse with their own high costs to repair and rebuild places of worship. St Chads complained that they paid half of their budget to support what they described as, 'paupers and bastards and other parasites,' a very Christian response Jasmine had thought.

Correspondence often took place in free time on Sundays, when a few inmates would queue to use the solitary ink pot and pen to write letters. One day a month family visits were allowed, but under strict supervision, as in a prison. Expression of feelings that survived the disintegration of family life had to be suppressed, but things sometimes got over-heated.

On the opposite end, resentment, blame, and ill feeling were equally displayed, by desperate people in the absence of future hope. This was the only contact many had with the outside world. The high walls in the yard permitted only muffled sounds, smells and smoke to enter, there was no gravel, grass or even a tree or visiting bird or mammal, to relieve the monotony felt in the confines of their surroundings.

Jasmine was given a strange look and her letter put to one side, when she wrote to her parents to her future address. Her home in Belle Vue was an old property but would not yet be built for another half century.

With so little food to go round and not exactly a choice of menu, it was eventually picked up by some folks in the Workhouse, that Jasmine was a 'Pythagorean,' the pre-1847 name for the 'abstainers of the eating of the flesh of animals, fish, and fowl.' She had not heard of this title, but Beth was proving to be the fountain of all knowledge and told her it was named after the Greek Philosopher Pythagoras (580 BCE), well known for his contributions to mathematics but barely known as an early non-meat eater.

'Oh, he was a vegetarian,' Jasmine had stated, which was a new word to Beth that Jasmine was able to share with her which made her look puzzled. Pythagoras's belief in the 'transmigration of souls,' with the possibility of eating an ancestor or being reincarnated as say a pig and getting slaughtered for bacon, had influenced his eating habits.

Beth said he also objected to the many wild animals, murdered at the hands of gladiators in the name of sport and spectacle, believing slaughtering animals brutalised the human soul. Instead, he was an eater of fruits, grains, nuts, and other products of the vegetable kingdom. It made her smile that she now knew more about Pythagoras's meat-eating views thanks to Beth, than his theory on right angled triangles.

There was a family cookery book, 'Golden Rule Cookbook: Six Hundred Recipes for Meatless Dishes' (1907) by Maud Freshel, passed down on her mother's side, over several generations with a quote that Jasmine had never forgotten. 'The true vegetarian will not be seen or adorned, by any of the reaping's from a dead body, whether they be feathers or furs, for these have no beauty in the sight of those who see them in thought, dripping with blood from which they can never be truly cleansed.'

Her grandmother had been the first Vegan she had known, objecting strongly to the slaughtering on poultry farms of the superfluous male birds and the hens as they become unprofitable layers. She voiced a similar humane objection that applied to the use of cow's milk by man. The calves are deprived of part of their natural food, the deficiency being perhaps made up by unnatural farinaceous milk substitutes.

Many of the calves, especially the new born bull calves, were torn away from their mothers, still covered in their birthing fluid, without even one feed and killed, thus leaving all the milk for human use. When cows cease to yield sufficient milk, they too are slaughtered. In 1905 the Vegetarian Society published A.W. Duncan's 'The Chemistry of Food and Nutrition,' a well-thumbed book in her grandmother's collection, now sat on Jasmine's bookshelf.

Despite Jasmine's own views, fresh fruit and vegetables were still thought to breed worms in this era, and perhaps they did, because night soil was still used as fertilizer. Potatoes were the only vegetable that was felt to be appropriate for children and a working-class child's diet was based on bread, potatoes, and water.

With children's diet so restricted in quality and quantity, diseases of deprivation and tooth loss were rife and many of the working class did not have the teeth to chew dark bread. Jasmine had seen pictures of the damage of Rickets, a disease caused by phosphorus and calcium deficiency, that left children with bowed or knock-kneed legs; but she was also seeing the end result, of adults with small, painful, misshapen frames. Rickety girls grew into women with narrow, boyish hips that led to difficult childbirth and high mortality rates.

Struggling to eat a balanced diet here whilst remaining vegetarian was impossible at times, but Beth must have had a word with Helen, as one day she was sent down to the kitchen to see her. Jasmine loved their time together, Helen always welcomed her with the love of a sister, and the secrecy of a best friend, but she was confused at times as to whether the intimacy she perceived was just that and the infatuation one-sided, on her part.

'Why didn't you tell me you don't like to eat meat?' Helen scolded Jasmine, whilst giving her a huge smile and hugging her tightly. Jasmine lingered in her warm embrace, briefly nuzzling into her neck before pulling away sharply, as she realised how familiar she was being. She stepped back, rubbing her eyes to conceal her embarrassment.

'Sorry, I'm so tired and missing my mother,' she said not able to meet Helen's eyes, but instantly regretting her words, comparing their encounter to maternal affection.

Helen paused, making Jasmine peep through her fingers to gage her response. She seemed to smile knowingly, even gladly, but Jasmine was still confused and regretting showing her true feelings without obvious reciprocation.

'Come,' Helen said assertively and reaching for her hand, led the way through the back-kitchen door down to the vegetable garden. 'I can make you vegetable juice drinks with spinach, cucumber and celery and maybe one with apples, carrots and parsley.'

'Now you actually sound like my mother!' Jasmine injected wittily and they both laughed as Helen linked her arm, clasping her hand again. 'Come, lets sit together under the weeping willow and talk some more, about you and I.' She half whispered, smiling intensely at Jasmine who suddenly felt very shy and naive, but filled with anticipation.

The tree was at the furthest part of the garden, behind the greenhouses, looking down to the river but hidden from view. It was a warm, sunny day and Jasmine was glad to sit in the shade of the branches after the heat of the house. Helen surprised her, pulling out a flask of home brewed, sparkling elderflower wine from her bodice. They took turns to gulp it down laughing as the aromatic bubbles sprayed up into the air, tickling their noses. Any awkwardness was diminished as they resumed their sisterly friendship, but there was 'an elephant in the room.'

Jasmine decided to speak first, 'I don't really think of you as my mum at all.'

'I should think not, we're the same age!' Helen laughed, but beyond the twinkle in her eyes, she studied Jasmine with a deeper, more serious, gaze.

The spell of the intense eye contact was broken when a small, but annoying fly buzzed into Jasmine's eye, and seeing her trying to remove it, Helen leant over to help. Both suddenly became aware of the effect of their very close proximity and it was as if an electricity was passing between them. Jasmine had never felt anything like this before, always repressing her feelings in past near encounters with other females, in case she had read it wrong. She had never felt anything sexual with the opposite sex, but had not let on, just avoided it and made excuses with any male admirers who made a move on her.

Helen remained close, after gently using the corner of her hanky to wipe her eyelid and move the annoying culprit to the corner and out. They both laughed, Jasmine nervously, unsure of the next move but Helen seemed confident and experienced and tenderly brushed Jasmine's hair away from her face and stroked her cheek, tracing her finger around Jasmines lips. With their eyes once again fixed on each other, Jasmine felt the heat radiate in her cheeks and instinctively tilted her head as Helen moved in slowly, their lips brushing, which awakened a long suppressed, sensuous desire and powerful, physical arousal. She felt a giddiness, as if floating in another universe as their lips locked and tongues touched, slowly exploring each other's mouths, the intensity and urgency gradually increasing as their excitement rose.

Helen's response to her own insistent mouth sent tremors along her nerves and she moaned, feeling hot and breathy. It was as if they were seeking an intimate fusion, a timeless, passionate moment, where they shared one breath, wrapped in their own magic, before the outside world inevitably pulled them apart.

Undisturbed, hidden amongst the wide spread of graceful, arching branches, they were able to lie for a while in an intimate embrace in the long grass under the Willow. The warm sun filtered scattering light through the trees drooping boughs and elongated leaves, and the soft breeze made a rustling, whispering sound bending the branches effortlessly. The beauty and elegance of the Willow evoked feelings and emotions that changed from melancholy to magic to empowerment.

Helen told her they sometimes harnessed salicylic acid from the bark and milky sap to treat headaches and fever. Jasmine was filled with wonder at medicine even from Willow trees, everything she was encountering here held enchantment and mystery. They lay together talking more about how to get extra vegetables, eggs and potatoes into Jasmine's diet as a 'Pythagorean, or vegetarian,' but their passionate encounter had led to an intimacy and closeness that they both felt so comfortable with, it would be difficult to keep secret and impossible not to repeat. The thing she was encountering here held enchantment and mystery.

10

LAUNCHED INTO ETERNITY

One night, lying exhausted in her bed, unusually waiting for sleep to come, Jasmine found her mind wandering, as if trying to work something out. She worried for a second that her illness was coming back. And then it hit her; 1784 was the last year Emily had given her and had been confirmed by others since and it was definitely the year date on the odd newspaper she had picked up in the day room.

So how had she got hold of a book by a Bronte sister, not yet born for another thirty-two years? Had another 50 years gone by? She was sat bolt upright, eyes wide and whilst most were snoring, one woman, Liza whispered, 'What's up?' Doing the maths quickly, Jasmine asked 'Is the year 1834?' Quiet laughter was followed by 'Of course! For one so shrewd Jasmine you're so forgetful!'

Lying back, her heart beating loudly in her chest, she closed her eyes and smiled to herself, she was now into the next century, having survived the 1700's, and although she appeared no older, she hoped it meant she was closer to going home. Another pauper inmate, Sally, had given her a woven purse that she had made in the spinning room. Jasmine kept it safe on her person most times or hidden away from the temptation of others when sleeping. She also had a warm shawl that Beth from the Luna ward had given to her. She wore this when able to get outside, taking great care of it, especially when she was involved in pumping water from the River Severn.

Her prize possession however, was a silver green-eyed owl pendant, sat on a crescent moon that Helen had given her. She had been quite taken aback by the owl initially, the strong association with her brother's death, but Helen reassured her.

'The owl is a symbol of Athene, goddess of foresight and knowledge. Also, the symbol of the female and fertility, with the moon's cycles of renewal. It will protect and bring you greater wisdom, insight, and help you see the whole truth.'

It made sense to Jasmine and as she could not wear it on display at the Workhouse, she threaded it on a string and tied it around her waist.

Although even the able-bodied paupers owned few possessions, most things were sold off before they arrived, the dormitory often felt overcrowded, with the women very protective over their precious links with the outside world. Worthless objects in material value, but priceless now, held memories of better times gone by, or played a comforting role in their empty, desolate lives. Paranoia in the layman's sense, over ownership of space to keep treasured memorabilia close, led to angry accusations and physical fights at times.

A rather strange woman named Rhona, who virtually slept clutching on to her mountain of sentimental, but worthless possessions on her top bunk, leapt down from her bed one night following the crashing on the hard floor of a clay ornament. It clearly shattered on impact judging by the clatter, into what sounded like a thousand pieces.

Her immediate sobbing and high-pitched cries were incessant, and when her bunk mate Jean attempted to comfort her, Rhona lashed out viciously, causing her consoler to fall awkwardly, banging her head loudly. The full moon was shining brightly through the barred window, the only available light with all candles snuffed out hours earlier, but a stream of dark liquid could be seen to run away from under the head of Jean's still body.

Although in obvious shock Rhona, as with the others, who had remained motionless for what seemed like an eternity, taking in the surreal scene before her, started to pound her fists into Jean's face and proceeded to deliberately bang her head into the ground repeatedly.

The disturbance caused such a commotion throughout the long room, with women screaming and either crowding around trying to stop Rhona's madness, or hiding away, back in the recesses of the dark dorm; as far away as the confinement of the walls would allow for.

And then the banging started, as if at a large sporting event, it spread across the room with multiple voices calling help in unison. Something similar had happened before Jasmine thought, lying close enough to see and hear everything, but cowering in her bunk, before pulling the musty blanket over her head, to escape the horror in plain sight.

The racket made by the women, got the attention of an attendant, who slept in separate quarters nearby. There was a hushed silence as heads turned at the sound of the turning of a key in the huge oak door at the far end, and the attendant cautiously entered, carrying a lantern. Within seconds, the woman turned tail to get assistance and half an hour later, Jean's battered, bloody body, was taken away by an undertaker, as was Rhona, who was handled with less care and harsh words by two Police Constables.

The town's Sheriff attended several hours later, barely a wink of sleep achieved by any of the women and dawn still not fully broken. Jasmine had lain shuddering throughout the early hours, despite the stagnant warm air and the coal dust that filled her lungs, she felt icy cold and a fear that was palpable. All women were questioned individually by the Sheriff and work started late that day, with breakfast forgotten.

Rumours over the outcome of the investigation spread like wildfire in the dorm over the next few nights, the subject banned with threatening consequences during the daytime. Jasmine did talk quietly to Nurse Beth about it on the Luna wards, whilst making beds. Beth was a calming influence on Jasmine, and did not have a liking for idle gossip, preferring to wait for facts rather than 'make mischief.'

The lunacy inmates were oblivious to the incident, either too far gone, or so far removed to have any knowledge or opinions on the dire situation. Jasmine wondered if Rhona was detained in the prison she had been held in, prior to being transported here, but then remembered a whole century had passed since that journey, which had only strengthened her belief that she was in some kind of historical time warp that would lead to the future.

It was the lecherous Workhouse Master with his sneering wife present, who finally addressed the women that evening after supper time. The two empty bunks of poor Jean and Rhona had been quickly filled by two more desperate women, but the blood stain was still visible if you knew where and what it was, despite vigorous scrubbing and the many tears fallen upon it.

Ironically, all the precious bric-a-brac items that Rhona had treasured so much, had been quickly gathered together and thrown away. They were informed she had been found guilty of the Capital Offence of Murder and had been tried by a professional judge at the Assizes court. Jasmine knew from her studies Rhona's trial would have been quick, solicitors were rarely present, and prosecutors, judges, and jurors exercised their own judgement in how they interpreted the law, with none of the safeguards that protect against wrongful convictions that exist today.

It was considered an advantage, if the all-male jurors had prior knowledge of the background to a trial, and any information they had on the community, particularly of its more disreputable members, which would then be used when making major decisions. Grand jurors for the Assizes were ideally, 'the best figures in the county.'

A local paper the Shrewsbury Chronicle, reported some details of the Workhouse Trial.

'The well-known elderly Judge, the Right Honourable Peter Hodges suffered from gout and was in pain most of the time and very grumpy.

The Prosecutor Adam Wright was a religious man, who felt that crimes against God and humanity should be punished severely. Members of the grand jury consisted of middle ranking professionals, including merchants, wealthy tradesmen, and artisans.'

The judge had apparently placed on his head the 'black cap,' a nine-inch square of black silk, and proceeded to pronounce the sentence.

'Rhona Evans, you stand convicted of the horrid and heinous crime of murdering Jean Taylor, from the Workhouse where you resided. This Court doth judge that you be taken back to the place from whence you came, and there to be fed on bread and water till Wednesday next, when you are to be taken to the common place of execution, and there hanged by the neck until you are dead. After which your body is to be publicly dissected and anatomised, agreeable to an Act of Parliament in that case made and provided; and may God Almighty have mercy on your soul.'

As was standard practice, a local journalist Thomas Aston had attempted to visit the condemned Rhona to pen her last words. These would have then been printed as handbills and sold on the morning of the execution for 1d. However, it emerged Rhona had tried to take her own life the night before but had been revived enough by the prison doctor to meet her punishment.

Last words of another convicted prisoner Ann Harris Shrewsbury 1828.

Hark the solemn prison bell

That tolls my destiny to tell

Hark distant feet they come to tell

That I am called to die

Joseph had managed to get hold of a newspaper that reported on the execution the following day.

'The three condemned that day, including Workhouse murderer Rhona Evans, were greeted by a large unruly crowd of over six thousand, who had come to watch the spectacle. It was deemed an excellent day out. The carts were each backed under one of the three beams of the gallows and the prisoners were positioned at the tail end of the cart and tied up to the beam with only a small amount of slack left in the rope. The Ordinary prayed with them and then the hangman, who was dressed in an oilskin hat and smock frocked coat pulled white night caps over their faces. When everything was ready the horses were whipped away, leaving the prisoners suspended as they were, 'launched into eternity.' They only had a few inches of drop and thus writhed in agony for some moments.

Rhona Evans apparently struggled violently for over a minute, her body convulsed, and stomach heaved strongly twice. Relatives pulled on the prisoners' legs to hasten their end, but there was no-one there for Rhona, other than those jeering, so the hangman did the same for her, putting her out of her misery.

Receiving his fee of 10 guineas plus travelling expenses he was also entitled to keep all the hanged prisoner's clothes which he could wear or sell. In the case of these three destitutes, ragged clothes ruined by body fluids, from languishing in gaol and losing control of bladders and bowels and their guts due to fear, they were left fully clothed, dignity at least partially intact. Today, no bodies were left to rot and fall to pieces; all had been sentenced to medical dissection, so therefore cut down and dropped heavily into the cart that had reappeared and taken to the Royal Salop Infirmary.'

From what Jasmine could work out the prison was in the area of Ditherington, near the Flax Mill and the gallows, on what was now the patch of grass at Old Heath where the shops in Mount Pleasant would be next to in the future. She knew 'dither,' meant to 'shake and quake,' and described the fear in the condemned prisoners, taken down that route to meet their maker.

It emerged that the precious, broken clay ornament, had been made for Rhona by her seven-year-old child Sarah, who had died of Cholera as had her husband, Michael. Left alone in the world, Rhona had fallen on hard times and rather than prostituting herself, she had entered the workhouse. One of her dearest but most doleful items, almost discarded after her arrest, was the post-mortem photograph, taken of her dead child and spouse, who had passed away within an hour of each other. Before Rhona had arranged their pauper burial, with one simple unmarked grave, and a bunch of wildflowers, watered and wilted by her salty tears; she had spent her last penny on the photograph. A final, lasting depiction of what had been her whole world, the only photographic evidence existing that they had ever lived, which was so common in those days.

Stella, who spotted it whilst cleaning the area, passed it onto Beth, via Victoria, who had access to the outside world, and could get it to her in the prison. She was said to have had it tucked down her top, close to her heart when she swung. Fortunately, there was no macabre photographic image of Rhona in her final death dance, but likely ones taken after her execution by the surgeon or anatomist.

11

REBELLION

One day Emily reappeared, a shadow of her former self and as her story became known, it took all of Jasmine's strength to stop herself from attacking the Workhouse Master each time she laid eyes on him. Beth had been away for a few days visiting her sick aunt, but she'd overheard Eddie the porter saying she had also been meeting with Helen and Joseph in the back kitchen.

She had always suspected they knew more about Emily but wondered now if they had been somehow working covertly to secure her release and could not risk speaking about it. It was so busy without Beth; Jasmine could not slip away to see Helen. Despite the exhaustion of her work, Jasmine began to struggle to sleep again, her head becoming full of unwanted images of her friend's ordeal and the anger she carried towards the perpetrator. The Master had abused his power and authority over Emily who was so vulnerable, for his own amusement and satisfaction. He had also spotted Jasmine running errands in the corridors on more than one occasion and stopped and leered at her like she was a piece of meat.

Emily's previous enthusiastic chatter was now reduced to one-word replies, her pitch low and flat and she had somehow lost the light in her eyes. Despite her harsh existence, she had been bright and cheerful before. Although it was such a happy relief to see Emily after she was discarded for a 'younger model,' it soon became apparent how much psychological damage had been done.

Two days after her release, Emily started shaking, developing quite a coarse tremor, which meant she couldn't hold a cup herself without spilling the contents. Beth had immediately returned and whipped Emily away from prying eyes, to provide around the clock care on

Luna Ward, where she installed Jasmine's help.

Beth had to know Emily, but at the same time there appeared to be no recognition. It impressed Jasmine how much understanding Beth appeared to have for her condition, in a century where mental illness meant being locked away and trauma was barely recognised or hidden, swept under the carpet.

Although she had not said very much from the onset, Emily began to struggle to speak at all, turning her head away from food and drink and alternating between audible distress to a trance like state, staring up at the ceiling blankly. Emily seemed to re-experience her ordeal daily, if only in her mind's eye and her emotional pain was blatantly obvious to all who saw her. She relived the abuse when awake, haunted by distressing memories and again, via nightmares when she collapsed, exhausted into troubled sleep.

It was what Jasmine's mother Jacquie would call an acute stress reaction leading to Post Traumatic Stress Disorder in the modern world, but Jasmine felt even with her own layman's knowledge on the disorder, she could potentially help her friend. She would draw on what she had read, experienced and seen in the modern world. It took several weeks of full physical nursing care, combined with patience, reassurance and understanding, just to help Emily relax. She began to feel less anxious and able to feel safe enough to trust them, which led to a visible improvement.

Emily had not remembered Jasmine at all on her return. Although the pair had only met briefly before Emily was separated and taken by the Master, she had made a huge impact on Jasmine. She had made it her mission to try and find her and then warn others, seeing the damage done and how Emily was almost unrecognisable, an empty, traumatised shell of the person she once was. Emily did not appear to know anyone else either, a dissociative amnesia enveloping her, despite Jasmine being sure the others knew of her from concerned looks exchanged between them when she first mentioned Emily. They had promised to help find her and Helen had urged Jasmine to let them do so quietly, without mentioning her too much for Emily's safety.

There were similarities between how Emily presented now to how Jasmine recalled herself, when she was in Shelton Hospital. Memories of that time were now unlocking, unconsciously repressed due to the high level of distress attached. Something they had both had in common.

Jasmine did something that a night nurse named Jane had done for her, she just sat and spoke gently to her about anything and everything, in a soothing, reassuring voice. In the day, attempts at therapy with Jasmine had sometimes felt like interrogation, she had truly believed she was detained in a prison, on a life sentence for allowing her brother to die. She knew any attempts to get through to Emily would work better if perceived as a distraction and not to illicit painful information from her. So, she told her stories from the future, which were fanciful fairy tails to Emily's ears, and dangerously remote from reality to anyone else listening, who might think her mad. Loving her history, and wanting Emily to feel empowered following her suffering, Jasmine told her the story of the Suffragettes and the subsequent women's vote. She talked about the impact of the feminist movement in bringing about reforms in family life, wages, work, and educational opportunities.

She told her about her grandmother's sister who was involved with Greenpeace and how other women's political activism brought about changes including reproductive rights, childcare provision for wage-earning women, laws against rape and sexual harassment, and consciousness-raising about women's oppression.

Beth was often close by and overheard her at times, she would either respond by smiling, frowning, or looking in amazement, and would ask her more about some subjects when they were alone, like the stories of the suffragettes and votes for women, which Beth seemed intrigued by. She never once questioned the validity of Jasmine's stories, nor saw them as imaginary tails. Her occasional frowns were only if she considered the subject matter too much for the recuperating Emily, whose head was still in another place at times. Slowly Emily responded, her far away frightened eyes and distressed expression relaxing somewhat, as she began to build trust in her narrator. Her attention began slowly to focus on Jasmine, eyes widening or crinkling into a subtle smile and her lips slightly curling up at the corners.

Soon she was interacting fully, asking questions and Jasmine told her all about her life, and how she found herself spiralled into the past. She never mentioned her mental health problems or Joe's death though, just amusing and happy anecdotes to make Emily laugh. Coaxing her to function and live again, they distracted her, occupying her mind with diversions. It was then that she started to produce new, positive thoughts and happier memories, which strengthened her recovery and helped her move forward.

Laughter was also one of the best medicines and Emily responded well to Beth and Jasmine's antics and 'gallows' humour. They had no choice but to laugh or else cry, making light of the serious situation, where they were powerless to undo what had been done. But this helped them all get through each day. It was also the experience Jasmine had received from one of her favourite hospital nurse's Lisa, who had gently coerced her out of her own trauma and psychosis into reality and living in the real world again. At least it had worked, until she had relapsed.

Jasmine was over eighteen when she was sectioned, so had ensured her confidentiality was respected and information withheld as requested from her parents once she had mental capacity to make some decisions. When she disclosed to her nurses Jane and Lisa and social worker Angela, that her brother's death was all her fault, she was met with surprise and shaking heads. They had not seen it that way at all and spent hours gently challenging her negative beliefs. Family therapy had been suggested, which Jasmine vehemently declined but then a meeting including her parents was reluctantly arranged, but Jasmine was too guarded and paranoid to disclose anything. It wasn't that she didn't want to admit that her brother's death was all her fault to her family, it was because the 'voices,' had told her not to. They whispered to her and each other, that other family members would come to a 'grisly end,' if she did and it would be her fault yet again.

Beth was secretly astonished and had learned a lot from her young assistants' apparent skill in nursing Emily back to good health. Beth still regularly pondered where this strange girl Jasmine had come from and had found no records when she decided to discreetly investigate.

Jasmine had been sent to the Workhouse Lunatic Asylum from the prison, but had no memory of what she had been originally apprehended for and again the report from the gaol had not come with her, unlike the other women. On several occasions, she had quietly insisted she was from the 'future,' but Beth had always discouraged this talk, believing it would be viewed as part of her 'madness,' that needed to be pushed aside. Most of the time Beth could see Jasmine was lucid although far from 'normal,' which wasn't a bad thing. Beth had an inkling though that Jasmine might be like someone else she once knew who had said similar strange things before disappearing...

It worked both ways, Beth had also surprised Jasmine, her skills and manner in calming Emily and in fact the whole ward was astounding, given the lack of treatment for mental illness in these times and next to no recovery rates. Sometimes Jasmine heard Beth whispering to Emily and other patients, and the calming affect was almost instantaneous, like a drug or hypnotism, but Beth just said she was just reassuring them to help them relax. She had seen Beth get frustrated with the doctor at times when he visited, but when he disagreed with her, she would face him and shake her head slowly looking into his eyes. He then appeared to suddenly retract his comments, changing his mind, and came around to her way of thinking, which got far better results.

Alternatively, Beth would sometimes nod and agree with one

particularly arrogant doctor but do her own thing once he had left. Helen and Joseph sent up tinctures and lotions that calmed and comforted, if not cured the patients and Jasmine had started to help them make them. She noticed that even in the early days, they individually sought Emily out, rather than just dropping off the healing potions, showing concern and compassion towards her, but sometimes, it was as if they knew her well.

Nursing Emily back to health, Jasmine learned of her love of children and deep sadness, having cared for a baby whom she said had died of Smallpox. Beth had looked away, her face seemingly pained, but said nothing. Not long after, Beth made a few enquiries that led to a job for Emily to look forward to, as a pauper's assistant in the nursery at the schoolhouse. By now, six months pregnant and unmarried, Emily was made to wear a red dress by the corporation, the uniform of shame and humiliation for unmarried mothers.

She never spoke of the Master who had raped and impregnated her, even though it was common knowledge for fear of recrimination, suspecting severe punishment and being cast out. Remarkably, Beth had uncovered the pregnancy very early on, even before the morning sickness began. As her pregnancy progressed, Emily gained lots of support in many forms from the pauper women and even some female attendants. Emily began to look forward to welcoming her innocent child into the world.

The women sewed, knitted, and passed down baby garments and tiny, warm blankets. With all the knowledge and promise of support and help, which a mother would usually provide, Emily was given the strength and determination to overcome her own ordeal for the sake of her unborn child. Although the trauma she tried to hide was never far from the surface of her mind and could be seen in her eyes at times, lurking in the shadows and lying-in wait.

Jasmine naively thought justice could be achieved if the truth was only known, she underestimated the abuse of power within the establishment. She had made it her vocation to warn and protect other young women to stay clear of the Workhouse Master and avoid all eye contact. In fact, to avoid being anywhere within his vicinity, if possible, but she declined to follow her own advice. Beth warned her to be careful, in case word got around about what she was doing.

Beth had an anger in her eyes when they mentioned Emily's treatment and predicament, but in front of her, she was always reassuring and calm. She met with Helen and Joseph regularly to go over supplies needed, but they whispered and seemed to plot at times, telling Jasmine She was risking so much already, warning others and to leave certain things to them. Jasmine managed to steal more precious time with Helen alone, but although they would laugh and talk about almost anything, there was a mysterious barrier when it came to discovering some of the secrets her friends seemed to hold.

But Jasmine's ignored their warnings and her anger and determination, now made it possible for her to almost confront him without words or fear. This demeanour being what she thought was her 'protection,' as she believed he only selected the most vulnerable young women, knowing her could get away with it. He made no more advances towards Jasmine, but she knew he was aware of her presence and would have detected the hate she carried with her towards him. This appeared to make him feel uncomfortable and he frequently turned, shiftily, away from her glare while she tried to maintain eye contact.

12

THE SHOW

Life had become an established routine, with each day very much like the one before. Apart from Sundays, when Jasmine had started to earn enough privileges to go outside of the house for short periods. She had to be careful, as wearing the clothes of a workhouse inmate, she was often looked down upon by women and ogled by some men. Beth's shawl helped her hide her pauper's uniform and sometimes she would lend her a dress. As she found her way around the Workhouse, Jasmine searched for a way home. She knew now that it had to be via a portal as had appeared through her mirror, but could not find one anywhere in the pauper areas. She asked Victoria to show her again the rooms and areas not permitted to paupers, but they were mostly locked or in use when she had time to check.

On Shrewsbury Show Day, Beth got cover for a few hours and agreed to take Jasmine whom she had grown very fond of. She was constantly amazed by Jasmine's naivety and lack of knowledge of certain things, most of the young inmates had old heads on their shoulders because of their hard lives and were street wise. Yet some of Jasmine's ideas and methods on the wards were quite

Revolutionary and had improved things for everyone. Jasmine had found it hard to contain her excitement at the prospect of a day out and having been careful with her earnings she saved in her woven purse, she had some money to spend and intended to enjoy herself.

She had gone with her mother in 2004, when opera singer Katherine Jenkins sang to the crowds, and wondered how different it would be this time. In the future it would be 'Shrewsbury Flower Show,' with over 300,000 flowers on display, from Alstroemeria to Zantedeschia, as well as celebrity gardeners, TV chefs, arena events, headline music acts and show stopping fireworks.

Today Jasmine would literally witness and experience history in the making, which in her time, was already made, the future unknown to the crowds today. Beth had warned her to keep her 'chatter,' about her being from another time to herself; or she would be having Jasmine as a patient after all, instead of a helper.

The day before, Beth had presented Jasmine with a package wrapped in brown paper. She was told not to open it until the morning of the Shrewsbury Show and had struggled to sleep with excitement the night before, keeping it hidden under her sheet in case it was stolen. She had been told to not make a fuss about going to the show, for fear of questions or a jealous uproar from some of the other women. Those working in essential services at The Workhouse, had some free time on a Sunday, but tended to do what would now be termed 'split-shifts,' due to essential cleaning, caring and meal provision roles.

Jasmine had told Emily and Nadia had tried to arrange cover, but it was not possible, and she didn't seem to mind as she loved caring for the pauper children and orphans. Nadia told Jasmine she'd been many times before, and of ways to 'sneak in,' without a ticket. Helen could not come which would have been perfect, but was excited for Jasmine and made her promise to tell her everything on return.

The morning of the show, Jasmine quietly and slowly opened the parcel whilst it was still half under her covers, to conceal the content from prying eyes. Her gasp and wide smile attracted some brief attention, but it was Janette, a tiny stooped woman two beds down who approached her. She gazed up smiling inquiringly, so Jasmine held the dress up for her to see. It was a beautiful, dark pink print, cotton-edged dress, with satin piping, lined with linen. It had a wide flaring neckline, and short, very full puffed sleeves, with the bodice fitted to waist. She had heard Beth talk about her aunt Anne, a dressmaker, and guessed the garment came from her as it was too small to fit Beth and looked brand new.

Despite her gnarled fingers and bent frame, Janette helped her into it, puffing out the flattened sleeves. She then reached into her own hidden box of treasures and taking out some vintage hair pins and ribbons, expertly styled Jasmine's hair, parting it in the centre and dressing it in elaborate braids and loops over each ear, gathered into a topknot.

'Oh, thank you Janette!' she whispered happily. With no mirror available, she explored it carefully with her fingers and swished her head gently, the curls tumbling around her ears. Remembering her green-eyed owl pendant, she secured it openly around her neck rather than her waist.

Looking down curiously into the sweet, lined face of her friend, Jasmine wondered about the story behind her speed and skill. Janette knowingly answered the unspoken question.

'Keep it to yourself, but I used to dress the Ladies at Attingham House in all their finery.' She beamed proudly, despite her dire state of poverty and poor health. Jasmine hugged her, wondering if she had just got too old and of no use to them. Discarded, ending up on the streets and ultimately in the workhouse. She remembered mentioning her to Victoria, who said she was only fifty-six years old.

Jasmine had cleaned her boots until she could see her face in them and gathering her woven purse, she headed off to meet Beth, who would be waiting for her outside at the bottom of the back stairs. On her way down, she had a spring in her step, but hearing a deep cough she didn't recognise and footsteps coming up the winding stairs, she hesitated, nervously. With nowhere to conceal herself, she stood sideways against the wall to allow the man to pass. Her heart sank.

It was the Master, who had kept Emily out of sight as his so called 'personal maid,' for the first month here, before he replaced her for a new, less broken sex slave. Jasmine had either stared angrily or kept her head down on the occasions when he had passed her or addressed a group of the paupers that she was amongst, but now he had her full, individual attention.

He stopped, looking puzzled initially, but soon turned his thick rubbery lips into a leery smile and is if she was his property. Reaching over into her body space, he greeted her with a squeeze of her arm, uncomfortably close to her breast. There was no eye contact now, as he looked her up and down from the neck to feet and his breathing became faster. He was so close now she could feel the heat from his sweaty body and nearly heaved at the sour smell on his breath and spittle around his mouth.

'I'm just running an errand for Beth Sir,' she stated quickly, her head lowered and body turned away in the direction of heading straight down the stair way.

'There's no rush surely?' he said with a thick voice, squeezing her arm again, so that her instinct was to push him down the stairs or use a modern breakaway technique, that her mum had taught her in case this ever happened in the twenty-first century.

Just then, she heard Beth calling up and he hesitated as if still in two minds as to whether to enforce a change in her plans for that day, but thankfully he stepped away and she excused herself. 'What's your name young lady?' she heard his voice above her call, but she ignored him, and tore down the stairs, trembling as she fell into Beth's arms.

It was ten minutes before she calmed down and could thank Beth for the most gorgeous dress she had ever worn. But it was all slightly spoilt now after that experience and she held a deep fear now, which Beth could not reassure her was unfounded, that this powerful evil, predator, would seek her out next time.

As they walked on, her mood lifted slightly as she read a poster displayed on a streetlamp, on the tree-lined path by the river, which announced the Show. 'Roll up, roll up,' it began expectantly, with promises of unmissable festivities. Kingsland's fields would hold 'fun shows,' described as 'shindies of every sort,' with theatre, shooting, dancing, wines, cakes, comfits, beef and ham sandwiches, coffee, brown stout and beer.

They made their way first with the throng of spectators to the Castle, and she discovered talking to Beth, that many of the street names had remained unchanged for centuries. These included Butcher Row, Longden Coleham, Dogpole, Mardol, Frankwell, Roushill, Grope Lane, Gullet Passage, Murivance, The Dana, Portobello, Bear Steps, Shoplatch and Bellstone. If only the road to her home existed now, but what was the use? Her mother would not be sat there waiting for her.

Originally, the Shrewsbury Show was held at Whitsun, the seventh Sunday after Easter, or sometimes the second Monday after Trinity Sunday, which commemorated the descent of the Holy Spirit upon Christ's disciples and was a grand and solemn religious occasion.

The procession then was led by priests carrying the Holy Sacrament. The guilds followed them, each in their own colours, accompanied by minstrels and candle bearers. After High mass in old St Chads, companies divided to their own halls, to celebrate with feasting and drinking and other medieval entertainment. Even then it was thought to go back as far as the thirteenth century.

St Chad's was founded by Offa, King of Mercia, in 780 AD and rebuilt in the thirteenth century. Unfortunately, in 1788 the chiming of the clock caused the tower to come crashing down upon the church, so demolishing it. During the Wars of the Roses and the Puritan era, the Show disappeared, almost forgotten for decades. Revived with the restoration of the Stuarts, the show reappeared with much more emphasis on entertainment and the focus on the regalia of individual guilds and companies.

Beth explained that some Victorians looked down on the show in its current form, deeming it a pleasure fair now, as opposed to a trade one, so thought it had become pointless and was the cause of immorality.

'Some folks say it draws a lower sort of person, and much drunkenness, bringing injury to the town.'

The Shrewsbury Chronicle described the Show as a 'ridiculous pageant,' with its 'usual array of drunken kings and factory queens promenading the streets.' They approached the castle where the Guilds assembled from noon to one o'clock before heading to Kingsland, the course of the procession being lined with excited crowds. The bells of the different churches sent forth their melodious and enlivening peels.

The Guilds paraded through the town with their decorated flags and banners to the tune of their own music. Masters and Apprentices for all the companies, including the Butchers, Carpenters, Fish sellers, Brickmakers, Shoemakers, Tilers and Plasterers, with streamers and emblems. There were also Tailors, Skinners, Cabinet Makers, Hatters and Flax dressers.

The Master Butchers were led by a 'King,' dressed as Henry VIII wearing a scarlet mantle and embroidered vest as they paraded to their music, 'Roast Beef of Old England.'

The Master Tailors were dressed in long gowns of leaves sewn together, representing Adam and Eve, and there was an enchanting, figurative representation of the apple being offered from the forbidden tree.

Jasmine's favourite was the Apprentice Hairdressers and Weavers, headed by their 'Queen,' with a long flowing train, riding on a grey horse led by a Paige. She appeared working at a spinning wheel. Jasmine wished her friend Janette was up there with the entourage, smiling down having dressed the Queen's hair. Beth squeezed her hand affectionately, enjoying the procession as much as Jasmine.

The Combrethren of Saddlers, Painters, Glaziers, Plumbers, Curriers, and others, had a horse caparisoned with blue tapestry led by a dressed jockey, booted and spurred with a flag, emblazoned with the armorial bearings of each of the trades.

The Hatters had an Indian Chief in a magnificent Eastern costume and the Master Cordwainers, makers of leather shoes, were adorned in leather surcoats, a loose, sleeveless robe, worn over armour, the insignia of an order of knighthood. The uniform of an officer from the century before, on horses led by Squires. It was impressive, even to Jasmine who had seen the developments that the future would bring but never history in the making.

The Guilds were followed by the Town Mayor and Corporation, proceeded by the Town Crier, Marshall, and Sergeants of Mace, along with County MPs and the Earl of Powys, adorned in their robes of office. They were accompanied by their wardens, all high up on horseback.

The crowds would follow down to Kingsland common land, all dressed up ready for feasting and entertainments, returning to town for further evening celebrations later. Each company had its own arbour, surrounded by trees and built of timber, brick, or stone, with tables and benches, where townsfolk would assemble.

The mayor and his entourage, stopped at each stall, to pay respects and sample the wares. Each arbour had a dejeuner and refreshments were liberally provided by the respective trades. It was an annual treat of hospitality and good cheer and a day of recreation and feasting in Kingsland. A man playing a banjo sang loudly, one of the lines seemed very fitting for today, 'The poor were fed with plenty, and the rich sent empty away.'

Beth had shown her a poem, published in 1770 that had afforded some idea of what The Show was like during that period.

'Shrewsbury Quarry'

What friendly forms in social pomp draw near,

With thankful smiles to bless the bounteous year,
In glad procession, brotherhood, and bloom,
Like Flora's festals near thy walls, oh Rome,
To Kingsland Arbours once a year they go,
In ordere'd elegance serene and slow;
The bodies corporate in classes bright-
In different classes, but in one delight;
There blend with mutual hands the friendly bowls,
There blend their wishes, and there blend their souls;
Their yearly Archon over all presides,
Their state he governs and their joy he guides,
There mixing jovial, with each other jovial band,
To each his heart he gives, to each his hand;
With each he quaffs the invigorating cheer,
To friendship sacred and the hallowed year.
The sun would gladly in his course delay,
And stretch beyond its lengthened bound the day,
To gaze with rapture as each blossom glows,
On these rich blessings, which his beam bestows;
His prone career, his cadence they behold,
His western stage in crimson clad and gold,

The march in happy order to town;

There polished pleasures teem with new delight,

There balls and banquets crown the genial night.

By 'Mayor.'

Jasmine had already considered that the town's most famous son and most important citizen was 'currently' alive, born in 1809, Charles Darwin; who would go on to write in 1859, 'On the Origin of Species,' with his theory of evolution. He was now twenty-five, the same age as her. She thought of the statue of him as an older man, outside the library, currently a school in present day, and almost willed herself to be walking past, only in 2006. He was presently a young man, who had studied at both Edinburgh and Cambridge University. She wondered if he would come home for the Shrewsbury Show, as a university student might do, whatever the era. Interestingly, she had read that his lifelong health problems were now thought to be possibly part organic and part psychological, owing to his self-confessed 'episodes of abdominal distress, especially in stressful situations.' So many great findings made by him, still studied and talked about centuries later and yet no knowledge or help at that time for his probable irritable bowel.

Money raised from the Show would lead to The Salop Horticultural Society in 1836 presenting the event as a 'Carnation and Gooseberry Show.' By 1857, the first 'Flower Show' evolved, which went on to attract over 50,000 visitors to the town. In 1924 Shrewsbury Castle was bought from show profits for £2,621 and presented to the town. At present, the castle was owned by Sir William Pulteney, the town's MP. A wealthy but generous man, who also built Laura's Tower for his daughter.

Events advertised today, included the familiar Punch and Judy puppet show, a Circus, magicians, and exotic menageries, as just some of the entertainment on offer in the 1834 Shrewsbury Show. Meats hung, in the butcher's stalls, partly preserved by salting, smoking, and curing in brine to keep it edible for as long as possible.

Breathing in all the new sights and smells around her, Jasmine walked up and down, not taking her eyes off the stalls and barely aware of the whereabouts of her companion Beth at times. Vendors sold fried fish, hot eels, pickled whelks, sheep's trotters, peas'-soup, hot green peas, penny pies, plum 'duff,' meat-puddings, baked potatoes, spice-cakes, muffins and crumpets, sweetmeats and brandy-balls. One of the most popular dishes sold at the fair, attracting a crowd were the jellied eel, or as it was being called here, 'eel jelly.' She watched through the gap of eager people thrusting coins, as the eels were chopped and boiled in fish stock with various herbs and spices. She had never tasted them before, but the flavour was similar to rollmops, cheap but nutritious.

After sampling some of the salty, fried wares, finding her appetite had returned rather than just pure hunger, she felt incredibly thirsty. Tea and coffee, ginger-beer, lemonade, hot wine, new milk from the cow, asses' milk, curds and whey were on sale. In addition, she saw a beverage advertised as 'sherbet,' and some highly coloured liquids, that had no specific name, but were introduced to the public sold as 'cooling' drinks. With so much choice, she asked Beth to select for her and hot wine was handed to her. It tasted much stronger and sweeter than the mulled wine she'd had at Christmas at home, but it 'warmed the cockles,' as Beth said. She smiled contentedly, experiencing genuine pleasure and feeling at ease with her surroundings, albeit very different, for the first time in as long as she could remember.

The entertainment was not completely alien and she was drawn to watch the players on traditional Victorian stalls like Hook a Duck, the Coconut Shy Stall, Hoopla Stall, Cork Shooting, Darts and 'Milk Churn.' Prizes were not cuddly toys or goldfish, but little wooden animals and porcelain figures and there were wrapped sweets like liquorice, barley sugar and marzipan fruits. It would be another thirty years before the revolution of the Victorian fair, which would bring with it candy floss, carousels and steam-driven swings and roundabouts.

Yet still, her mind boggled at the thrill and entertainment value of the rudimentary theatrical performances staged on makeshift platforms and popular games, all but vanished in the future, replaced with technology. Board games rapturously played and cheered on by all ages, like chess, drafts, and backgammon. For the well-off, gambling in card games was going on, with large amounts of money being placed extravagantly on tables. But people of all ilks seemed to be placing bets, within their own budgets or not as the case may be.

There were human acts on display, and Beth told her about others from past years like conjoined twins, midgets, people with multiple arms or legs, extremely tall people, obese people, people born with facial or other deformities, and 'tattooed people.' The two women were covered in heavy intricate inked designs, which was unusual in this era and appeared to be attracting a lot of fascinating stares and pointing.

She thought of her own discreet tiny owl and pussycat, delicately applied on her lower back, and wondered how she would have been received if she had more visible ones, like her university friend Gemma.

The most popular attractions were oddities with extraordinary talents. Entertainers today included a mimic and ventriloquist Captain Austin, who shared his stage with Oanita, the double-jointed Indian squaw and Amy Dot, a 26-inch tall 'fairy queen.' Also, attracting a crowd was a performance by the 'The Female Christy's a 15-strong group of armour-clad lady artistes, who performed complete with spiked helmets and jewelled breastplates.

Thrill acts on display today included fire eaters, sword swallowers, the human pin cushion and knife throwers. Another area they passed had a sign, 'Bare Knuckle Fisticuffs.' Boxing without gloves seemed extremely popular and prize fighters waited their turn, drawing jeering and cheering crowds who placed wagers.

Animal oddities such as the two-headed calf and the miniature horse, were featured in the freak show as well. The Victorian's had a peculiar taste for the love of exotic animals, the highlight being a giraffe paraded around the square named Jenny Lind, apparently after the famous Swedish opera singer. The poster announced her arrival as 'Queen of the Animal Kingdom.'

The day was flying by, exhausted, Beth and Jasmine sat on the grass during the late afternoon, enjoying the warm breeze and people-watching, conserving their energy as they had the early evening yet to enjoy.

As if all the surrounding new sights, sounds, and tastes weren't enough, other stranger sensory experiences, were occasionally entering Jasmine's consciousness and physical awareness. For example, on closing her eyes as she lay back on the grass, there was complete silence, with every sound restored on opening them again. She repeated these actions three times and on blinking wide the last time, found her arm was being shaken by Beth, who had apparently been talking to her and thought she was unconscious as unarousable. She hadn't heard or felt anything until peering into Beth's concerned face.

Previously, when walking around the stalls, surrounded by the hustle and bustle of the fair, she had sensed somebody watching her and on turning around, felt their presence was close and hiding quickly in the shadows away from her. Beth had noticed her uneasiness at times but put it down to her chilling encounter with The Master and tried to take her mind off it.

When Jasmine finally glimpsed her stalker as he quickly took cover behind a stall, she recognised his face. It was impossible, her brother Joe's hit and run driver was here and judging by his expression, he was mouthing inaudible threats at her. Feeling very scared but not too unsafe in the open, she grabbed Beth's arm and urged her to follow her back to where the man half crouched to conceal himself. He didn't try to flee, this was her opportunity to confront him, after all he had put her family through. He picked something up off the floor and she cautiously approached. He made eye contact as he rose to his full height and smiled, holding an owl on his gloved hand.

'Meet Jonah,' he said kindly, assuming she had come to see his bird as she abruptly approached him face to face. He no longer had the features of Joe's murderer and although she looked around the vicinity swiftly, she knew he wasn't really there, it was all her own paranoia. But as she walked away, she pondered on the name he had used to introduce the owl, 'Jonah.' Wasn't Joe's slayer called Jon Hannah? It seemed uncanny and he'd vanished when she turned around again.

13

EVANTIDE

A dancing bear in the square was attracting a throng of spectators, most of them stupefied on liquor having been supping all day. The bear's custodian had the great beast chained by the nose and Jasmine could see by old scars and fresh welts, that it was treated very badly. Folks were paying a penny for the dance, and cheered as it moved rhythmically, but she was really starving and just trained to beg for food. A sad, scared, skinny animal, with bloodshot eyes and a sticky tear on her cheek.

It sickened Jasmine to think how so many people in these times enjoyed cruel so called 'sports,' like cockfighting and bull baiting. In Shrewsbury, Bear Baiting had once been a horrific blood sport, where a post would be set in the ground and the bear chained to it, either by the leg or neck. Several well-trained fighting or baiting dogs, usually Old English Bulldogs, would then be set upon it, replaced as they got tired, wounded or killed. Bear pits would be dug to conceal the vile practice, taking it 'underground,' literally after it was finally banned.

The Bear Steps was in one of her favourites of the many well-known narrow passages, passing between buildings from one street to the next. Also called 'shuts,' a short-cut, where folks could 'shoot through,' from one street to another and were still in use in Shrewsbury centuries later. This well-known shut named Grope Lane, connected the town's main market places from High Street to Butchers Row to Fish Street.

As with many towns in England, where there was an area associated with prostitution, it was previously named 'Grope Countelane,' mentioned as early as 1561, to indicate a place of 'scandalous lewdness and venery,' according to author Thomas Phillips' History and Antiquities of Shrewsbury (1799). The reference was to female genitalia and debauchery and whores and the word 'cunt,' originally considered vulgar and not obscene as it is now. She remembered that half-way up Grope Lane, victims of the Black Death were also buried at the site of a long-gone old chapel in a plague pit.

Where the narrow alley met with Fish Street, stood the famous 'Bear Steps,' where the miserable spectacle of bear baiting was supposed to have once been hosted. However, when Jasmine asked Beth, she knew nothing of any recent practice at this spot, saying it was named after the Bear Inn, but probably had bears dancing there at some point. It would be the following year under the Cruelty to Animals Act 1835, when Parliament would prohibit all such mistreatment, including cock fighting. Of course, it still occurred, but took place covertly.

Years before, Shrewsbury's own MP, William Pulteney had brought in a bill on 3rd February 1800, to prevent bull baiting, however was defeated on 18th April. It was like walking through a history lesson. Dates, Acts and quotes popping into her head connected to life as she experienced it now. Jasmine had always looked up at the magnificent old buildings as she walked though her home town, wondering about the lives of their former occupants back then. Yet here she was, walking past the same familiar Tudor dwellings and late Georgian architecture, the latter of which was quite recently built.

On passing through the town in the prison cart on the way to Kingsland, she had discovered the start of time leaps in multiples of fifty years, which appeared to match the changes in her surroundings. However, the mystery was why did the time leaps not alter the ages of her or the people she was with? It was as if she was imprisoned in a time warp.

Crossing what is the town's existing Welsh bridge now, she remembered how on arrival, she had crossed the ancient St George's Bridge, an impressive fortified structure. Longer and further west, with Mardol Gate at the town end and a smaller, square Welsh Gatehouse over the first wet arch on the Frankwell side. Improvements were evident though, since Jasmine had passed through from the prison in the last century, with nineteenth century powers to start to pave, clean and light the streets of Shrewsbury.

That evening, the companies and guilds were returning to town by nine o'clock, but by a different route to attend town balls, theatre and dinners. The ordinary townsfolk were heading back for continued merriment and frivolity at the Inns and taverns, where street sellers also lined the cobbled paths once again. There were groups of men inhaling snuff and smoking clay pipes and the clouds of smoke made her cough. The nineteenth century men wore trousers now, replacing the knee length breeches and had waistcoats and coats. Jasmine looked around at the women, all ages and shapes and sizes, from different classes, but most in their best, Sunday clothes. She smiled, thinking she also no longer looked like a pauper.

The wealthy, in all their expensive finery, many driven by coaches to the door, entered the town's upmarket establishments, whilst the commoners filed into the local Inns, where plays were staged and jugs of ale were poured. Assembly rooms filled up with card games and dances and there were clairvoyant evenings, astronomy displays and illusionists, catering for every taste and pocket.

After walking past and peering in through the gas lighted doorways and widows of establishments, from halls of splendour, to houses of disrepute and everything in between, Beth urged them to make haste as they needed to get back sharpish. They were inadvertently heading in the direction of the red-light area of the town. The 'scarlet women,' were out on every corner selling their wares and appeared to be getting a fair amount of attention and trade. With men carrying more brass than usual in their pockets, the euphoric moods and alcohol intoxication made for increased interest and disinhibition.

The ladies of the night, who could be seen front of house on the street, appeared quite able to handle themselves and were just as rowdy as their punters and completely inebriated. Distinguished by their heavily rouged and powdered faces, disguising their hollowed cheeks, they wore shortened dresses displaying their ankles and low bust line, some revealing cleavage, others heaving bosoms. She wondered about the more vulnerable young women and the violence that could be going on behind closed doors, in the houses of ill-repute.

Sleeping in the dorm, she had listened to women comparing their lives on the streets to that in the Workhouse. It was often the new arrivals who spoke the most disparagingly of the effects and lifestyle from prostituting themselves. They described seedy brothels, where they were forced to sleep with men chosen by the Madam for them. Some had regular clients who chose them, which could be either a familiar encounter or else a violent, sadistic experience, that left them shaking with fear at the prospect.

Stories were told of institutionalised depravity, women beaten into submission, enduring every type of debauchery and fetishism conceivable, from which breaking free from was impossible. This was the era where men were not encouraged to express their sexual desires and fantasies within the confines of marriage, as wives were not encouraged to be at all sexual and basic intercourse was supposed to be purely for the purpose of procreation. It was not the done thing for a married woman to show anything but quiet submission.

Both working and living conditions were very poor. One pauper inmate Martha, described staring up at mould spots and mushrooms growing on the peeling, damp ceiling, to block out what was happening to her. She went off in her mind on a journey into her own fantasies of being 'Lady of the Manor,' instead. She was fourteen years old when she got away. Others glorified their street walking days, recounting only the good times where free flowing gin and the camaraderie of the working girls made life more bearable. Memories of abuse and suffering repressed as they now endured the tiresome, dull drudgery of daily life as a pauper.

Making her way to the 'new' Welsh Bridge rebuilt in the 1790's, on foot with Beth, Jasmine noticed it looked almost identical to the time she came from, other than the road surface, which despite some paving, was still covered with rocks of very uneven sizes, pushed aside by traffic, leaving deep ruts and mud holes in the road.

With permission to pass through and travel arrangements already arranged with a relative of Beth's from Frankwell, they travelled in a clapped-out horse and cart waiting to take them up to the ferry man with his punt-pole by the Kingsland Bank. Jasmine could tell Beth knew and liked the man, there was an obvious romantic connection between them, so she gave them as much privacy as was possible on such a small vessel, to make small, flirtatious talk with one another.

Once across the river, she and Beth began running up the bank to the doors of the Workhouse, giggling, as it was close to 10.00 o'clock, having enjoyed every second of their free time. The doors were normally locked at 8.00 o'clock, but Beth had arranged for Victoria to let them in by the back staircase. Jasmine's heart sank again, at memories of her worrying encounter on that same stairway earlier that day with the Master.

Making it to safety with relief, she topped and tailed with Beth that night, in the attendant sleeping area of the Lunacy Ward, and as her head hit the hard mattress, she was so tired she didn't hear another sound.

14

A DICKENS TALE

Jasmine awoke to find herself lying on the very edge of the queen size bed, Beth taking up three quarters of it and lying flat on her back snoring loudly. Turning to face the window she smiled to herself, as the memories of the day before floated back and the happy sights, sounds and smells filled her head contentedly. Her dress was beautiful, it had been such a surprise. The soft feel of the package before unwrapping, had made her think it was another woollen shawl, she felt so fortunate having Beth by her side in this inexplicable new world.

And then suddenly, in the blink of an eye, a very different memory entered her head at the exact same time as she caught sight of numerous dirty streaks on her gown. Balling her hands into fists anxiously, she winced in pain and stared down at the cause, her battered, dirty finger nails. Her heart pounded loudly in her chest, as what had first appeared like a vivid, frightening dream, became a reality. The events in her mind seemed to unfold before her like a story.

The beginning was Jasmine lucidly recalling a visit alone to St. Chads Churchyard yesterday. She could clearly see herself wandering away from Beth and walking towards the church which stood high above The Quarry that sloped down to the river and the grounds of The Show. But she could not understand why she would have left Beth's side for more than a few seconds or at least without telling her.

A completely different chain of events then unfolded in her mind like a series of flashbacks that fitted in with the evidence of very real soil markings on her clothes and hands. She shivered as she realised there were two parallel versions of events from yesterday, running alongside in her mind.

The newly remembered story moved on as more details came to mind. Although it was a hazy, dream like sequence that made her hope that it was one. It was all coming back to her, she had wandered away, leaving Beth to talk with her cousins and a young girl they called Lorraine. Seeing the new St Chads opposite, she had curiously approached the cemetery and looked in at how well kempt it appeared. She knew where she would have been heading, to the 'fake grave,' of 'Ebenezer Scrooge,' a fictional character of Charles Dickens whom in this era, was yet to write his book, 'A Christmas Carole,' in 1843.

Jasmine was well versed on Dickens. He held strong views about child poverty and had been dedicated to social reform, using the novel to put forward his arguments against it. Completing the book in six weeks it was published just before yuletide. A film was made of the story in 1984, set in Dickens' beloved Shrewsbury.

As a child, it was a real thrill for Jasmine to stand back watching some of the filming with her mother. The skating scene had been made using polythene sheets and washing up liquid. The Square, used for the opening scenes of the film, covered in fake snow with people walking about in Victorian dress. Shrewsbury's own Town Crier, author and tour guide, Martin Wood, played the body double for Michael Carter, who was the Spirit of Christmas Future.

The graveyard seen was filmed at St. Chads at 2am using special effects, including a raised railway placed above the headstones, to allow the spirit to 'float over the graves,' and hover above Scrooge. Dickens gave his first ever public reading of 'A Christmas Carole,' at Shrewsbury's Music Hall, staying at The Lion Hotel, a sixteenth century coaching Inn, where he wrote to his family.

"...we have the strangest little rooms, the ceilings of which I can touch with my hand. The windows bulge out over the street, as if they were little stern windows in a ship and a door opens out of the sitting room onto a little open gallery with plants in it where one leans over a queer old rail and looks all downhill and slantwise at the most crooked old black and yellow houses…"

With scenes from the 'Spirit of Christmas future,' recorded in St. Chads disused graveyard, permission had been given to carve 'Ebenezer Scrooge's' name on an actual period headstone, deteriorated to the point that it was unreadable, left there for all eternity. But others insisted it was a prop and made to look old. Jasmine wanted to see if there was an original grave.

As a child, whose family loved the film, her mother had taken her to make a crayon rubbing with tracing paper to detect the original, hidden name in the worn away letters, but without luck. As always, her mother had made the trip fascinating, using silver foil presses and flour and then water to darken, highlight, and clean the area which was fun but all to no avail. Writing up her adventure in the Quarry Park later with an ice-cream, had eventually led to first prize at school, for the 'most exciting day of the summer holidays.' It wasn't of course, but even then, she included historical facts and interesting anecdotes in her school essays. It was just as well they had local picnic days out, as her brother Joe's antics often deterred her parents from going away to a caravan, or abroad on a plane like her friends. Poor Joe, always troubled or in bother and now lying in a cold, boneyard himself, Jasmine remembered shivering despite the afternoon heat.

Standing at the entrance of the iron gates of the cemetery, she looked down the stony path, through the leafy trees, at the neat grass and clean grey headstones. The moon was full and brightly lit the ground, tinting the landscape with an icy blue wash and beckoning her in with a seductive light. The sounds of a pair of Tawny owls emitting their courtship call, 'twit-twooo,' filled the area she looked onto. Confused at the change and seeing her breath in the cold night air, she turned her head around slowly towards The Show, where the noise of people having fun returned and the sun shone brightly, the river glistening under its rays.

She then looked back again at the moonlit church yard. As if drawn in by the gravitational pull of the moon and midnight blue sky, sparkling with brilliant stars, she found herself stepping over the threshold between day and night, from cheery noise to desolate silence, into an eerie terrain. The atmosphere was extraordinarily calm and alluring, but lacked reassurance.

Always curious as to whom the headstone originally belonged to, she wandered dreamlike, down the track from the gate, the light fading fast as a dark cloud crossed the path of the moon between the trees. As the wind rose, a gust lifted a pile of brown, crispy leaves, spinning them around in a funnel which headed towards the stone she sought. With seasonal change from summer to autumn and now calm to stormy, the air embodied spiritual and psychological forces, moving the tree branches as if they were creaking zombies. Powerful, swirling gusts seemed to rush around the stones, making her cover her face from its sting.

Mist, rising from the ground was above her ankles now, the cold air emanating from the tombstones, chilling her bones. As the cloud passed by, the moonlight gave everything a bluish haze again. Tree branches seemed to beckon her with bony, pointing fingers that she couldn't oppose, casting elongated shadows ahead. The cemetery was no longer a tidy, well kempt site, but a disused churchyard once more, a retched, lifeless place. The church clock struck two with a piercing chime, it had to be two in the morning and not the summer afternoon she had stepped out from on the other side of the gate.

Approaching Ebenezer Scrooge's well-known headstone, situated in the shade of a tree, Jasmine found herself staring down at what was now a freshly dug grave. The tree above her seemed to scatter gloom and despair and with sorrow and anguish Jasmine fell to her knees, clawing the earth as her eyes took in the wording on the stone. Dark clouds now seemed to lower themselves over her like a menacing spirit in a black hooded robe, as if a visitation from the grim reaper, a symbol of death floated over her. A strong sense of despair, misery, torment, suffering and sadness, enveloped her. The sensation of being suffocated and pressed down by an unseen dark force made her feel like she had to accept her fate and not look up. As quickly as it came, the veil of cloud appeared to shrink and collapse, a fear of 'what is yet to come,' shrouding her in the calm again after-glow.

Once more, the grave inscription was unreadable and ancient, and the grass was long and dewy over the soil. Crying and shaking her head in disbelief, she scratched at the moss-covered headstone, her nails scraping and tearing as they removed centuries of layers of dirt, desperately trying to uncover the name that had to be a mistake, but had appeared to her as clear as day. Sobbing uncontrollably over the headstone for an undefined moment in time, Jasmine found she was pulling herself to her feet with a sense of urgency and survival instinct and backing away, she turned to run at full speed.

A Tawny Owl was hooting in a tree above her, her richly mottled feathers merging with the boughs of the tree. She peered down at Jasmine, from her roost where she guarded her eggs, laid on a nest of old pellets. The undigested feathers, bones and fur of her prey, a grisly bed for the soon-to-be owlets. The male owl swooped down from his perch, on a rotten ash tree, the smell of the powdery, mouldy timber, clinging to his wings. Protective and defensive, his Autumnal, territorial howling penetrated her skull. She was amongst the creatures of the night, thus of danger and magic.

Leaving the perimeter of the grave yard, she ran blindly into the darkness through tear filled eyes, in an effort to escape the horror. Once through the gate, she realised she had brought the night with her, the showground empty. Her journey took her through an infamous part of the town alone, full of misery and crime and grimy rag and bone dens. She found herself in an area with vaguely familiar landmarks. There were closed shops with shutters up, stables, manufacturing premises and an abundance of pubs, but it was a scene of bawdiness and disorderly contact.

Judging by the covert behaviour of some of its inhabitants, it appeared to be the centre of vice and crime. She was somewhere between Roushill and Mardol, where the prostitutes had drifted to, after their homes near the castle were compulsorily purchased from their landlords, to make room for the new railway.

There was much drunkenness and noise, from every direction around her, women's cackling laughter, men crooning old welsh drinking songs, and the intermittent din of taunts, threats, and abusive shouting from both sexes. Moving cautiously, down the area that stretched from Mardol Head to the riverbank, she passed numerous shuts in between. One called 'Masons Passage,' now Phoenix Place, led from Mardol to Roushill. 'Alleys of evil repute,' like Kings Head Passage and Sheep's head shut, led down from the bottom of Mardol to the riverbed. Here, she almost stepped into low lying flooded shuts, with filth and no doubt, attendant diseases from the over flowing, open drains.

With the Smithfield Road, yet to be constructed, there were shuts in appalling conditions that no longer existed in her century. One day all that would remain would be the decaying facades of cottages, the passages used as thoroughfares. Prostitutes occupied overcrowded dwellings in Kings Head Passage, Caernarvon Lane and between Mason's Court and Mason's Passage.

She remembered reading there was once more than two hundred shuts in Shrewsbury, compared to just over twenty in her day. Unfamiliar pubs, like The Sun, the Couriers Arms and further up The Horseshoes, but there in front of her was the still existing King's Head, a place in these times, where thieves and prostitutes assembled on their premises.

Brothel keepers were known to keep a 'vile den of infamy,' under the guise of lodging houses. She knew many prostitutes assumed an alias to hide their activities, like milliner, dressmaker, silk weaver, household or 'occasional' servant, until the 1861 census, when every prostitute and brothel keeper were named as such.

At this time, Mardol was the main thoroughfare to the old Welsh Bridge and route for travellers to Wales and Ireland. The approach had long been the traditional haunt of 'women of easy virtue.' Some clients resembled simple farm workers, hawkers, pedlars and itinerant labour passing through town. Many in search of work, would board up to twelve to a room in lodging houses.

Meeting the woman in alleys and pubs, some were respected regulars, other victims themselves, selected by prostitutes who ensured they were plied with drink and robbed, in the darkness of the passageways. If gullible country folk reported the theft, it meant exposing themselves to publicity. The women if caught, were condemned and punished with imprisonment and hard labour, but their punters got off as little more than innocent figures of fun.

The age of consent was still only twelve years old until 1875, and many young girls on the game led short lives, over within ten years, killed by venereal disease, poverty, destitution, or prison. Impoverished females, driven to the oldest profession just to earn enough to live, were regarded with scorn or amusement, the origins of their plight neglected by those in better circumstances. There was very little charitable help other than Salop Penitentiary, a harsh, uncaring regime with religious indoctrination in a refuge for fallen women, or The Workhouse.

Walking more quickly, two raucous, drunken men, stepped out into Jasmine's path from the doorway of a bar, their loud laughter and strong smell of ale, hitting her senses and halting her, before she bumped into them. Lewd suggestions were made and hands grabbed at her, missing due to inebriation and her squirming away, as though her life depended upon it.

A gentleman appeared, but only in appearance, making the men leave her alone but now propositioning her too, with no intention of accepting 'No,' for an answer. With one hand tightly gripping her arm and the other hand aiming to force a strong-smelling handkerchief across her face, whilst pulling her down a shut, she knew what she had to do. Twenty-first century self-defence classes came into play and turning sideways on, she kneed him in the groin, with all her force and swung her arm down hard releasing his grip and leaving him doubled up, almost on the floor.

Running out of the passage way, looking behind in case he was in pursuit, Jasmine ran straight in the arms of a night watchman, who was guarding a man held in stocks under a street light.

Thinking he would help her as an early form of Police, she was wrong. Having no sympathy for her tale of woe nor any intention of seeking out the man who had attacked her, he held her to blame and chained her by the arm to the street lamp. Looking down at herself she realised she was wearing the uniform of the workhouse now, muddied by the graveyard debacle and not the pink dress.

'You low life, scrounging paupers should be in by 8 o'clock and looking at your shameful, dirty state, you've been selling your wares to men. What would my good friend the Workhouse Master think of your ungratefulness and flouting the rules of the house? What's the punishment for that I wonder? We'll see what the sheriff has to say.'

Trembling at his words and the thought of what was 'yet to come,' she slunk down to the floor sobbing, the chain sliding down the post, so she was seated on the cold floor by the man in stocks.

Jasmine jumped at the shriek and hiss of a barn owl perched above her, at the top of the street light, its white heart-shaped face with dark eyes stared down on her almost accusingly. A Luminescing Barn Owl, that seemed to light up the night sky, as it flew past them on its slow sloth wings, its bright reddish centre 'resembled a carriage lamp'. Purdy (1908). Taking off on his buoyant flight, embodying the freedom it possessed, like the Lord of the night. Staring up, Jasmine recalled its underside, the prey's-eye view, was the shade of moonshine and as it turned, its back like spun gold. And that was all she could remember.

With her mind back in Beth's room, re-joining her body, she pondered the end of her parallel memory. It didn't make sense, which dress was she wearing? Her pink gown that she had worn with Beth was dirty and yet she had been recognised and apprehended as a workhouse inmate in the uniform of shame.

Had this nightmare really happened and she had been brought back here to the Workhouse by the Sherriff to await the Master's wrath and if so, she wondered if this meant her punishment was 'yet to come?'

Or had she run up the back stars giggling with Beth, falling exhausted into bed next to her, sleeping top and tails as the communal dorm was locked? The latter would indicate a safe, uneventful journey home and St Chads a bad, terrifying dream and after all, she had woken up next to Beth. It must have been a dream, it had elements of her love and knowledge of history, childhood memories in her home town and a very real experience related to her favourite story, 'A Christmas Carole,' almost brought to life but with herself as the main character.

Had she bargained with the night watchman, as Ebenezer had with a warning spirit, begging for a chance to make amends? She had woken up in the workhouse, with vivid memories that could be a dream, but what of the evidence of the soil on her clothes and under her finger nails? And how could this have been her own grave, when she was from another time in the future? In the novel, the tombstone bears Scrooge's name and sobbing, Scrooge makes a solemn promise to the ghost that he will change his ways to avoid this outcome. What did she need to do to stop this happening to her?

She guessed she must also be a selfish and a cold-hearted miser with a lesson to learn. The voices had told her this before but were silent currently. She wondered now if this destroyed her hopes of ever returning home, altering the passing of time. As if this was her place of burial, it meant she would never even exist in the twenty-first century.

Beth was slowly stirring and Jasmine feeling shame about the state of the dress, quietly crept from the creaky bed, taking the soiled garment down and folding it so the marks were hidden beneath it.

Seeing her black, broken finger nails, she tiptoed to the staff washroom where she soaked her fingers in the tepid water, feeling the pain of them scraped down to the quick. She closed her eyes tightly, which only enhanced the images of her clawing at the headstone in disbelief, to unveil her own name again and next month's date.

The significance of the owls hit her, opening a wound so deep it had never healed, its sepsis poisoning her body and soul and destroying her ability to function when brought to the surface. Nearly always suppressed and buried deeply, a trauma that was relived when allowed to emerge. Her dead brother Joe, the white van man, 'Active Owl Security,' with the gentle snowy bird depicted on the side pitted against the gore and horror of the bloody hit and run, the true disregard for life and justice.

Her own part to play, pushed down as always with the main missing part she had failed to tell. It festered away, so that in her old life, her brain had created 'voices,' to ensure she was always reminded of not what she had done, but what she had failed to do. Omission of a duty of care to her own brother. A perpetual punishment, endured to protect her from the guilt of her parents knowing the truth and looking at her with disgust, disappointment and questioning eyes that would always ask 'why?'

Her freedom of psychotic symptoms and insight in this century was unfathomable, but she was pretty sure now she was on a quest of some sort, to make the necessary changes to return home and be of sound mind again. Feeling more positive, Jasmine got herself together, splashing water over her face, but was on guard, half expecting to be apprehended at any second. She joined Beth who was up now and getting prepared for the shift change, to look after their charges for the day on the Luna wards.

Beth was tidying the sleeping area when Jasmine returned and had moved the dress to place it with her woven purse on the ottoman. Holding her breath, Jasmine searched Beth's face for signs of disapproval or anger, but there was only a sweet smile. Seeing Jasmine looking so worried, she offered reassurance, assuming it was related to yesterday mornings' unwanted attention from the Workhouse Master.

Deciding to come clean, having made some connection and realised that her own web of lies and cover-up had only led to her becoming mentally ill in the twenty-first century and trapped in the past now, Jasmine held up the ruined dress. She had to try and explain what had occurred to Beth and also to unravel yesterday's events.

Bracing herself, she gasped. There was not a mark on the dress, turning it around examining the fabric closer her gaping mouth made Beth laugh. Realising it would cause confusion and make her sound crazy, Jasmine turned to Beth with a smile, 'Thank you for this beautiful gown and such a lovely day,' she said with the conviction she truly felt and the relief that it must have been a dream, one that carried warnings and insights and messages, but even less bona fide than whatever strange reality kept her here.

Beth grinned and briefly hugged her and then as if embarrassed by her words of gratitude, she hurried Jasmine through to the wards. Tying their aprons on the way, they made the swap with the weary night nurse and pauper helper, who had done a double shift to allow Beth and Jasmine to go to The Show.

Next year the plan was that it would be their turn, that's if the fast-spreading Tetanus hadn't wiped them all out. Tetanus was one of the biggest killers of this time. A highly infectious disease where bacteria enters the body through wounds, causing respiratory paralysis, tonic spasms, and rigidity of the voluntary muscles, especially those of the neck and lower jaw causing lockjaw.

15

MURDER BOTTLES

The workhouse bell rang at six o'clock and the slumbering children were required to rise, make beds, attend prayers and wash and clean their shoes before breakfast and then it was recreation followed by school at nine o'clock. Able bodied mothers had to attend to themselves and their babies and infants as part of the strict routine. On the days Jasmine slept in the dorm, she noticed there was a system of mothers helping each other to accommodate different work schedules. Starting at different times, the kitchen workers had to be downstairs by half past six, laundry at seven and workrooms and household maids at eight o'clock.

Emily took Jasmine to see the school rooms one day. They had small square windows which were always slightly open, giving a chill to the room. Although some light filtered in, they were far too high for anyone to see out. In the nursery, one wall had a lower window that looked out on to an adult ward, so was whitewashed, giving it a dreamy celestial glow to the otherwise dreary room.

The cold, stone floor was unwelcoming and the few books they had were old and out of date, but Emily said it was more than some of the poorer children living outside of the Workhouse were getting. The toy cupboard was often locked, its access dangled like a carrot on a string with high expectations of the children in return by some teachers. Dominoes had been donated and they had a shabby rocking horse, two cloth peg dolls, ten marbles, three soldiers and some chipped wooden bricks. There were bats and balls and skipping ropes for the junior children, but they were rarely seen out of the cupboard.

Older children were taught sewing and knitting, a quiet pursuit, easily taught and supervised and thought to deter the opportunity for idleness, although it was dull and repetitive. The nursery was full of knitted blankets donated for the comfort of the young children by middle class Christian do-gooders.

As soon as they were able, school had to be attended every morning and afternoon, where the children were taught to read. The physical conditions of the workhouse were thought to have a 'malign influence,' so the schoolrooms were situated as far away as possible from the main areas. The house itself represented dependency, which was thought to be contaminating. Although the pauper children were deemed to have little or no interest in their lessons, there was no recognition of the hunger, cold and separation anxiety that was often the cause of them being disruptive and unmanageable.

Jasmine remembered from her history lectures that even in 1901, the journal of the Poor Law Handbook stated, 'Pauperism is in the blood and there is no more affectual means of checking its hereditary nature than by doing all in our power to bring up our children as to make them God fearing, useful and healthy members of our society.'

This very year in the 1834 Poor Law Act, the principle of 'Less Eligibility,' set a requirement where you only had to teach pauper children to read, and not necessarily to write. It determined a lower quality of education for pauper children, with basic instruction in reading, elementary writing, fundamental arithmetic and the principles of Christian religion as sufficient.

It culminated in reinforcing the poverty trap, with deprivation merely passed down from one generation to the next. It would be eleven years later, before they finally changed the legislation, which would mean fewer children would ultimately need poor relief, or enter the perpetual cycle of poverty.

The older girl's education was quite different to the boys, with more emphasis on household tasks. They did learn spelling, tables, and dictation, but the boys had extra curriculum like map reading, learning time with 'use of clock dial,' and 'reading with explanations.' The workhouse schoolmistresses and masters were poorly paid, had no formal training and only a basic level of education themselves.

Other forms of education were directed towards the trades, boys did carpentry, tailoring and shoemaking and girl's had needlework, knitting and domestic service. As soon as their ages would permit, they were 'put out,' as parish apprentices or boys joined the armed forces.

Once a year the school received the following provisions which were often shared between several children.

1 reading sheet, 2 boxes of slate pencils, 3 dozen pen holders, 1 box pen nibs, 1dozen slates, 6 dozen exercise books, 2 squares of blotting paper and 1 bottle of ink.

It was mostly women whose labour was the mainstay of the workhouse; Beth had always said working in the poor-law service was a reliable, if not 'unbecoming' choice for a working-class woman. Mrs Inglehart was one of the few middle-class women who gave their time to visiting the more vulnerable of workhouse inmates, preaching religion, recommending improvements, but best of all providing treats. She was the children's favourite, as the sweets and small toys she provided, were always given directly to them in their grubby little hands, so none of the attendants or teachers could snatch them away. Not that Nadia or Emily ever would. Mrs Inglehart was rumoured to be a friend of Florence Nightingale and applying to be the first female to go for election as a guardian of the poor.

Emily relished her job as pauper nursery nurse, an assistant to Madam Nadia Fabron, a kindly French, grandmother figure, who nurtured the younger Workhouse children. Although Nadia had separate sleeping quarters, she would never close the door between them, and often opened her eyes in the night to find two or three little ones, not much more than babies, curled up with her.

Emily was sleeping back in the dorm at night with Jasmine when not on night shifts and they now shared a bunk. On the first night of separation from their mothers, Emily would stay too, as the 'poor little urchins,' would usually sob themselves to sleep, a heart wrenching sound like lambs separated from the ewe for weaning, or 'Lambs to the slaughter,' Emily had said, judging by the sound of some of their bleating.

Those motherless plus under seven were cared for at night with the very young ones, but in the day, the class was too big, so a schoolmistress was needed for the children aged five to seven, which left the under-fives with Nadia and Emily as her helper.

There were segregated classes for boys and girls aged seven to thirteen, taught by a schoolmaster, and girls up to fourteen by a schoolmistress. Boys would be expected to be in local employment or apprenticeship around thirteen, or if not to join the Army or Navy.

Emily and Nadia ran the nursery in the day with firm, but consistent boundaries, but had a natural warmth and compassion that the children responded to and thrived on. With their mothers either winding yarn from dawn 'til dusk, or absent altogether in the cases of orphans and deserted children, they were completely dependent and at the mercy of their carer's from as young as one year old. Nadia treated them all the same and regarded all her motherless babies and infants as 'God's petite Angels.' For many, their futures were determined before they even left the womb, many categorised as 'bastards' or the spawn of either 'idiots, lunatics, cripples or felons.'

Unbeknown to Nadia and Emily, things would not change until 1867, when Dr Thomas Barnardo would lead the way in setting up proper children's homes, having stated that workhouses were the wrong places for children. But as Jasmine knew, the 'future history' of children's homes would remain plagued with the occurrence of hidden abuse and cruelty for as long as they existed.

Orphaned infants forced on the parish from birth, were originally put out to a wet nurse where they remained until, 'of age sufficient to be admitted into the house.' The foster mothers were required now and again to bring them in, to present the baby to the directors so that they may observe what care is being taken of them.

Then, one afternoon a change took place to solve all of this, when Nadia and Emily received a case delivered containing a new product to try. Babies old enough to hold a bottle, especially those with no mother or wet nurse, could be handed a glass banjo shaped bottle, with a length of rubber tubing and a nipple. Two different types had been delivered for Nadia to try, so some bottles had labels with the make 'Mummies Darling' on and others had 'The Little Cherub.' Mrs Inglehart had kindly put a word in before the governors meeting and the idea was embraced, as the delivery would be funded by a charity set up by a benefactor of babies rather than the parishes, who in turn saved money on wet nurses.

The bottles were becoming popular with all classes, as the fashion of women's corsets made it harder to breastfeed. Difficult to clean, the advice given was, 'wash the nipple every two or three weeks.' Unbeknown at the time, these bottles were the perfect incubators for bacteria, which flourished and became deadly without sterilisation. Infant mortality rates were already high before the product was widely used, but these 'Mummies Little Helpers,' another brand of this novel creation, would all be known as 'Murder Bottles' in the future, with only two out of every ten infants living to see their second birthday.

Jasmine was not aware of this at the time, when Emily excitedly told her about them and found she was starting to accept many things she encountered as 'the norm.' She did not really have that much knowledge, formulas, or instructions at hand, for sharing the secret to future 'ground breaking' inventions. But her eyes had widened at Emily's description of the lack of sterilisation or even daily washing.

'Please say you'll wash them all thoroughly at the end of every day.' Jasmine pleaded with Emily after she had told her.

'There's no need honestly, the delivery man gave us full instructions.' Emily replied reassuringly. 'Check with Nadia if you wish.'

Jasmine realized it would be difficult to convince her friends, when few people from each millennium over the centuries, had rarely questioned what was said and handed to them at the time, treating it as gospel. So, she approached Beth, who had already taken on board some of her improved hygiene suggestions with good effect, even if they were not exactly aseptic technique. When even Beth tried to question why they would need to do differently to what it said on the box, Jasmine knew it was time to say something or forever hold her peace.

She reminded Beth firstly, that she never did exactly as the physicians prescribed, either turning them to her own way of thinking or doing it entirely her own way. At the end of the shift, she decided to be very brave and forthright and asked Beth to come down to the kitchen with her, as she wanted to tell her something important with Helen and Joseph present. Perplexed and weary Beth agreed, always somewhat intrigued by Jasmine's perspective on everything, and so accompanied her down to the back kitchen. Helen was expecting Jasmine anyway, as they met at the end of most of Jasmine's shifts now, but she greeted Beth with a warm welcome, getting three glasses out and a large bottle of cooking sherry from the cupboard.

'This is all very nice', said Beth, 'but I think our Jasmine has another reason for getting us all together isn't that so my girl?'

'Oh, yes?' asked Helen jiggling Jasmine's folded arms affectionately. 'I must say you look very serious my dearest,' she stated. 'Is it top secret?' She laughed, but Jasmine looked worried.

'Is Joseph around too?' she asked solemnly.

'Whatever is the matter?' Helen asked concerned, standing up to cradle Jasmine's head which made her smirk.

'It's nothing that serious!' she exclaimed amused at Helen's reaction.

'I'll get him, is he outside?' Beth asked, starting to sound impatient with fatigue.

Joseph returned with Beth less than a minute later, wiping the soil from his hands as he studied Jasmine's face with an anxious frown.

'Are you ok Jasmine?' Suddenly aware of all eyes watching her with somewhat anxious anticipation, she decided the only way to tell them, was to just say it.

'I'm not from this era,' she blurted out before pausing briefly, 'I don't know how, but I was pulled back to the past, from a time in the future.' They looked down quickly and around at each other, the speed of eye movement and averted gaze, somehow telling Jasmine this was not altogether a surprise. It was Beth who answered her after the other two turned to her, Helen still had her arm linked through Jasmine's, but appeared to freeze and tense, which was not the response she was expecting. She'd imagined they would smile, reassure her it was impossible, and discuss tinctures that would clear a possible 'brain fever,' but never the words Beth spoke.

'Jasmine, we had another who came before you once, who said the same thing and disappeared, suddenly.' Helen shuddered, but Beth continued. 'She was only young, but before she left, she said her granddaughter had come for her.'

Jasmine froze now, thinking of the mirror and its ancestral connections. Her beloved grandmother's gilt framed mirror. She wondered if it was her grandmother they spoke of and Jasmine had followed her through the portal and shown her the way back.

'Did she mention her granddaughter's name?' Jasmine asked.

'Jaygee, I think,' said Joseph. 'I remember thinking it was not a name I'd come across.'

Jasmine stood up, staring ahead, 'JG, Jasmine-Grace. I was always known as 'JG,' to my grandmother, the initials of my name. It had to be me. Was my grandmother Ellen-Grace here once? I knew I'd been here before!'

Helen jumped to her feet now and excused herself as she hurried away, eyes wide and hand over mouth as if distressed from memories flooding back. Jasmine was confused and looked to Joseph for answers.

'Helen was very close to Ellie. It upset her greatly when she vanished. All of us in fact, but they were very close.'

'My grandmother told me she had special friends once who called her Ellie. Are you then the friends she told me about when I was a child? I honestly thought it was just a story. My mum, her daughter, used to hush her.' Jasmine found the memories were coming flooding back.

'We believed her Jasmine,' Beth interjected, 'she came like you with no papers or background and appeared to carry knowledge that did not seem possible in these times.'

'Helen will now be thinking you're gong to leave soon, suddenly and never return,' Joseph spoke sadly. 'It was a woman alleging to be her daughter Jacquie who came looking for her first, but Helen could not part with Ellie.'

'What? How old was my mother?' Jasmine was shocked.

'She wasn't a child Jasmine; she was about the same age. That is why this is all so strange; how could we believe this woman was our Ellie's daughter.' Beth interjected.

'So, if I also came looking for her as a child here, how did this young woman Ellie, believe I was her granddaughter?'

Beth looked at Joseph who lowered his head. 'Ellie, came here quite normal Jasmine. But developed a madness that nearly destroyed her and also those here who had great affection for her, seeing her decline. If you were her granddaughter and she recognised you, she must have been convinced to follow you home.'

Jasmine paused remembering her grandmother being like a revolving door patient at the local psychiatric hospital as she grew up, with long periods of intractable depression and at times given long courses of twice weekly Electro-Convulsive Therapy.

She hesitated trying to take it all in. So, Joseph was saying her grandma went mad here? Whereas Jasmine felt pretty normal here, whatever 'normal' was, but had been plagued by mental health problems before at home. Or was she following the same path as her grandmother and destined for recurring bouts of psychotic depression on return? Or whatever the latest label for her was.

Jasmine wanted to run to Helen feeling her pain, but then something struck her. Had her grandmother taken pleasure in a relationship which was more than just a friendship with this same woman Helen? The idea was preposterous, but picturing Helen's reaction to her grandmother's name again, also plausible. She sat back down abruptly. There was so much to consider, she turned to Beth to guide her.

'We will meet and talk every other day about this, and how best to help you my dear.' Beth said reassuringly. She turned to see Joseph's eyes focus on the area behind her. Helen had returned and stood motionless, but nodded, smiling weakly at Jasmine, seemingly trying to hold herself together. Jasmine went to her, her own heart breaking at the thought of leaving her behind, yet lifted at the prospect of perhaps one day returning home.

She thought about what she knew of her Grandma Ellen's battle with mental illness in the twentieth century and the special, secret friends she spoke of, whom she thought her mother knew nothing of. There was a 'friend' she had mentioned often, whom she had a nickname for, was that Helen? She looked up into Helen's face, remembering.

'Helen, did Ellie call you Nell?'

Helen nodded briskly, the unexpected connections hitting them all in different ways. Three generations had been here, Jasmine twice. The question was, how did they actually get home and what about the people and relationships they had to leave behind?

What shocked her most though, was that her mother had apparently been here too and never said anything, or had her mum thought it was all a dream? She knew her mum had always disliked and been almost fearful of her grandma's owl decorated mirror. She had hated Jasmine inheriting it and hanging it in her bedroom. But if they had been here and got back home before, then so could she. Jasmine just had to find the way or be discovered by a loved one and more importantly maintain her sanity.

Beth changed the subject bringing up the new bottles and Jasmine was relieved too at the change of subject. Two days later, Beth went with Jasmine to the nursery, to talk to Emily and Nadia about the importance of the cleaning of the bottles. Her secret was safe, although Jasmine had told Emily many of her 'future stories,' when she was nursing her back to mental health, but she had thought they were all make believe. It worked, and Emily proudly told Jasmine some weeks later, that she had made it her task to ensure that all the parts were thoroughly washed daily and left to air dry. Two days later Jasmine also realised Helen was avoiding her.

16

THE UNDESERVING

Jasmine spent the next two weeks working only day shifts as Victoria had needed every day off to care for her dying mother. She found herself seeing more of Emily because of this and they chatted at night where they shared their bed space. Beth had told Jasmine that Helen had gone away for a few days to see a cousin, but she knew this avoidance was due to the awkwardness of the situation. Her own grandmother had to have been Helen's lover and she recognised time was needed for both of them to come to terms with this. Emily's friendship was a distraction and she could talk to her about anything without judgement, although she never mentioned Helen or her brother Joe. The latter was too painful. Emily's pregnancy was progressing well and she was so happy working with Nadia in the Nursery.

One day, Jasmine found Emily staring into space on the edge of her bed. It quickly emerged that she had been suddenly moved to work with Miss Morley, schoolmistress for the over age-seven girls. Here, she was also expected to go into the over-sevens boy's class, to be witness to punishments handed out by Mr Woodcock or to help deal with any incidents. She hated both classrooms, unable to get the authoritarian teachers to see anything from the children's point of view or be corrected or listen, when they wrongly accused a poor child and chastised them horribly.

There were strict rules on behaviour and corporal punishment was meted out daily. As for all inmates of the workhouse, there were cellars underground where you could be, 'lock'd up,' for two days or dinner could be completely withheld or replaced with just bread and water. Paupers of any age could be deemed disorderly or 'refractory,' for 'slightly worse or repeated offenses,' if something they did was interpreted as disobeying the strict, rigid rules.

Some of the toughest penalties imposed were for simply making a noise when silence ordered, usually during compulsory prayers. Other rules prohibited swearing, threatening, striking or insulting another, not washing, refusing or neglecting work, pretending sickness, playing cards or gambling.

Many families got caught out attempting to make contact with a spouse or sibling they were separated from. You were prohibited from going into a ward or yard assigned to a different class of pauper and segregation was by age, sex and physical or mental ability. Permission was required and rarely given in-between set times, as deemed to 'unsettle' the inmates. Only elderly, infirm couples were permitted to stay together.

Since her arrival, Jasmine had seen a woman made to sit for two hours wearing the scolds' bridle and a man whipped and sent to prison for two months hard labour, but child beatings were even more common place. The description of punishments documented in the big official book, were very different to the ones so cruelly inflicted on an almost daily basis. Emily believed the children, particularly the boys, were willfully ill-treated, with unnecessary and needless pain and suffering.

The rules stated 'No child under twelve should be punished by being confined to a dark room or sent to the Refractory,' yet it was always used as a terrifying threat. Also, 'No corporal punishment shall be inflicted on any male child until two hours have lapsed from the commission of the offence for which such punishment is inflicted.' This was supposedly to control excessive force made on children in anger, but Emily witnessed immediate, barbaric attacks on pupils and also, long drawn-out threats of punishments causing major distress.

Another, 'No corporal punishment shall be inflicted on any male child except by the Schoolmaster or Workhouse Master.' Followed by, 'Whenever any male child is punished by corporal correction, the Master and Schoolmaster, if possible, shall both be present.' This seemed to be no problem, as Mr Woodcock and the Master appeared to take great pleasure and satisfaction in attending and dishing out the harsh, ruthless punishments, which they inflicted on tiny children as young as seven. If the Master was unavailable, Emily was called in from the girl's class to be witness, 'in case of any complaints,' certainly not as an advocate for the child.

'No male child shall be punished by flogging whose age may be reasonably supposed to exceed fourteen years.' Meaning flogging could be administered to boys under fourteen.

Any complaints dared to be made, were either dismissed, not investigated or found to be false. A child was often flogged again or targeted every day if they objected to being unjustly beaten. As vulnerable voiceless victims, with a fear of their oppressors and a shame attached to their abuse, they had no choice but to accept it.

'No corporal punishment shall be inflicted on any male child except with a rod or other instrument, such as may have been approved of by the Guardians or the Visiting Committee.' It appeared to Emily that everything must have been approved and the more humiliating and painful the better at times.

She had seen Archie Phillips beaten with a birch broom, naked, across a table, for leaving a little dirt in the corner of the room. Other punishments Emily was forced to witness included, heads shaved, warm clothes removed and boys being made to wear girls' clothes in school.

William Furnace aged seven was made to step into a sack and crouch down and the cruel schoolmaster hung the sack up on a high beam for two hours because he was, 'annoyingly scratching,' but this was due to scabies.

'No corporal punishment shall be inflicted on any female child,' but this rule was ignored by the schoolmistress, who was sadistic and indifferent to suffering. Eleanor Turner aged ten, was beaten on her bare legs with fresh stinging nettles that had been brought in by the schoolmistress. Emily suspected Eleanor was always the intended victim, as she had watched Miss Morley get more inpatient and irritated with the child, who could not remember her numbers. She was even deprived of water for the rest of the day. Emily later found Eleanor with cupped hands, attempting to collect and drink the water running down the mossy gutter in the girls' toilet.

One day Lucy was made to stay in and scrub the floor on her hands and knees. She had spilled a tiny drop of ink, but was ordered to clean a much larger section of the schoolroom floor, missing time out in the yard. Her twin sister Jessica, hid low behind a desk, discreetly hanging back to help her, as the others filtered out.

Emily had tried to remain with the intention of aiding Lucy, but Miss Morley had guessed this and had ordered her out of the room. Unbeknown to Emily, she had also figured the twin would stay, as the girls were inseparable since their mother had died and had a cunning plan to catch them both. Emily noticed the schoolmistress kept checking her fob watch and after about a quarter of an hour, Emily was summoned from her break and told to follow her.

Without warning, the schoolmistress's imposing frame darkened the classroom doorway. The girls froze as they looked up and met her sneering gaze. Without a word, Miss Morley stood over them and kicked over a scuttle of coal, then turned over the pail of water and rubbed both girls' heads in the sooty, wet mess. Emily could only scream silently inside, her hand pressed against her mouth as the twins cried pitifully. Although she was allowed to help them clean up, seeing their distress and humiliation and the satisfaction on Miss Morley's face, led to Emily not sleeping and a haunted look returned permanently to her pale face.

In the next fortnight, Emily witnessed Timothy struck by a bunch of keys for daydreaming, Jane's head banged hard head against the wall for picking up a dropped pencil, Sarah's face slapped twice for crying, Hetties's hair pulled viciously for turning around, David struck with a pan and Samuel given twelve strokes on each hand for questioning something. Emily and Jasmine approached their friends and a covert meeting was arranged with Helen, Beth and Joseph.

Just like the time when Jasmine had been freed from the callous Mrs Lewis of the Casual Ward, Schoolmistress Miss Morley also received an impromptu visit, exactly one day after Emily went for help.

Hearing footsteps entering her schoolroom, she turned round, ready to scold an unfortunate waif whom she assumed had forgotten something. At the same time, Mr Woodcock entered from the adjoining boy's classroom, asking 'Did you call me Miss Morley.' The unintentional rhyme making Helen and Beth smile. Emily watched on from the back of the room silently and Jasmine had been permitted to watch from behind Beth.

The colour drained from the schoolmaster's face and Miss Morley abruptly sat down, holding on to the desk, her knuckles white. Not a word had been uttered, the teachers did not know the two women who stood before them, but the power in the atmosphere around the room was charged and terrified them.

'Emily will be returning to the nursery to work with Madam Fabron only, as from tomorrow and will not be called upon by either of you again.' Beth spoke slowly, but with authority and the schoolteachers just nodded silently, unable to avert their gaze from the faces before them.

'From now on you will feel any punishment you bestow onto others tenfold.'

Helen stepped forward and the teachers froze, taking a sharp intake of breath.

'Kneel here and pray to your god you will not go to the fires of hell for your mistreatment of these poor, wretched children.'

Standing on shaky legs, both the tyrannical teachers were spiritually forced to kneel on wire netting over hot water pipes, where they assumed a meek praying posture. Just as they had done to little Mickey Carter yesterday and Elsie Nicholls the week before. With palms together and eyes closed, their whispers and whimpers of requests for forgiveness to save their souls could just about be heard.

Charles Dickens had once commented on the trial of an abusive schoolmaster who was absolved of all guilt as, 'brutally conducted, vilely kept, preposterously inspected, dishonestly defended, a disgrace to a Christian community and a stain upon a civilised land.' It was rare for a cruelty charge to ever be tried in court, so with no justice for most pauper children, this was one way of stopping them for good.

Beth and Helen left the room unnoticed and would not be remembered, but the fear implanted in the inner souls of Miss Morley and Master Woodcock would forever alter their practice, as the risk and consequences otherwise, were far too great for them to bear.

17

'MAGICK' GARDEN

Spending much more time with Helen again, Jasmine knelt in the walled kitchen garden by her side, selecting the most succulent sage and rosemary leaves. This area had the means for botanical remedies galore, in the form of produce to make teas, tinctures, infused oils, and balms. Beth used them in many different ways, to soothe, reduce fever, pain, and stop rashes. As a keen gardener who had always helped her father, Jasmine had started to assist Helen in her spare time to pick herbs, weeds, plants and seasonal fruit from the borders.

With Jasmine's extra help, Helen and Joseph, infused, strained and bottled more than ever before for later use. The containers and jars were stored in the tall pantry but some were consigned to a box tucked away under the bottom shelf. Those remedies and bottles that required a warm, sunny windowsill to ferment, were displayed or concealed in the greenhouse. Both Joseph and Helen seemed afraid to keep some of them in plain sight and were often looking over their shoulder nervously. Helen would always reassure Jasmine when she enquired, changing the subject to one about their relationship, her smiling eyes deeply penetrating and almost bewitching to Jasmine. When she tried to dig deeper, curious, Helen whispered, 'Some potions are not meant for everyone's eyes.'

Jasmine was well aware that Joseph and Helen had protected themselves by changing their names and disguising their relationship as one of a married couple, to avoid detection. They were from a family of accused 'Witches,' whose maternal relatives had been tried and hung as 'cunning women.' Although distinguished from Witchcraft, cunning folk remained potentially vulnerable targets for accusations when something did not go to the customers plan.

If any cunning folk were felt to be causing harm to others, the penalty was now long, harsh, imprisonment, and malicious complaints were not always fairly heard. Only professional Witch-hunters and theologians out to make money, continued to proclaim the 'cunning craft,' as being the same as Witchcraft. It was assumed that if they possessed healing powers, then surely their powers could be used to do harm.

On the whole, they were left to their own devices and ignored, avoiding the wrath of laws against magic and witchcraft, except in the case of an actual complaint. But resistance from certain religious groups could lead to unwelcome public attention, when their practice could be labelled as diabolic or heretical. However, many poor and desperate people viewed them as essential and the only way to afford and obtain treatments and cures, so they were left to quietly resume their work, practicing their magic as an open secret. Certainly, the tinctures and teas were herbal and natural, but Jasmine had seen her friends add some strange substances and utter words as if whispering chants.

Helen was known to be a 'healer,' and often summoned by the Mistress for personal use or requested by workhouse nurses to help provide relief for ailments. With fever, a sponge bed bath was the norm, with cool water, using damp cloths particularly on the forehead and back of neck.

Beth would brew a cup of yarrow tea, supplied by Helen, which opened the pores and triggered perspiration. A large spoonful of the herb was steeped in a cup of freshly boiled water and once cool, the drink was offered again, until the person started to sweat. Elderflower, when in season was used in the same way. For sore throats, the inner bark from slippery elm was steeped before straining.

For dehydration, Jasmine encouraged regular cups of cooled, boiled water and set up fluid charts, which Beth and Elsie found very novel, but took this on once they saw the results from monitoring. The hot water pipes around the walls now had bowls of water on them, as a dehumidifier, to stop the air from drying out. This appeared to improve symptoms of asthma and other breathing problems, by reducing mold and mildew. Beth had encouraged Jasmine's relationship with Helen and Joseph, enabling her to meet up regularly, after seeing both differences and similarities in their knowledge and techniques, which seemed to lead to even better recovery when combined.

Jasmine was at her most fulfilled just lately when working in the shrubberies with Helen, learning about the different herbal remedies. She discovered she could offer some ideas herself regarding plant extracts that she was aware of from 'future learning,' with her father. At times, she was suddenly aware that she used modern language or mentioned herbs and spices that had not yet even arrived in Britain, as were imported around a century later.

This sometimes went unnoticed, but often Helen and Joseph would look at Jasmine peculiarly or with intrigue and Jasmine would share something quietly with them. This included stories about future medicines and vaccinations. Joseph was more cautious about being overheard, but Helen loved and embraced any new information.

Gathering handfuls of nettles to steam, the tea when steeped acted as an antihistamine, a diuretic, a treatment for anaemia and also, helped arthritis and rheumatism. Stinging nettles seemed to improve respiratory and urinary problems. She knew from her father that they aided in the recovery of eczema, asthma, sinusitis, and rhinitis, he and her brother Joe were sufferers of these ailments and nettles were regularly on the menu back at home, in soup and even nettle wine made by her parents once. She discovered from Helen the entire plant was of value including the leaves, roots, stems, and flowers.

Helen would stand looking up at the heavens and accurately predict the weather, based on the behaviour of the moon and formation of clouds. She said the different presentations were omens for frost, rain, or fine weather on the way. Jasmine told her about future weather stations and satellites and did funny impressions of weather presenters on television. Jasmine loved Helen's predictions; she was so enthusiastic and captivating, but the feeling was mutual and each brought a smile to the others face.

Walking through the small orchard one day, Helen told her, 'If the sun shines through apple trees on Christmas day it will be a good crop, if it does so on Easter morning, it heralds a warm summer to come.' Also, plants like Parsley sown on Good Friday were believed to thrive, the soil alleged to be 'redeemed from the Devil's power.' They laughed and joked together and Jasmine forgot about her plight to get home, when in Helen's company.

More ancient folklore beliefs were shared one day when Helen showed Jasmine her treasured paper 'Almanac' book. Here she had recorded all of her herbal secrets, advice about animals and prophetic conjurations. She read some to Jasmine as they sat weeding the flower beds one afternoon. As a lover of gardening, Jasmine knew about seasonal planting but Helen obeyed the ancient lores like sowing blooms during the waxing of the moon to make them thrive and dealing with weeds during the waning of the moon, to help them pass away.

'If the scent of flowers is strong, and the Marigolds have not opened by seven o'clock, it means rain,' she continued, 'and when they're fully closed it indicates a storm.' A cat washing its face also apparently indicated rain and a spider prepared for high winds by shortening the main filaments of its web. They giggled, as Helen pretended to present her with a spider up close, to make Jasmine jump and squeal and then chased her around the kitchen garden. This followed with scattering fallen rose petals on each other, laughing contentedly and forgetting their wider fears of separation.

Joseph too had become a good friend and confidante, it was ironic another 'Joe,' should come into her life, after losing her brother Joe so tragically. The next day she was walking past the pond and as she gazed in to the mirror surface, hoping it would suck her back in to her twenty-first century, Helen's face appeared in the water behind her. She jumped, startled by her sudden appearance and Helen laughed, gently squeezing Jasmine's arm reassuringly and resting her chin on her shoulder. Feeling a warmth and contentment from their contact, that seemed to obliterate the loneliness and sadness inside, Jasmine leaned into her, enveloping herself in the tender feeling of safety and trust. Aware of their sudden physical intimacy, she went to step away, but Helen drew her closer to her and they stood motionless for a while.

The moment was interrupted by Joseph's announcement of, 'There you both are!' and he walked them back up the path, pretending to be oblivious to observing their brief, tender encounter. He turned the conversation to the lemon seeded balm, he wanted them to help him prepare, now it was ready for the treatment of hysteria and melancholia.

There was a tiny woman stooped over with old age in the back kitchen, who looked up as they entered, 'Meet Mrs Medlicott Jasmine, she's our Aunty Grace. Blessed be,' he bowed respectfully to her.

'Merry meet and Blessed Be Dear Jasmine, healer from another time yet to pass.' Jasmine stepped back in astonishment, almost tripping over Helen who steadied her and rubbed her shoulders. She felt Helen's energy pass through her and knew she was smiling and had admiration for the elderly woman. It was all too surreal to hold in her head, so she spoke out aloud.

'You know who I am and where I'm from?' she questioned, seeing her nod smilingly, Jasmine added, 'My middle name's Grace and my mother's maiden name was Medlicott.'

Joseph smiled too with a hint of bewilderment. 'Shrewsbury is a small place, perhaps we are all distantly related?' he questioned, but it was unconvincing. Joseph might have told Grace Medlicott about her, but something made her think the knowledge she possessed was more powerful than hearsay. Right now, friendship, acceptance and the strong, warm feeling evoked within her and from every person in the room was enough to feel safe. But Jasmine had one more important question she felt compelled to ask.

'Will I ever go home?' she bravely asked this elderly lady, a stranger, but held in high esteem by her new friends and whom she now saw as an oracle.

'My child, of course you will when it is time.' Jasmine gasped and smiled, 'Blessed be,' she bowed to Mrs Medlicott, immediately liking their aunt, 'and Merry Meet.'

Her delight was mixed with a bitter sweet taste, which she also saw in Helen's face too, as she turned sideways to study her, knowing her return home would mean their parting.

Joseph changed the conversation, explaining they often sneaked their aunt into the back kitchen, to help them make some potions. Herb infused oils, seeded balms, and tinctures, prepared with lavender, wild garlic, apple cider and vinegar. Lemon and rosemary, with alcohol, sugar or vinegar were added to preserve the herbal harvest.

Arnica was bottled, for sprains, bruises and wounds, and gin-soaked raisins for gout and pain relief from arthritis. Beth in particular, had made requests for a tincture to use for sleep aids, to soothe stress and 'nerves,' which included lemon balm combined with valerian root, catnip and chamomile, which was found also, to be calming for restless children as a sedative. The leaves of the Jewelweed plant smeared over a rash helped greatly, as did rubbing an onion over a sting.

Elderflower, when in season made into tea, steeped, strained and drank helped the sick 'sweat it out,' and a salt water gargle with dried garlic relieved sore throats, the latter having antibacterial and antiseptic properties.

Honey was in short supply when Jasmine first came to the house, but she had suggested they keep bees and it was now used for everything from healing wounds to fighting off infections. Honey had always been considered nature's elixir for health and energy. It all helped but Jasmine had never seen such suffering in the absence of modern treatments, and was seeing first-hand, the destruction to the body and mind, caused by diseases that had been wiped out for decades in her lifetime.

Helen and Joseph remembered talk of there once being a large farm here, with twenty acres of good land when it opened in December 1784. The workhouse had been almost completely self-sufficient and made profit, but greedy embezzlement would lead to land sold off, and future inmates would not be offered much in the way of employment. It would be just accommodation for most, unless you had a trade or skills that were useful or you were a vagrant, literally earning your bed and bread and butter.

The grazing farm covered fifty acres, with twenty cows for dairy produce, and pigs kept for selling out once three months old. There were much less animals here now.

In 1796, a windmill had been constructed and flour ground for the house, which had its own bakery, producing bread and beer. The entire surplus would one day soon be sold off for profit, saving the taxpayers thousands, but serious fraud would mean Shrewsbury's experiment in poor relief would be abandoned and the parishes would take over once more.

But with the large herb garden and beehives, combined with healing, Witchery and some 'future' knowledge thrown in, there was at least some symptom relief for many ailments.

There were countless deadly diseases, drifting around in the early nineteenth century. Many paupers were sent to the infirmary, but the Workhouse hospital ward took in many of its own cases. At any one time, there were patients suffering from a wide variety of complaints, from broken legs, measles, typhoid fever and smallpox to blindness, scarlet fever, diphtheria and dysentery. Sage was considered good for most ailments, especially the liver and blood and it would stem bleeding wounds and cleanse ulcers and sores.

Smallpox was beginning to be controlled by the new practice of vaccination but infant mortality-rate was still high. Many of the workhouse children contracted it too late, to escape the horrors of the symptoms and it spread like wildfire. With transmission through inhalation of airborne droplets from the mouth, nose, and throat, through prolonged face-to-face contact or contaminated bedding and clothing, infection was widespread. Separated from their mothers once aged two, they turned to each other for comfort, so the transfer of disease became almost impossible to prevent with the young children.

Scarlet fever had also suddenly begun to recur, in a serious, cyclic and often fatal epidemic. Again, the younger children were most vulnerable, developing sore throats and chills, with body aches, loss of appetite, nausea, and vomiting. Next, the rash followed, like itchy sunburn with tiny bumps. Arriving first on their necks and face, it spread to the chest and back, then the arms and legs. Their little 'strawberry tongues,' became very red and lumpy. Incidence with complications and high mortality had risen dramatically, with no antibiotics, low immunity, and with poor socio-economic conditions on top.

News of a local outbreak struck fear and dread into the heart of the workhouse community. In the worst case, a whole dormitory of children had previously been wiped out in a matter of a week or two. If the rash faded by about the sixth day and the skin and tongue peeled, a sigh of relief could be breathed, as it was a sign of hope and recovery.

Jasmine knew there was no vaccine even in her future world where it was rare, but it still existed. She had no medical or nurse training and sometimes wished her mother were here instead, as she felt she could help more and give advice, but she then felt guilty to want her mother here when Jasmine knew the reality of living through this time. Knowing the basics helped, she had picked up a lot from her dual trained mother and knowledge of prevention helped, like frequent hand washing, not sharing intimate items, and staying away from other people when sick.

She had to find more way to help her charges in the Luna Ward and Emily with the young children. This was not easy, without the antibiotics that would prevent many complications in the future. Jasmine kept thinking that if outcomes could be improved, she would achieve something worthwhile and believed she may even find an opening to her birth century again.

Outbreaks of measles, fever, typhus, and whooping cough still regularly took the lives of tens of thousands of people, young and old. It worried Jasmine sometimes that she had not had the second dose of the MMR Vaccine that is measles, mumps, and rubella, due to having a seizure after the first, but in her own time, she was protected by 'the herd,' a different population altogether.

Diseases spread by contaminated water like Cholera, were much more prolific in the overcrowded, poorer districts outside the walls of the Spike. With public water sources fouled with effluent, Cholera caused profuse and violent cramps, vomiting and diarrhoea. Dehydration was so rapid and severe the blood thickened, the skin turned a deathlike blue, and death followed often in a matter of hours.

There were new Laws however, street-side butchers and fish vendors could not dispose of innards and unwanted flesh into street gutters. It was rare now for householders to throw refuse out of tenement windows, into the streets below.

Jasmine shivered and almost gagged at her memories of the sights and smells of Shrewsbury in the 1700's. Although waste matter disposal and sewage had improved, the water supply and drainage amenities were still insufficient to eradicate Cholera. Night soil disposal was being addressed, but still built up by the River Severn, causing a slick of human sewage and the streets were covered with horse dung.

One of the more prevalent illnesses that Jasmine first heard of was TB, which was known by several different names, including 'the robber of youth,' which Jasmine was soon to discover was quite apt. She also heard it referred to as 'the captain of all these men of Death', as well as 'the graveyard cough,' and 'the King's-Evil.' Beth called it 'Consumption', which Jasmine knew to be Tuberculosis, and having witnessed the devastation it caused. It was a comfort to look down at her shoulder at the protection of her own scar from the BCG or 'Bacillus Calmette–Guérin' vaccine that had only become available since 1921.

Jasmine learned quickly about the classic symptoms of active TB, a chronic cough with blood-containing sputum, fever, night sweats, and weight loss, which was how the term 'consumption,' came about. The Spike moved patients from the Lunacy Ward, when possible, to reduce the risk of contamination and infection. It was one of these deceased, female, patients, whom Jasmine had helped carry down the steps to the mortuary one night. The relief she felt for the poor woman, quickly replaced with the horror of the overcrowded mortuary. It would be later found that at least a quarter of all deaths in the first half of this century, were from Tuberculosis.

Beth tended to use the lotions and potions produced by Helen and Joseph to treat ailments but at times when Physicians when called, aggressive treatments like bleeding, leeches, burning the skin or the less evasive treatment of opium were used. The Workhouse became a grim and forbidding place during an epidemic.

Influenza spread like wildfire, through close contact with those already infected. If flu symptoms persisted and there was inflammation of the lungs, treatment was a course of four or five leeches, or a blister applied to the chest, to relieve the 'oversupply of blood.' The bowels were kept completely open and patients, already weak with fever and infection now also suffered from dehydration, a serious case of diarrhoea and anaemia. Headaches were literally treated with vinegar and brown paper, bandaged around the crown like in the nursery rhyme Jack and Jill. The brown paper heated by fire, and dipped in vinegar.

Jasmine read in a pamphlet that Beth had on the ward, about treatments for influenza of the 19th century, where a physician wrote, 'The influenza, when it attacks young and nervous females, frequently gives rise to great depression of spirits, for the effectual removal of this symptom the following mixture is found to be extremely serviceable.'

Aromatic spirits of Ammonia 2 drams

Compound Spirits of Lavender 2 drams

Compound mixture of Camphor, 1 oz. and a ½

Mix and give a teaspoonful in a wine glassful of chamomile tea

Three or four times a day

Many of the ingredients proved to be quite toxic to humans, or acted as purgatives, which brought about diarrhoea. Other substances used, had a highly corrosive mineral acid, like sweet spirits of nitre or nitric acid. Camphor, when taken orally, was poisonous in large doses, although it could be beneficial when applied to the skin as a vapour rub or used to inhale as a steam. Calomel or mercury chloride, which when taken internally, worked as a laxative and disinfectant was also used in teething powders for infants, with no one yet aware that it caused widespread mercury poisoning. Also used to treat syphilis, it was given in such toxic quantities that hair and teeth fell out.

Rumours were true that the Master had Syphilis, and the Mistress suffered many more of the symptoms herself. Helen knew that he took Mercury treatment, and had a painful skin sore, called a 'chancre' on his groin. It was the reason for his twisted gait and would eventually grow into an ulcer. The Mistress had also contracted it, and had been through the stage of sore nose, throat, and rash and was now at the 'tertiary stage.' Her face had three prominent soft, tumour-like balls of inflammation and her balance was poor, with painful legs and seizures. She wore a wig that was lopsided when drunk or 'drugged up,' and had bald spots and no back teeth.

Jasmine hated the master and once dreamt she had poisoned him, with a philtre she concocted from powders and unguents kept in Helen's locked boxes and chests. She felt panicky on waking, as she was not sure if it was true, with all of her recent experiences of being in and out of touch with reality. On confiding in Helen about the dream, Jasmine was met with a reaction that told her the truth was not that far off fruition, but she was hushed about the matter, leaving her feeling a mixture of awe and trepidation.

With no access to anaesthetics and antibiotics, salves for easing pain were made from natural products. Hogs lard used as an ointment and lotion was made from boiling bramble leaves in water, adding honey and a little wine. Jasmine's namesake 'Jasmine tea,' was brewed for Beth's patients for catarrh, and hot boiled onions and blackcurrant tea aided colds. Onion poultices drew out inflammation and a raw one left in a room collected and retained bacteria. When an onion was tied to painful corns, foot swellings and bumps, it seemed to do wonders.

Eyes were bathed in cold tea or warm milk, and Rue, an astringent herb, was felt to be effective for clearing the sight. Rheumatoid sufferers would have mummified potatoes sewn into their pockets and would wear a piece of Elder close to their skin. During pregnancy, plant Sage was given to help stem infant mortality and ensure healthy blood. Raspberry leaf tea or again Jasmine tea, given to ensure a quick and easy labour. Sick children were passed through the soft branches of an Ash tree, known for its healing powers.

Rosehip syrup was considered even then to be a good healthy remedy, coltsfoot was alleged to have medical properties and Valerian was credited with curative powers. With burns currently treated using white of egg or soap and dandelion juice from the stems and leaves for chilblains, ailments were slow to heal, but Beth and Helen seemed to add something extra, that could not be grown in any herb garden.

One summer evening in the garden, Joseph showed Jasmine the Mandrake plant, considered magical, the berries used for opiates but also love potions! Helen was with them and both women smiled, Jasmine tired to stifle a giggle and Joseph knew for sure. He also smiled to himself, reddening slightly.

18

THE GREEN APPLE MARKET

There was a plan to cover Jasmine's nursing shift with the help of Beth and Victoria, so she could join Helen and Joseph on their weekly trip to the town Market. Supplies needed for the Workhouse, as they were no longer able to produce everything required for meals and the upkeep of the house on site. Previously self-sufficient for most of the produce used, there was now a lengthy list of regular fresh produce needed and as kitchen gardener and cook, Helen and Joseph were in charge. Travelling by horse-drawn cart with Jimmy, a lazy porter at The Spike, who acted as their driver and as usual was quite happy to pull-in next to the Market Vaults and spend most of his weekly 9 and 6 wages on ale at the 'Bloodtub' (9 'Bob,' or shillings, 6 pence and 3 farthings- 9/6 ¾).

As Jimmy checked his fob watch and conferred with Joseph on the time of their planned rendezvous, Helen observed Jasmine looking up at the building intrigued. She explained it was known as the 'Bloodtub,' and the building housed two separate pubs. The entrance off Gullet Passage was the sixteenth century 'Gullet Inn,' originally a debtor's prison. Jasmine knew it as The Hole in the Wall from her day, but found out before that it had also, changed names from the Market Vaults to the Star Vaults after the 'new' Market Hall opened in 1869. It was originally only nicknamed the 'Hole in the Wall,' which made sense now, as its name was probably connected to its previous pre-pub usage of the building's cellars as a goal. Jasmine had been to The Cellar Bar area for live music nights with her friends and read about some of the historic pub's history, but was fascinated to see it as it was then.

The Apple or 'Green Market,' having two names also, was reached via a shut past the pubs, to The Square. There was an abundance of cheap seasonal vegetables like onions, cabbage, leeks, carrots, beetroot, Jerusalem artichokes and turnips on display. Bunches of watercress were available, formed into posies and eaten like that for breakfast as it came, or if you were lucky, between two slices of stoneground bread, smeared with dripping or lard, the watercress, rich in vitamins and nutrients. Joseph called it the 'the poor man's bread,' but when he bought them a large one to share, and broke it up she became aware of her hunger pangs and devoured her portion with relish. Walking on, he told her to expect cherries today as it was summer, with plums in autumn, and the apples in abundance in winter.

Despite all this, the children running around appeared undernourished with tiny frames and looked pale and rickety. Their staple working-class diet was worse than that at The Spike, on bread, gruel, and broth made from boiling up bones. They ate offal including brains, heart and 'pluck,' the name for sheep's lungs and intestine, as well as the bowels, guts, innards, and entrails. Sheep's head was cheap and on full display in Butcher Row and around the Market Hall, sold by the country butchers.

Christmas dinner at this time amongst the less affluent was known as 'poor man's goose,' and was apparently a mixture of sheep's liver and heart, with sage, onions, and potatoes. Helen informed her the Workhouse would be luckier and have turkey or beef boiled with onions and veg, served with forcemeat balls, bread, celery sauce, carrots, cabbage, and 'stoved' potatoes. All cooked slowly by the fire, in dripping and water. Pudding would be mincemeat and plum cake plain, with marzipan rather than sugar icing and sweet oranges.

The streets were picturesque, the produce on sale giving it a country feel despite the chaos and overcrowding on market day. Outside the hall in The Square, the market thrived, but with no shelter, the sellers and their wares were exposed to the open. The Costermongers wore large neckerchiefs and stood behind baskets, barrows and carts filled with fruit and vegetables outside the Old Market Hall. Drawing customers in with their singsong poems, spiel and chants, the most charismatic getting the sales. Young coster girls sold cut flowers and small bunches of herbs in shallow baskets, older girls had baskets full of the now extinct Costard apple, a medieval variety, large and ribbed.

Inside the hall, there was little space and it was too small to provide anything but corn on the bottom and woolen cloth produce on the top floor. Jasmine derived comfort from seeing the familiar building even though this was in a different time. She knew the history of her home town well. The Old Market Hall was built in 1596 and made of stone and had not changed much over the centuries, except the usage. In front of it in the Square, there was once a bog, known as the Bishop's Pool once used as a 'ducking pool,' for 'nagging wives,' and dishonest traders.

In the 1870s, the upstairs would house two courtrooms until 1995. When public hangings were the fashion, many were held in the Square, and condemned criminals would be led from the holding cell in the Hall to be hung in front of the building. During the Second World War, the undercroft would become a brick-built air raid shelter. She placed her arm around one of the columns and closed her eyes, willing herself to open them in 2006.

Brought back abruptly from her daydream, there was sudden shouting and a loud whistle, blown close to her ear. Feeling a tugging on her skirt, she realised she was being pulled around the pillar by a young, strawberry blonde-haired girl, who was one-step ahead of the officer of the law. Almost losing her balance having had her eyes tightly shut, Jasmine stared down at the grubby but cherubic child, who made no attempt to run now, but evaded capture, stepping backwards or sideways, every time the officer tried to grab hold of her.

Jasmine noticed the market sellers and customers paid her no attention. It was as though this had occurred before, the constable knew her name, addressing her as 'Lorraine,' and she seemed to be mocking him, as she laughed, looking directly at him, whilst biting hard into her forbidden fruit, a stolen Costard apple. She was a pretty, cheeky, little thing, raggedly dressed in clothes that were too big and ripped. Helen appeared by Jasmine's side and whispered with affection.

'She's as thin as a lath that young urchin, and always mischief making.'

'I'm sure I've seen her before.' Jasmine pondered but her memory was faltering. As they were speaking, Jasmine spotted another man in close proximity, creeping up behind the child, carrying a menacing looking hook and a large net on a pole; the sort used to catch butterflies. Wearing all black, with a long-crooked nose and sinister expression, he was a replica of the tertiary antagonist; the Child Catcher, in the film Chitty Chitty Bang Bang. The scariest villain and 'boogieman,' of the silver screen, who had regularly entered Jasmine's own nightmares as a child, after watching the film.

Helen stepped forward and Joseph moved to the side, surrounding Lorraine, but unobtrusively. Following their lead, Jasmine moved to the other side, until they formed a wide, but protective circle around the girl. Jasmine was mesmerized as she could see a shimmering sphere of gold and white light that appeared to join the three of them, creating a high-energy space that only they appeared aware of. Joseph silently mouthed some words, and the man with the hook and net seemed to stop in his tracks, looking around as if confused, scratched his head and ambled away in the opposite direction.

The constable also stopped, looked up at the sky as if a drop of rain had fallen on him and with a puzzled expression on his face, he turned away to make small talk with a nearby street seller. The only other person who seemed to notice was Lorraine, who giggled, took another bite from her stolen fruit, and said quite brazenly, 'Ta very much Mistress Helen and Master Joseph and whoever the other nice lady is.'

With that, Lorraine scarpered, ducking and diving through the busy market square, through the mass of produce and people, until out of sight. Helen and Joseph smiled at Jasmine, but Helen looked slightly unsure and glanced quickly at Joseph who nodded reassuringly and beckoned both women closer. Jasmine was not sure what had just occurred but sensed she had taken part in something 'magical,' which had protected the girl and distracted her pursuers.

'She's safe now,' Joseph began, 'You have a natural innate gift Jasmine to protect others.' And with that, he walked on smiling. Helen hung back slightly to walk beside Jasmine and started to tell her a little about Lorraine. 'She's a little thief that gal, one day we shan't be there to save her.' Jasmine shuddered thinking of the harsh punishment of children in the 1800 and 1900s.

Although children between the ages of seven and fourteen were considered incapable of forming criminal intentions, they could be found guilty where proven beyond doubt. If convicted of serious felonies they faced the full penalty of the law, namely sentences of imprisonment, transportation or even death.

'Who was the man in black with the hook and net?' Jasmine asked, almost mentioning the film which would not be made for another one hundred years or so.

'Who? The Constable?' Helen replied, 'I did not see a hook or net.' Jasmine realised she was either seeing things again, or the future was seeping into the past, as the 'Child Catcher' was fictional and from another time, but then so was she...well, not fictional as far she knew. Feeling a mixture of confusion and panic well up, she was about to express and confide her fears, when they turned into a quaint little cobbled street, which Jasmine knew as Princess Street. Lloyds Mansion, a large private dwelling, situated proudly on the corner.

It was there in place, of the future dreary Princess House, containing the twentieth century job centre. In her grandmother's time it would have been Della Portas, Shrewsbury's first department store. Here, the

Music Hall and The Square met 'Candle Lane,' and Jasmine looked for her favourite old book shop, Pengwern, which was presently separated into two rundown houses. At this time, candles were made here and soon, the street would be upgraded and renamed to commemorate the visit of Princess Victoria.

Ironically, Helen slowed down as they passed the premises of the future book shop. Jasmine had read of the horrors that had allegedly occurred here in the past, the fourteenth century timber framed building, held the blood curdling tales of several tragedies. In the 1500s, five children burned to death on the upper floor, as their mother perished below. Sometimes the smell of smoke and sound of children playing and laughing upstairs could be heard by customers in the shop and the one next door. It was also the site where a maid hung herself and Elizabeth Bickerstaff was murdered on the stairs, chopped up by her kinsman Thomas, and buried in the house. He reported her missing, but the landlord's dog dug her up in the cellar, several months later. A malevolent spirit is alleged to pass evil on to another by striking others in the torso on the stairs. Jasmine had even entered the shop with a friend once, who had rushed out feeling sick as she began to mount the stairs to the second floor of books.

'This is where little Lorraine lives, Beth's cousins take care of her as Emily can't.' Helen said sadly.

'She's Emily's child?' Jasmine asked in shock and disbelief.

Joseph, who had walked on with another townsman in front, hovered and re-joined them, hearing Jasmine's question, which had been louder than she realised.

'You didn't know?' he asked gently.

'No!' Jasmine was still quite alarmed, she had thought she knew everything about Emily, after their long confiding chats following her escape from the Master. She had even told Emily more about herself than anyone else, as although just as close to Beth and Helen, Emily seemed to accept and even embrace her stories more, with the intrigue they merited.

'It's well known by those who knew Emily years back,' he began almost apologetically,

'She was made pregnant by the master of a house where she was a maid. That's when she first became unwell and we got her to the Workhouse. The baby taken away, but then mysteriously left upon the doorstep of The Spike one cold night. Beth recognised her by her distinct birth mark. Beth had her smuggled out to the safety of their cousins before she was sold on to goodness knows who. Emily can't cope with even hearing her name or speaking of what happened.

'They're cousins?' Jasmine retorted perplexed.

'Beth and Emily are sisters Jasmine,' Helen stated as if telling her something she had stupidly forgotten. Jasmine needed to sit down, recognising the light-headed feeling of a faint. Helen guided her to some steps, seeing her swooning and sat her down next to her, arm around her shoulders.

'Some things are kept very quiet Jasmine, for good reason in these wicked times, Beth and Emily trust you, but have not had the chance to confide in you all their secrets. The walls have ears!' she exclaimed smiling reassuringly.

Helen cradled her head and whispered, 'Poor Emily was later taken to the reformatory, a refuge for fallen women. Deserted women who are raped by so called 'respectable gentleman,' are treated the same as prostitutes. It's run by a religious lot, they believe that women act out on their own selfish desires. Worse than jail, you're supposed to stay for two whole years to 'cure' you. She had to show a deep sense of self-hatred for her 'evil actions,' and ask for forgiveness from God for her sins. They woke them at 5 o'clock, made them pray four times a day, attend church twice a day, the work was hard labour and they'd be locked in their bedrooms by 8 at night. She ran away and ended up thrown into gaol before we got her back again. And not long after, baby Lorraine was returned, albeit dumped on the steps.'

'And then the Master got her in his clutches. No wonder she's traumatised.' Jasmine said quietly, now able to make more sense of what she already knew. Although there was no explanation as to how she could had first met Emily in 1734 at the prison, which then became 1784, followed by 1834 initially at the Workhouse and now a jump to 1884. It was a complete mystery and as it did not make any sense, it still gave her hope that this was not real, but part of a journey forward and home to her family in 2006.

Joseph handed her his liquor flask, and she coughed as the neat gin hit the back of her throat, but laughed at their startled expressions. He smiled down at her, proffered his hand to pull her to her feet and linked her arm, as Helen led the way towards St Alkmunds, the high spire visible above all the Tudor buildings, for their next purchases.

Poor Emily and the other young women, Jasmine pondered sadly. They were so vulnerable and had no basic human rights or choice in what happened to them. Joseph told her of one of the early female paupers there, who was found to be pregnant and alleged the Master to be the father.

An inquiry heard that she was of 'dissolute character,' who had repeatedly allowed a male pauper to sleep in her bunk and was drunk in the middle of the day. The Directors concluded that the Master was deemed entirely innocent of making the pauper pregnant, and the focus was to change the regime to put a stop to the system of management which could give rise to such complaints.

Since then, he said, 'other methods have to be employed to limit his abuse of power over innocents.' He winked, and Jasmine smiled knowingly. The magic they shared with her was starting to emanate from her also.

They continued walking up Grope Lane, past the Cross Keys on High Street, now her favourite Costa coffee shop, where 'women of the pave' loitered, as they sold their own 'personal wares.' Walking past the burial site of the plague pit which made her very thankful she was not visiting in that era. She had been in this area on The Show Day but it had a different feel today.

Following her nose down Fish Street, Jasmine noted that little had changed, with the familiar churches and the Bear Steps. Her senses however, were immediately startled by the pungent waft of fish. With no refrigeration and the supplies being the catch of yesterday, many customers approached with a hanky over their nose and some women had a posy of dried herbs or flowers tied to their wrists. Vocal fishmongers, insisting their produce was the freshest, from north Wales, Cheshire, or Bristol, moved around with boards and stands full of mackerel, herring, sprats, eels, oysters, mussels, cockles, whelks, haddock, John Dory, and cod roes. Helen was interested in the Herrings, as they could be 'soused', dried, pickled, or smoked. Despite the scant portions allowed at The Spike; Jasmine had noticed the diet of these times was so much richer in vitamins, minerals and plant nutrients and imagined their immune systems would be stronger if only supplies were more plentiful.

Apples and onions both cooked and raw, were a large part of their staple daily diet as well as oily fish, and seafood, and they ate the whole fish, head, roes, and all. She had also noticed most working-class Victorians did not smoke excessively or drink much alcohol, other than weak, yeast-rich beer with meals.

Walking on to purchase The Spike's meat rations, she observed the country butchers, who erected their 'standings,' beyond Fish Street and the Square. Town butchers had their permanent fixtures where they lived and worked at the Shambles,' and 'Flesh Stalls,' in Butcher's Row. They headed there next, as the Workhouse got a discounted price for going local. Joseph said it was the most popular with townsfolk too and had a good reputation, but there was call for an indoor Market Hall for shelter and better conditions. All the windows on the ground floor were rented out as butcher's booths but the noise was deafening as they tried to out shout each other, and the filth and stench was worse than the fish in the next street, to Jasmine's delicate senses.

They bought their meat at the flashboards, thankfully all stove ready today, and with no slaughtering to witness, but the cobbles were red and slippery. Earlier, livestock was driven through the streets, leaving behind trails of slippery, pungent manure and cruelty often ensued. Slaughtered on the premises or even in the streets, the blood of pigs ran down the hill leaving cesspools containing rotten animal matter. Flies polluted the carcasses, turning them rancid.

Thankfully Reforms would take place in 1860, the date stamped on Jasmine's brain through her studies as the situation led to numerous complaints of it being, 'Injurious to health and offensive to common decency and prejudicial to householders adjoining the locality.'

Market traders and penned animals now blocked the streets around Pride Hill and The Square, on market days. Deals sealed by drinks in public houses rather than by Auction. A long row of carriers' carts lined the streets, farmers setting up their stalls and standings, blocking the route. Streets were covered in dung after each livestock fair, which led to complaints, from the churchgoers of St Mary's, who passed that way in their 'Sunday best,' on their way to their sermons.

One woman, Molly Crompton, who was a regular at The Workhouse sold 'nosegays,' tiny posies of lavender, for the genteel ladies to hold beneath their noses to combat the abhorrent smells. It would be another fifteen years before the town had a proper Smithfield, although The Streets Committee formed ten years before, had made improvements to 'clean, drain, pave and light,' the town. Horses were now forbidden to be sold in The Square and sheep and pigs were now sold at Castle Street and 'Swine Market Hill,' now St Johns Hill, and Claremont Hill.

When the dung was collected and sold as manure, Molly went back to her main occupation, the 'world's oldest profession.' Eventually, murdered, in the cellar below the Old Post Office pub, her body found dumped in the river. Helen said her spirit remained there inhabiting a room in the hostelry, accompanied by the distinctive lavender scent of her wares.

Another regular at the Spike was Mary, a 'Knocker-upper,' whose job was to shoot dried peas at sleeping worker's windows to rouse them in the morning. She would leave her four young children tucked up in bed to do her job, but once when one was sickly, she was told to sling her hook for time taken off her work. Helen laughed saying she quickly got her job back, as she was the best around. However, she was still regularly seen queuing outside the Workhouse, with a trail of young infants in tow, a babe in arms and a belly full of arms and legs when destitute, having to rely on poor relief, only obtainable inside the House of Industry.

The saddest case Helen had told her about, was Bridget Doherty, an Irish girl, from a London match factory. There were many flamboyant tales of how she came to be in Shrewsbury, having been the 'maid of a countess,' to a 'stowaway on a barge.' The attention her colourful stories brought her seemed to compensate for the avoidance she received on another level, due to the ghastly hole in her face. She was hard to look at, with a large deforming necrosis in the bones of her face, which Helen said was Phossy jaw. She was really an impoverished girl who had made matches dipping the ends into a mixture containing white phosphorus.

Exposed to fumes from the mixing, spreading, drying, and boxing of the matches. The vapour slowly destroying her bones. First, Bridget suffered painful toothache and gum swelling, before abscesses formed and the jawbone started to glow green in the dark. Without surgery, serious brain damage followed, and she spent her last lingering weeks in the infirmary, dying from organ failure. Helen had told Jasmine those 'saved,' often died of malnutrition as unable to eat. The discovery of red phosphorus would one-day lead to the eradication of the disease and the London Match girls themselves, would hold the biggest strike some fifty years from now, which would improve working conditions no end. Jasmine thought about another favourite film, 'The Little Match Girl,' remembering how she had sobbed, her heart breaking as the child froze to death on the streets, too afraid to return home, as she had not sold enough matches and would be beaten. Jasmine then a young girl, watched avidly, delaying her Christmas dinner to see the very end.

Mardol and Roushill went straight down to the river where the Mortuary was. Walking past, just before the door closed; she could see the inhabited autopsy slabs, lit by gaslights. Moved from Pride Hill, The Circus Yard, now Morris and Co; had a Butter and Cheese Warehouse on Bridge Street, close to the banks of the River Severn, it was ideal for the trading of Welsh dairy produce and where they went next. An intimidating route for 'respectable females,' to pass though, with verbal insults from drunken prostitutes who congregated around these stalls, their trade coming from the riverboats. Eventually it moved to the 'Butter Market,' in Howard Street, known by Jasmine as a nightclub in her time and next door to the 'Dana' Prison, built over and on top of the Georgian prison where she woke up in the 1800s.

Jasmine observed the change in behaviour when Helen and Joseph walked through, a clear sign of respect as well as familiarity, in the women's demeanour, many known well to the Workhouse at one time or another. Their future already contaminated by the cycle of prostitution and pauperism from which they had no hope of ever escaping.

19

ROSE COTTAGE

Jasmine was shocked to see the dilapidation behind the respectable facades of the houses on the main streets. Cutting through, they passed cottages built behind stylish shop and public house fronts. Layer upon layer of homes that looked more like slums, built on the rear of those facing the street. There were holes in roofs and broken drains, but noticeably overcrowded. Others empty of residents but full of squatters and vermin. Alleyways had been driven through the ground floor of existing dwellings, dividing them into two smaller properties.

One-up, one-down and practically falling apart, the dwellings were less like houses and more like rat holes. All available space filled, numerous cottages crammed behind and added to, as monies became available to profit making proprietors. With many built on downward slopes, some families lived in a yard, below ground level. These were hidden pockets of poverty, the living conditions dire.

'Like hovels, a breeding ground for fever.' Helen exclaimed, as all three passed through, hankies pressed over mouth and nose.

Outside, the damp, warped masonry and scant ill-fitting windows signalled the ramshackle, neglected state of the area. Blocked outside lavatories and slops poured into improperly trapped open drains leading to backflow. This left inches of human excrement with overflow discharged into the yard and cellars instead of running down towards the river. She remembered reading these outside lavatories were often shared by over one hundred people from large families and often blocked and unusable.

With no gardens, some tenants had homemade chicken coops and rabbit hutches attached to the walls for eggs and stews. One area, with a courtyard between the cottages had a shared piggery. Joseph told her residents purchase a piglet to fatten and slaughter it as soon as grown. Neighbours who helped feed it would come to watch, and get a cut of the meat. When the slaughter man came, the poor squealing pig would be hung up by its back legs, its throat cut and blood drained off to make black pudding. After splitting its belly open, intestines removed and washed, they would throw the bladder to the kids to use as a football. Every other part of the animal was used to feed or entertain the families.

Helen guided them down a shut and stopped outside a small dwelling with a rickety door. She tapped gently, almost timidly, but probably Jasmine thought, to avoid knocking it down. A tiny old lady, draped in a shawl and head scarf tentatively opened the door a fraction. Seeing Helen, she beamed widely, displaying her toothless grin and moved aside inviting them in. Jasmine realised it was Mrs Medlicott, Helen and Joseph's 'Aunt Grace.' Jasmine turned to Joseph who gestured for her to follow Helen. She was short, but had to bend her head to enter and inside there was no natural light and poor ventilation. The floor was uneven and cold. Joseph followed behind a few seconds later, carrying a heavy container filled with water he had picked up, and began stoking up the fire.

Jasmine noticed Mrs Medlicott's fingers were gnarled with age, and no doubt from the daily toil of hard physical work, taking its toll on her health. She imagined the hardship and poor conditions had brought about her premature aging. The one oil lamp and two candles hardly touched the bleak interior, just enough to be aware of the earthen ground and gaps in the walls where you could see from one room to another.

It was a shack, not unlike a sheep shed, but the room size was more like a rabbit hutch, with barrels catching drips as the roof appeared to leak when it rained. The only other room was a small scullery at the rear and there was a narrow staircase to presumably, a single bedroom.

Helen dug deep into the pockets of her apron and produced a surprisingly large assortment of fruit and potatoes and a fish wrapped in newspaper, which she put on a wonky table before turning to hug her aunt tightly. Looking up, Mrs Medlicott welcomed Jasmine also.

'Jasmine-Grace, how lovely to see you, welcome to Rose Cottage,' and stepping towards her, arms outstretched she embraced her too.

'Come, please come with me,' signalled Grace and beckoning them to follow her, she climbed the short, decrepit steps to the top of the house. Jasmine followed intrigued and reassured by the expressions of her friends who smiled knowingly. She wondered why they were going upstairs, as when her eyes had become more accustomed to the dreary darkness and dim light, it merely resembled another cramped, damp room from down below. On climbing the last step Jasmine stood wide-eyed, almost frozen to the spot.

'How can this be?' she exclaimed, gazing around her and thought if the room below was like a slum, this was more like a palace! The walls up here were lime washed. She'd read once that this was done as a natural antiseptic and deterrent to infestations of vermin that led to tubercular. It also made the room brighter and more welcoming. There were wall shelves, full of small bottles and jars, filled with ground up powders and whole, dried and infused herbs.

Her eyes turned to a pile of huge leather-bound, gold-leaf books, stacked on a chair in the corner. One book was laid open on a nearby three-legged stool and had elaborate hand drawn illustrations of herbs and planetary symbols. Seeing her curiosity Mrs Medlicott urged her to look more closely and permitted her to turn the pages. Jasmine could see strange mathematical formulas and statistics, noting the phases of the moon and aspects of the planets. This went on to foretell their influence on each sun sign in the coming astrological year, like a calendar but with dates for predicted sunspot activity, tidal action and planetary position. Many of these occasions such as the Equinoxes, Solstices and Sabbats were partly familiar, but others like the Night of the Watchers, White Lotus Day and the Feast of Janus were alien to Jasmine. Other dates indicated times to plant herbs and infuse them. Feeling a cold, but gentle hand around her waist, Miss Medlicott had stepped forward to share more information with Jasmine on what she was viewing.

'My 'Almanac' which holds the sacred tools of herbalism and mystical incantations passed down from ancient lore and legend.'

Jasmine smiled widely; her fascination impossible to conceal. She felt more at home in this strange and magical environment than she had anywhere, for longer than she could remember. Looking up there were plants tied in sprigs hung from the beams labelled yarrow, mugwort, lavender, rue, basil, sage, rosemary, mint, and thyme.

Mrs Medlicott grinned widely at Jasmine's mesmerised, open-mouthed reaction. Placing one hand gently on her back which now felt very warm and the other outstretched in front, she signalled for her to view the precious treasures she had, laid out around the room. On a series of small square tables lit by candles, there were arrangements of sacred items not unlike those she had seen in books on Wiccan alters. The first table had an alter bell, a wiccan wand, a pewter chalice and a number of dishes holding clear fluid and salt next to a mortar and pestle.

Intrigued, she moved on to another table that was in fact a large box, covered in an alter cloth with a triple moon pentagon, edged with lace. It was laden with seasonal twigs, dried flowers, feathers and shells. Her eyes turned to a stone with a pentacle drawn on and two ritual blades beside an athame dagger. The candle burning in a glass jar was made of red beeswax and next to it were a number of decorative wands, made of hawthorn and oak wood, stone and crystal.

Lastly, and most ornate of all was a small table holding a goblet, a candle snuffer and some scales. There was incense blowing sage smoke, and two tall candles of white and gold, burning in elaborate candlesticks. The only other object was a tiny ceramic thimble with an owl painted on. Jasmine's eyes widened as she recognised it at once and went to pick it up but stopped.

'It's yours,' Grace Medlicott said, yet she could not possibly have seen, her tiny stooped frame stood behind Joseph who was between them.

'I couldn't possibly,' she stuttered, 'I have one already just like it.'

'That is the same one child, take it now, it belongs to you,' Grace said in a matter-of-fact way. Helen smiled and nodded but could not disguise her puzzled expression. How did Grace know so much? A thimble identical to this had been the start of her childhood owl collection, but how could this be the same one from nearly two centuries before? She looked back at Grace again to check, but the elderly woman was beside her now and took the thimble placing it into Jasmine's cupped hands. She then closed her eyes and whispered something, her head tilted upwards and Jasmine heard her ask the Goddess for her blessing.

'For strength and protection,' she requested, a small ash wand now gripped in her arthritic hand, that she sprinkled with salty water and waved through the incense, 'a symbol of safety from harm,' she finished. Jasmine hoped this would work, she had asked too many questions at the workhouse and was a target herself now.

She remembered now, her grandmother had gifted her the owl thimble when she was only six years old, her mother had not spoken, but had shaken her head and rolled her eyes. Jasmine had thought her mother's disapproval had been because it must be very expensive or deemed too breakable for her, but the significance was becoming more apparent. And with so many strange occurrences, she recalled when she first met the elderly woman, in the workhouse kitchen with Helen and Joseph and discovered her name, 'Grace Medlicott.' Her surname was of course her grandmother's maiden name and 'Grace,' the family middle name, traditionally passed down.

Lastly, her attention was drawn toward a serene looking barn owl, perched on a high crevice in the corner of the wall. Soft brown eyes followed Jasmine's movements and she marvelled at her dazzling white front plumage, with soft downy edge feathers and golden-brown spots.

'Sophea, our white hoolet,' said Grace proudly as she took Jasmine's hand to lead her over to the magnificent bird. There was something so familiar about this great owl to Jasmine. It was as if they had met before and she felt this trusted connection from the bird as their eyes locked. Under the perch stood Grace's tiny wooden bed, embellished with a hanging canopy made from a embroidered cloth and a warm looking soft blanket

They left not long after, Helen's apron pockets and Josephs backpack emptied of the fish and vegetables in exchange for armfuls of herbal medicines made by this tiny, but very charismatic and powerful lady. She kissed them all farewell and looking at his fob watch, Joseph announced it was time to head back.

'How?' she asked Helen as they looked back at the dilapidated building with leaking roof and crumbling walls.

'Illusions!' she whispered back and the pair laughed, making Joseph turn and smile at them both. He had not seen his sister so happy in years, this mysterious stranger had entered all of their lives with charisma and possession of her own new magic, which along with the gift she had of their own kind, was a potent mixture, one she did not yet fully recognise in herself...yet. He was surprised Beth had not confided in her but Emily was not a shock, she was very sadly too far gone, her superficial exterior hiding crippling, suppressed trauma.

The relationship Jasmine had with his sister was of the kind he had rarely encountered, but knew if they perused it, they would have to live as cousins or companions. Helen had lived a lie for years pretending to be her brother's wife to avoid religious persecution. Joseph had enjoyed a few romantic and indulgent liaisons; it was acceptable male behaviour and he had wondered if societal disapproval was the reason Helen had not. There was another woman once of course, Ellie, who like Jasmine, talked of coming from the future before disappearing.

He hoped Jasmine would not do the same and break Helen's heart again, but knew he daren't hold out any hope. But although his eyes were wide open as regards their true relationship, he knew others would not blink an eye, seeing the two women laughing together. It was just knowing his sister so well, her love for Jasmine was blatantly obvious and seemingly reciprocated.

Joseph had to go into the 'Bloodtub,' to fetch Jimmy, who staggered out with a crooked smile on his face. Women weren't often seen in public houses in these times, unless you were a woman of 'ill repute.' The younger, genteel ladies were becoming socialites in the cities and more upmarket establishments, but most here favoured temperance and sobriety as a virtue.

Three of the street sellers met them too, with barrows carrying heavier items they had purchased throughout the day. Surprisingly, Jimmy loaded the goods onto the cart with a steady hand before they climbed aboard and started to head back.

'Talk to Beth, but be careful with Emily,' Helen said pulling Jasmine in close, as she felt her confusion and gloom, 'but I beg and warn you, not with anger, or within the hearing of others,' she smiled with a concerned frown. 'It's complicated.' Helen squeezed her hand and before long, they were joining in with Jimmy's drunken Irish songs, some written in the 1800s, but familiar to Jasmine, like 'Rare Old Mountain Dew.'

Jasmine knew every word as her dad had The Dubliners version. She missed her dad so much but sang away, crying with laughter as Joseph passed the flask of gin around and the mood lightened.

20

MEETING MAD JACK MYTTON

Not every workhouse was as clean and comfortable as Kingsland could be and the inner-city ones were notoriously overcrowded, breeding diseases that wiped out many inmates. Jasmine had once read about a county workhouse in nearby Wellington that appointed a Master, who kept a diary of his findings from his short time there. He was a long-time reformer and campaigner for social justice for the poor, proclaiming himself as the 'upholder of the peoples' rights.' His diaries described dangerous conditions and contaminated food, which the inmates were forced to eat, giving them diarrhoea. He said the smell of putrid mutton prepared for supper, made the night soil smell like 'eau de cologne.'

Master Edward Lawrence accused his assistants of treating the men like dogs, although he later turned on the male paupers himself, calling them 'bone idle' and the females, 'thieves, liars and false as hell.' She could see the article in her mind's eye and remembered the date was 1890. It was disillusioning to think that over fifty years later, even when the facilities had supposedly improved, many conditions remained unchanged.

The Local Atcham Workhouse at Cross Houses, had a reputation for having less than favourable conditions, and was essentially a prison-like structure, dark and foreboding. As with all Workhouses, inmates receiving relief were made to wear special uniforms that signified their demeaning status. Parishioners who had fallen upon hard times through illnesses, accidents and old-age, would often rather beg or prostitute themselves, than enter the workhouse there. But begging was a risky business also, as still illegal and those caught could be publicly flogged. Stealing still carried the death penalty.

Women who fell into street walking, catered for men from all classes and were better protected by bawdy-houses and inns that could be found up narrow shuts and down side streets like Grope Lane. As always, there were certain privileged sections of society, who believed that poverty was caused by the bad habits and poor choices of the poor, labelling them as lazy drinkers and gamblers.

Jasmine had been tasked to accompany a 'lunatic pauper,' who had been wrongly placed at Kingsland Asylum and needed to be transferred to Atcham Workhouse, within the funding of his own parish. This would later become the familiar Cross Houses Hospital, before conversion to apartments. Beth had stared wide eyed at Jasmine when she shared this with her. The cart was also stocked with other items for trade or exchange and as Nurse Beth could not leave the wards, and Victoria was on night duties, another attendant, not known to Jasmine and from the infirmary was to accompany her. The driver was up front with the horses. The woman named Rebecca, was sour faced and grumpy and took no pleasure in the trip which Jasmine was enjoying immensely.

The patient, Victor Astley, had spent two nights at Kingsland and remained quite disturbed appearing unable to take in the explanation she and Beth had given him of what was going to happen to him. Beth had whispered to him calmly, before leaving the ward, but it seemed to have had little effect. Incarcerated in a straitjacket, deemed necessary for the journey, he rocked back and forth, but instead of leaving him alone, the attendant spoke harshly to him and even slapped his face twice. Jasmine swallowed hard, feeling angry and upset at the state of this man and the treatment that befell him.

Although Rebecca was a paid attendant, being the pauper lunacy nurse, Jasmine decided to intervene. Leaning closer to the man, to reassure him, something made the horses suddenly rear and abruptly halt, throwing her forward as they entered the Atcham Bridge, that crossed the River Severn. As she regained her seating position, the man, alarmed by the commotion and fearful of the sudden movement around him, lunged forward and head-butted Jasmine, throwing her backwards, so she nearly fell out of the side of the cart.

At the same time, a funeral cortege was going past on the old, now pedestrian bridge, in the opposite direction. It appeared to make a planned stop mid-way across, but the men rushed to their assistance seeing the fracas on the cart before them.

Jasmine later read in the Shrewsbury Chronical the details of the funeral that had stopped near them. It described the final journey of 'John 'Mad Jack' Mytton, born 1796, who was a wealthy, eccentric, aristocrat and a phenomenal drinker who indulged in gambling, horse racing and hunting. He was known to consume eight bottles of port a day, topped up with brandy.' Jasmine was open mouthed reading this, he was a famous Shrewsbury man, whom most local townsfolk even two centuries later, had some knowledge of. She remembered reading in her studies, that in 1819 the squire was elected as a local MP, after offering a fortune of a ten-pound note, to every Shrewsbury constituent who voted for him. Once elected, he only attended parliament once for half an hour, as he found it 'boring,' and could not hear well.

He became known as 'Mad Jack,' for his recklessness, having rode a bear through a dinner party and a horse upstairs, which he then jumped over a balcony to win a bet. He was known to sleep with his horse Baronet by the fireside, and once set fire to himself to cure hiccups. This led to many believing it was more 'madness,' than eccentricity. Today, he might have been diagnosed with bipolar disorder, formally manic depression, or if he had been poor, he may even have ended up on the Workhouse Lunacy Ward with 'mania and melancholy.

As it was, he eventually ended up in exile in a debtor's prison, where he died in 1834 at only 38, but described in the papers as a, 'round-shouldered, tottering, old-young man, bloated by drink, worn out by too much foolishness, too much wretchedness and too much brandy.'

He had lived a lavish life abroad where he spent his fortune acquired at 21, feeding his dog's steak and champagne among other extravagances, before returning to England.

It was now 1834, and today's trip had been the same day this famous local man's funeral procession passed through on the way to his burial ground at Halston Chapel, near Oswestry. The horse drawn hearse had stopped briefly on the bridge as it was where 'Mad Jack,' stayed regularly in room 6 of the old Talbot Arms coaching Inn, now called 'The Mytton & Mermaid.' On reading about it later, Jasmine could hardly believe she had crossed the Atcham Bridge at that same moment, in this strange time loop.

It is now said by some that once a year, on the 30th September, his birthday, Mad Jack's ghost appears at the window of the old 1735 listed building. His spooky apparition is then seen to jump from the top room of the house.

The pauper lunatic on the cart had been secured by their driver and one of the men from the funeral coach, Jasmine had recovered quickly and on arrival, the transfer was made when two male attendants from Atcham Workhouse came out to take him, none too gently inside. She struggled later, to forget the image of the poor man on his arrival, knowing he had been confused and paranoid and reacted as he did, due to fear, mistreatment and illness. There was such a clear lack of understanding of mental health conditions in this century, but it reminded her that the stigma still remained, although less so in her own time.

Jasmine was equally horrified at the point of having to hand over Mr Astley's paperwork, as the smell of the unsanitary conditions and the noises coming from Atcham, were indescribable and even Rebecca was keen to head back. They returned in silence, Jasmine only getting a kind word and a cold parcel for her head once Beth greeted her on arrival at the other end.

That night, Jasmine was awoken by a familiar, but chilling voice calling her name. Pushing herself up on to her elbow, she looked around. Everyone appeared to be sleeping. It was joined by another voice, connected somehow and close by, disembodied and yet seemingly human, talking about her in the third person. Falling back against her straw pillow, she grimaced, seeing no escape and feeling forced to listen intently. She had both hands pushed hard against her ears in empty protest, to the tirade of insults and accusations. It had started again.

'She knows it's all her fault and now she's caused this too,' hissed the older, female voice.

'Wherever she goes, there's always a Joe,' a male voice mocked, the one she associated as the inadequate, but vindictive son of the female voice.

She gasped, her brother and her gardener friend having the same name had crossed her mind before, but these worlds were so separate and different. The trauma of losing her brother was partly suppressed here, but she wondered now if she was a danger to her new friend Joseph.

'There's nothing she can do to keep him safe and get herself home.' The female voice taunted.

Penetrating her mind, the voices were uninvited and unwelcome guests of the most despicable kind; making accusations and derogatory remarks, gossiping about her doing terrible things, knowing she was not strong enough to stand up to them. From previous experience, Jasmine knew she had to not argue or tell anyone, as they would become louder and more spiteful and disparaging. Also, she had to be guarded and not trust anyone when they occurred, or something bad would happen to the people she loved...again. Jasmine never recognised them at the time to be auditory hallucinations, they seemed so real and powerful.

It wasn't just an inconvenience, the type she could ignore and confidently reject. The 'voices,' caused a deep, emotional and physical pain in her head, throat and chest, that made her incapable of feeling anything good, just a mixture of sadness, shame, guilt and the heavy burden of loss.

The voices continued in the same vein, 'Look at her now, she thinks she's saving people, when she's sending them to their graves.' the female voice shouted. 'Ha-ha! Her own grave is ready and waiting, it will only stop when she's six feet under!' the male voice spoke with sadistic glee.

Suddenly an owl hooted loudly and she screamed as it landed at the bottom of her bed. Not realizing that she was already sobbing uncontrollably and had attracted the attention of a large number of women in the dorm, she found herself surrounded by soothing voices hushing her and hands patting her. But when she looked more closely, their faces were demonic and grotesque and she could hear them plotting to kill her and put her into her grave. The owl hooted again and took off towards the window, where she heard the screech of breaks and a loud thud. Her brother's hit and run accident, by the man in the owl van was reoccurring. Looking up, she could now hear Mad Jack galloping on his horse around the room but as her eyes searched to locate him, she was held down and could not move. She knew she had to break free from the multiple, murderous hands and get to Joe, to stop him from being left to die.

Unable to take a breath, suffocating under one woman's hand placed firmly over her mouth to stop her screams, her terrified eyes opened to see the welcome sight of Helen standing over her, and the inmates parted to let her get close. Jasmine immediately calmed from hysteria to quiet sobs, but responded to Helen's soothing words and allowed herself to be helped to her feet to leave with her friend. They went down the back stairs, supported also by Victoria who had suddenly emerged. She started to feel safe and calm and did not question that the internal door was unlocked and the disturbance had not attracted the paid attendant. What she did notice again though, as her head cleared and they exited the room, was the silence behind her. It was again as if nothing existed once her back was turned.

Jasmine spent three weeks recuperating under Beth's care on the lunacy ward, sleeping in the attendant's quarter. Daily tinctures of herbal teas and soothing balms brought up by Helen and reassurance and tender loving care; soon got her back on her feet again. During this time though, she became slightly wary of Nurse Elsie, whom she felt might not be all that she seemed.

21

THE ALMANAC

Jasmine made a good recovery with her friends caring for her and confided in Beth that she was worried about Joseph and needed to somehow save him to be free to return home one day. The difficulty was explaining why and where home was. It was a stone's throw from the Workhouse but only existed in another time. She was reluctant to tell Helen, as their relationship was blossoming and it meant admitting her strongest desire was to leave and go home. Plus, she still carried the shame of not saving her brother and continued to fear some unknown threat and danger to others if not put right. Having lost her own brother Joe, she felt responsible for protecting Joseph and Helen from the same nightmare, but did not fully understand why. In the absence of conscious reasoning and having been told for so long she was hearing things or 'delusional,' she did not entirely trust her intuition. Beth listened without judgement though and told Jasmine to leave it with her. What transpired shortly afterwards, demonstrated her trust and belief that would appease Jasmine and arm her with protection when most needed.

Soon after, one late afternoon, Beth received a message from Eddie the porter to say that Jasmine was wanted in the back kitchen to help with something and she was excused to take leave of her duties. On her arrival, Joseph appeared visibly excited about what he was about to show Jasmine, his face beaming as he opened the door at the back of the pantry and beckoned her through. Expecting a small cupboard like space, she followed him down three steps and stooped to pass under the low doorframe, surprised to enter a long, high ceilinged room with shelves and a stone table. Joseph's eyes looked down at a large book which he introduced to her as an Almanac and explained it held a mixture of spells, conjurations, natural secrets and ancient wisdom.

Jasmine gasped but not in shock. It all made sense now and strangely felt like a missing part of a jigsaw, in that this was what something she had always known but had forgotten somehow.

'The Book of Shadows,' she mouthed quietly and he stopped and looked at her intensely for a brief moment, more with surprise than shock. She listened attentively as he showed her hand written charms for healing and instructions on how to make a 'Hand of Glory,' which would render one invisible and how as a last resort, to take the heart of an animal and to pierce it with pins to do harm.

He told here about cunning-folk, who used a wide variety of different methods to cure their customers, from the simple laying on of hands to the use of elaborate magic rituals, pagan prayers and herbal medicines. Thereby appealing to the physical, psychological, and spiritual needs of the sick. There was a huge burgundy book labelled 'Grimoire,' on the lowest shelf that looked well thumbed and another beautifully bound book, the 'Petit Albert.' This he said contained a wide variety of forms of magic dealing in simple but powerful charms for ailments. It was brought to him from Paris by Madam Nadia Fabron, which had them both raising their eyebrows and smiling knowingly at each other. She felt Emily was truly safe now under the protection of the nursery teacher, as long as they could keep the master at bay and if it took magic to do so then even better.

Suddenly, her eye caught a dark shadow and sweeping movement around the legs of Joseph. Looking down she saw the swishing tail of one of the scullery cats and then became aware of the other two.

'Sathan,' he introduced, as if she was meeting them for the first time. 'Azula,' he said pointing to another cat, washing his face who paused and turned to Joseph, gazing at him for a long moment and then slowly blinking his eyes. 'And Luna,' he said affectionately, introducing a cat who was stood on a high shelf, inspecting Jasmine closely with narrowed eyes, but purring, contentedly.

'Your Familiars?' she asked smiling.

'In a manner of speaking,' Joseph replied his eyes shining but his finger on his lips.

'We'll introduce you to the imps and fairies later,' came a recognisable voice with a tinkling laugh from the doorway, belonging to Helen. Jasmine turned and embraced Helen warmly, feeling content and safe and also, honoured at the trust and inclusion she was being shown. She had a strong feeling of belonging and familiarity, like Déjà vu, but did not know if she had already experienced this in the past or the future or if it was imbedded in her psyche. It was clear from past meetings that Joseph and Helen purposely avoided speaking of the fate of their accused and executed relatives, too painful and risky perhaps still, but reference was strongly made to interventions they as 'cunning folk,' would never do.

'Unless the person in question was evil and needed to be stopped of course!' Helen interjected. She explained that they would never offer abortions as some did, usually via a poisonous potion that would kill the foetus. As there were cases apparently, where the potion led to serious illness or death in the pregnant woman and questions were asked or accusations were made of being 'Perverted by Satan.' Working 'fancied acts of magic,' was still a hanging offence. Jasmine wondered if this had been a practice their ancestors had employed to their detriment.

A less sad 'claim to fame,' was a story Helen once told of their mother's aunt who was a local Shropshire healer, labelled a 'Witch' by some, who could cure people suffering from dropsy, known now as Oedema. She would dose them with herbal tea, a recipe she eventually divulged to a doctor named William Withering from Wellington for a small price, after he expressed intrigue at the results she attained. Foxglove was the chief ingredient used, but on being told the secret, it was the doctor only who became rich and famous for his discovery of 'digitalis', extracted from the plant the cunning folk called 'Folkes

Glove' or 'Witches Glove.'

Jasmine was impressed, but sad that the doctor had taken all the credit. She remembered reading in her studies that many 'Witch's brews,' had been the forerunners of modern drugs. Helen beckoned her over to show her a page in the book, entitled 'Talisman,' a spell for fever and thought to be a magical protection against disease

'Take a small nut to be cut in twain, the kernel extracted, and a live spider placed in the shell, which was to be sewn up in a bag and worn round the neck, and as the spider wasted, so would the fever leave him.'

'Have you used this before?' Jasmine asked wide-eyed.

'Of course,' Joseph interjected and lifted a leather necklace cord from his shirt with a tiny cloth sac attached. 'For protection,' he said his own eyes lighting up. 'We'll make you one.' Helen turned to Jasmine who felt a hot flush and a happy, ecstatic feeling and realised her enthusiasm was not just for the magic she was being shown. Looking down, embarrassed at her almost lustful reaction, she realised it had already been noticed. Joseph turned away slightly, a smile on his face and Helen clasped Jasmine's hands with her own.

'I want to show you so much, for you to be a part of what we do,' she said in a dreamy whisper now, her eyes fixed on Jasmine, her pupils enlarged and swirling. Instinctively, she edged closer and lowered her chin, her lips gently brushing Jasmine's forehead.

'Will you join us?' she whispered, her mouth moving down towards Jasmine's ear, sending shivers down her spine. Before she could answer, Helen was brushing her lips against her neck, with a passion that made her legs go weak. She felt herself almost lifted onto the tips of her toes; as Helen pulled her up towards her, her arms wrapped securely around her.

'We will teach you everything,' she said smiling down at her, her voice sounding more powerful now. 'Come tonight after supper and we will initiate you.'

Stepping away from her, she gazed at Helen in admiration. The atmosphere between them had been charged and intense, and the cool breeze that came now, as their bodies parted, made her eager to return.

'Okay.' She said stammering on the two-syllable word and turned to leave; reluctant to go she almost tripped, suddenly intoxicated with her feelings for Helen, hardly noticing Joseph was still in the room.

22

MALEFICIUM

Returning eagerly later to the back room, Jasmine found the atmosphere was more formal, with both Helen and Joseph present to welcome her, but seemingly wanting to get straight down to business. There was no mention of what had occurred earlier, but a charged warmth prevailed. Once they were down the steps and in the back room, Helen quietly closed the door and made several fast, but serene arm movements in the air, she turned to Jasmine to explain,

'I have thrown an inverted pentagram at the door to keep away unwanted visitors, the Goddess will contain and protect.' Jasmine looked up at the door and stepped back, the orange flames shining in her eyes.

'You can see it?' Joseph asked surprised.

Despite it being drawn in the air, Jasmine could see inverted triangles of fire, a pentagram denoting strength and symbolising spirit, air, fire, water, and earth, 'I certainly can,' she said softly in awe of her surroundings. Behind her, another fire stirred in the hearth, apple logs burned brightly with a smoky aroma. 'Considered lucky,' Helen said, 'also, we use them to keep out evil influences.'

'Stone cold, without light. Hold the shadow of the night away.'

The log fire suddenly crackled, its flames flickering brightly as if in response to the powerful chant. Jasmine was quite alarmed at how aroused she felt. Helen stood in front of her and smiled reassuringly.

'You seemed so relaxed for a moment then Jasmine,' she said, her eyes shining.

'Let yourself go, release your fears and the demons we all harbour.' She turned to Joseph who picked up a chain made of silver with a small dark green linen pouch and handed it to her.

'Your chain of protection as promised Jasmine,' Helen smiled and slipped behind her, reaching over her shoulders, to place the necklace on her chest and fasten the clasp at the nape of her neck under her hair. She uttered some inaudible soothing words and the pouch grew hot against her skin.

'Meditate until your mind is clear and you can focus and discard distracting thoughts.' Jasmine blushed, the heat from her chest rising, but remained as serene as possible as Helen and Joseph initiated a chant for protection, to surround the magnetic field with protective light.

'AD GURAY NAMEH, JUGAD GURAY NAMEH, SAT GURAY NAMEH, SIRI GURU DEVAY NAMEH,'

Which translated as, 'I bow to the primal Guru, I bow to wisdom through the ages, I bow to True Wisdom, I bow to the great, unseen wisdom.' Jasmine attempted to join in, finding the pace and rhythm almost hypnotic.

'Carry it through light of day

Out of sight and out of way.'

Helen extinguished the candle on her left and repeated the incantation,

'Stone of earth, stone of shade,

Into thee this spell be made

That no eye may notice me

Whilst traveling to wander free.'

Extinguishing the candle on her right, they were now in total darkness. The log fire had died down to smouldering ashes now, and only the light of the full moon shone through the window, allowing Jasmine to watch Helen pick up the stone in both hands, repeating the following invocation.

'Spirits of the night, Lords of the shadows, Guide my path. Envelope me in thine cloak of darkness. And let this spell be done.'

An incantation with a spell cast for an illusion was then chanted,

'Make them see what cannot be; flames that leap to make them flee.'

Both candles suddenly flared brightly, as Joseph continued,

'Dragon fog and chameleon sight, I command the shrouded sea. I bend the mist; I mix the light. Refract around behind me.'

Despite the formality of it all, they did pause to explain their words and actions, and Jasmine felt she was being given lessons almost as an 'apprentice Witch.' But she also recognised her importance in being a part of this, they needed her as much as she needed to do this herself, and it was all vaguely familiar, as if somehow part of her own heritage. The banishing spell she was told, would help rid them of harassment and cause the harasser to forget about his victims. A cleansing should be done as well, followed by some protection magic to help ensure the harassment does not come back.

Preparation came first, together they went through the first phase, which Joseph read from the book and from memory, and all three of them partook.

'First we Purify and Cleanse our minds and body of any doubts, demons, or spiritual impurities, which may distract us or make the spell go awry, leaving our bodies relaxed and minds clear.'

Following the other two, she cupped her hands to receive a small amount of a clear but pungent liquid, from a ceramic jug to cleanse her face and arms.

'We adorn simple but formal clothes that feel light, comfortable, and clean. We are asking the divine forces for a favour, so dress with reverence or nude.'

Jasmine gasped inwardly, unable to reply and was relieved when Joseph unfolded a dark green robe, which Helen took from him, and wrapped around Jasmine. As she did this, she squeezed her shoulders and let her fingers slide down Jasmine's arms, enveloping her in a soft, warm sensation. Jasmine closed her eyes, imagining being naked beneath the robe and how that would feel, and then quickly shook the thought away. Helen and Joseph then picked up two robes in midnight blue and a rich purple, and unfolding them, placed them around the shoulders of the other. Jasmine watched on intrigued at the ritual taking place before her.

'We anoint ourselves with oils on our fingers, forehead, hands, face, and chest. Visualizing negative and distracting energies dispersing as we rub it in.'

Helen opened a small bottle of Abramelin oil; she told Jasmine it was made using an ancient recipe including Myrrh, Cinnamon, Cassia, Calamus and Olive Oil. A ceremonial magical oil, blended from aromatic plant materials, described initially in a medieval grimoire called 'The Book of Abramelin.' They applied the oils on each other; Jasmine was relieved the dabbing on her chest was nearer her neck, as her body was already responding to the erotic tension in the atmosphere. They finished by anointing Thornapple, which apparently produced a state of trance.

'We purify our space spiritually by burning incense.'

Frankincense, was burned for purification and spirituality, Myrrh for healing and attraction, Copal for purification and cleansing and Pine, and Cedar to cleanse space of negative energy. Dragon's Blood, a red resin from plants, burned for love, strength, and courage, and used to add potency to the spell.

'We sprinkle storm water, collected overnight and blessed by the full or waxing moon.'

Jasmine noticed the moon was full, adding extensive natural brightness to the room. Helen explained the water they used was gathered during a thunderstorm, in the presence of lightening. It had been collected on an outside window ledge, where it had soaked up the moonlight, making it powerful and potent. She poured the storm water into a bowl, and sprinkled consecrated sea salt into it, symbolising the Earth element. Stirring, three times with a quartz crystal wand, she poured the liquid into a corked bottle, for intended use for spells, blessings, and cleansings.

Jasmine watched as Helen cast a circle with salt and she and Joseph placed a simple representation of each of the four elements at each corresponding point around the imagined circle.

A rock, representing Earth, was positioned in the north, a bundle of sage for Air in the East, a candle for Fire in the south and lastly a chalice with Water in the west. They called on the Spirits of Air, Fire, Water and Earth, envisaging the wind swirling around them, crackling flames and sun, waves and waterfalls and the feel of cold, rain-soaked earth beneath their feet.

Jasmine was transfixed at the site of the elements at work, the untouched log fire burning again, and wondered how on earth she could see them all. She could smell the rich, damp soil, their hair was whipping around their wet faces, covered in droplets of cleansing water falling upon them, and flames licked the circumference of the circle. They both turned towards her, inviting her to step inside, she found now that all the knowledge was within her, unleashed like an ancient memory. Standing in the centre facing north, she focused on her feet, curling her bare toes in the cold earth, grounding herself, she envisaged roots of light deep in the core of the Earth. Where the words came from, she did not know and no longer cared.

'Mother Earth, I call on you.'

A bright golden light seemed to shoot upwards from beneath her feet from the centre of the earth and into her body. Helen and Joseph turned to her as a column of light, like branches of a tree sprang from the crown of her head.

'Father Sky, I call on you.' She spoke with a voice she barely recognised, a confidence she had thought was long lost and a knowledge that appeared innate.

'From the earth's atmosphere and into the Infinite Cosmos, bring golden white light down onto us, protecting and containing us from all sides, as well as from above and below. We feel gratitude for this Divine support and thank you, thank you, thank you. The circle is cast. Blessed be.'

The circle encompassed the alter, where they began to meditate and work their magic. Jasmine was alternating between her gift coming naturally to her, to it all being only vaguely familiar again. It reminded her of her illness, where she experienced periods of reality and lucidity, followed by psychosis and dissociation.

Today she was told, they were going to make a waxen image of the Master and stick pins in it. He was already having sleepless nights, after they had tied a toad by its back leg, collected venom that dripped from it in an oyster shell, dropped onto his soiled linen, thereby bewitching him to death, making him feel like he was lying on sharp thorns or needles.

Joseph, seeing her face, assured her the toads were treated well and this was one who had died naturally. Like they, she had no compassion for the world's cruel and abusive humans. It occurred to Jasmine now, that their toads, cats, birds, and spiders were all 'familiars' in their own way, and alive or dead bewitched people, when the right spell was cast alongside.

Jasmine suddenly took a sharp intake of breath, as she remembered her grandmother making reference to the consequences of doing harm onto others, 'Harm none,' she had said, or it can back fire. 'What you send returns to you threefold, whether good or ill.' Her mother had tutted, but it had not been lost on Jasmine at the time; who saw it as more than sensible advice, after discussing her vengeful thoughts regarding a bully at school. Looking at her new friends with concern no doubt etched on her face, they appeared to read her mind, Joseph responding first.

'Jasmine, you have our word and promise it is quite safe to banish, bind, curse, or hex someone who has harmed you and yours in such a destructive manner. It is a myth that the effects will come back on you instead, the negative energy is just what we harness and send back to the perpetrator. It is the only way to stop someone who has harmed others and has no regret, remorse or plans to stop. We send that evil energy back upon him, that he has inflicted on our own; and all his present and future victims, or this will otherwise never end. He deserves all that comes his way, mundane and conjured.'

Helen continued by admitting to only occasionally performing bewitching or cursing for a friend, or friend of a friend. She said extreme care was taken to ensure it was secretively conducted, to avoid unwanted attention or reprisals. The intention was to conjure a supernatural power to inflict misfortune or punishment on a deserved target. Her only rule was the customer had to be the real victim, so the cursed was often a wife beater, adulterer, or rapist, which were all legal in marriage at that time. The magic was also known as a jinx, or dark spell, and could be spoken, written, or cast through an elaborate ritual. The aim was to see harm befall the recipient. Bad luck may dog them, death may take them, or any number of dire fates may plague them.

All was very still in the circle now, and pouring some salt around the 'envisaged' circumference, Helen looked upwards, to the Goddess, her hands raised, and spoke the following words aloud:

'To ward off evil, we mix the perpetrator's urine, hair, blood, and nail clippings which, when put together, will cause harm onto him.'

A lone raven landed on the outside window ledge looking in, and an owl was heard screeching close by. Jasmine shivered, wondering about the myth that they were harbingers of ill health and death. Owls had followed her everywhere since being here and she always associated them with her own brother Joe. The owl van that mowed him down and left him dying in the road.

The wax image had been carefully sculpted and the resemblance to the workhouse Master was uncanny. She began by carving the word 'Master' into the doll shaped wax, then using a sharp athame blade, she started digging deep little holes into it. Helen seemed excited as she sprinkled on some poisonous, soporific and narcotic herbs.

'Medicine from the meadows, woods, and graveyard.' Previously gathered hypnotic and tranquilizing herbs and soil from the around the headstones, were directly dropped onto the wax effigy, or 'poppet' as they called it, which appeared to recoil slightly as if charged, even though a lifeless object.

Joseph brought out a small pewter box, and slid it towards Jasmine nodding at her to open it, which she did very carefully and slowly. It revealed the selection of revolting, mixed personal items, including the Master's hair, saliva, blood and nail clippings, which partially floated in and soaked up a sample of his strong-smelling urine. Jasmine stepped back; her hand pressed firmly over her mouth.

'Jasmine this has to be done by you!' Helen urged almost desperately.

'But why?' she asked almost gagging.

'Three reasons Jasmine,' Joseph spoke more calmly but assertively but she sensed the urgency was there.

'Firstly, you have the virgin gift unused before, and we can guide you, secondly please think of the harm he did to our friend Emily and the others, last of all, you are at great risk personally.'

She knew all of this was true, it was starting to make sense when she thought back to the risks she was taking. Also, she now guessed the gift had always been there, but not harnessed, and came from her mother's side of the family. All the signs were there that she had come from a strong bloodline line of descendants of witches. After her grandmother had died, she had inherited the mirror and noticed its power almost immediately. She had even found a dusty old 'Book of Shadows,' an Almanac, in the attic once. She had read it under the bedclothes, somehow knowing her mother had chosen to push aside her own mothers' ways and yet clearly possessed some also.

There were so many clues looking back, the matriarchs of the family over the last four generations that she knew of were all dream interpreters, story tellers, and 'potion makers.' They all had strong superstitions, used homemade remedies and great cooks using herbs and spices in everything. All nature lovers, completely at home foraging in forests and by lakes, rivers and coasts, enjoying 'alone' time. They were all attuned with the cycles of the moon and sun, could identify trees, birds and reptiles, and employed certain rituals to events.

Finally, she realized they had all had witches' marks, 'it's only a birthmark,' her mother had insisted, but she remembered her grandmother had tried in vain to point out the significance, of them all having strawberry marks at the base of their necks. Looking back, her mother had attempted to deny her heritage, one which they all possessed, the magical imprint of the spiritual bloodline, in the genetic code.

Jasmine had seen herself as almost invincible, unable to come to any real harm because she was from another time. In Doctor Who, there was always an escape plan and a happy ending for the main character. But she was attracting attention to herself, by openly warning others. She knew Beth was worried about her and figured she had asked Helen and Joseph to help protect her. Also, if she was to save Joseph from an unknown danger, she needed to be safe herself.

'Most of the damage is already done as a reversal of Ancient Lore, by bringing Acacia into his room to worsen his condition of syphilis. The fluffiness of the flower is feeding on the vital forces of his sickness.' Helen said as if to reassure her.

'OK.' She stepped forward bravely with conviction and was met with wide smiles and encouraging nods from her friends. As Jasmine poured the bodily fluids and solids liberally over the wax candle, which literally squirmed, Helen chanted a spell.

'Creature of bees' wax thou art, now, creature of flesh and blood you be. I name you the Master of The Workhouse here. No more shall you do any harm, no more shall you take our women and offspring, no more shall you interfere in my life, nor in the lives of the helpless and my loved ones. I return to you the destruction you have caused others back threefold. By the power of the Gods and by my will, so mote it be'

Opening a small wooden box, she scattered the contents on the table, and began to prick the head and chest areas with multiple pins. Lifting the effigy with some ornate pliers, Joseph slowly passed the image of the Master, through the flame of a black candle six times, counting back and forth as one, releasing the powerful, negative energies.

Taking a pot filled with rotting compost and more grave soil, Helen used a knife to make a hole and the wax effigy was dropped in, spat on and covered with soil.

'Joseph will bury it tomorrow on a path the Master walks over daily and the damage done will be rightfully returned.' Helen said solemnly. At the end they thanked each element as well as the earth and cosmos.

'The circle is closed, but never broken. The love of the Goddess is forever in our hearts and souls. Blessed be. Merry meet, and merry part, and merry meet again.'

23

REFRACTORY

The task of burying the effigy had to be a tight, calculated plan, executed in such a way that Joseph and Eddie would not be caught in the process. What they had not banked on was the movements of the Master, who growing increasingly paranoid had begun to routinely change his schedule at the last minute, without informing even his closest confidantes. Also, his physical weakness from recent continuous, slow poisoning, meant he took the flattest routes and when going out had the coach brought as close to the door as possible. The spell was weakened tenfold as the Master did not tread over the ground where the poppet was hidden to release the spell. With so much going on this was not noticed by Joseph or Helen.

Meanwhile, news of expected pauper applicants who tended to be admitted in 'batches,' was privy to Marie, a young pauper woman who helped the Mistress with administration. This information was copied and sneaked to Jasmine as a list, with their ages so she could identify those most at risk. The board of directors met at the Workhouse with the Master in a handsome room, appropriated to their use twice in the week.

On Mondays they received the various applications of the poor and on Thursdays, they would audit the accounts and regulate the internal economy of the house. Jasmine had once stepped in and 'rescued' Marie, just before she landed in the clutches of the Master. Ironically, she now worked for the Mistress but although he had greater access, Marie was certain he would not dare touch her when she had daily contact with his wife.

Emily, who had been kept hidden from the mistress during her confinement, had been forced to perform lurid acts on the Master in the refractory cellar. It had only fuelled Jasmine's anger and hatred against the man further, when another inmate pointed out that some folks had probably turned a blind eye, as it meant less brutal punishment dished out to them when he held a woman down there.

Marie was partly educated, but her father was a gambler and was now incarcerated in a debtor's gaol, so she and her mother had ended up in the Workhouse as an alternative to extreme poverty or prostitution. No local shops or houses would take them on in employment, because of her father's unpaid debts.

One morning, Marie sent an urgent message up to the Luna Ward via her porter friend Eddie, to say that all the doors to the passageways around reception had been locked, and the new arrivals were being processed early, so Jasmine would be unable to intercept them. Knowing something was greatly amiss, Jasmine turned to Beth with a pleading look in semi-panic, as both guessed what was about to happen. Beth gave her a knowing, but worried look and gestured for her to leave down the back stairs that led to the makeshift mortuary.

Selecting the huge iron key, from the bunch tied inside her apron pocket, she unlocked the heavy door. Eddie the Porter, leaving by the normal route winked after agreeing that he would discreetly unlock the door at the bottom, plus the door leading to the kitchen garden where Helen would be, off the right-wing cellar. There was no turning back, Jasmine felt invincible and would somehow seize the opportunity to stop anything awful happening, installing the help of her cunning friends, Helen, and Joseph.

Taking a candle, she ran down the stairway, with Beth's words of caution ringing in her ears, followed by inaudible whispers, which put her in mind of her friend Helen's spells. Jasmine stopped to catch her breath and impatiently tried the door, but had to wait for Eddie who had gone the long way around. He had said he would need to 'bide his time,' as it was off his normal route and he would be questioned if caught. Her heart was beating fast as she heard the key turn in the lock, waiting for two minutes as agreed allowing Eddie to depart, before slowly opening the door, just a crack.

Listening for any signs of life around the morgue, she stepped into the darkness, her small candle wavering as a sudden draft tried to snuff out the flame. She had in the past assisted in taking several bodies down, but had not been there alone before. Unlike the very clinical environment of such places in modern times, there were no fridges, just ledges and openings in the walls, she could see several empty coffins stacked up resembling an ancient burial chamber.

Running quickly through, she noted the refractory cellar on the east wing was empty. If the Master had been bringing a young woman down here right now, she would be trapped as well, at the mercy of a sadistic tyrant. She had to get near to him alongside Helen, and somehow make their presence known. All before he made that turning below the ground floor, into the chilling underworld, that was his lair.

The risk was that he would capture them both. Two more unlocked doors to go to get to the back kitchen, where Eddie promised he would have Helen waiting to assist her. Suddenly, hearing loud footsteps and deep voices approaching, she halted abruptly; fear causing sweat to creep down her back and her blood seemed to run cold in her veins.

Crouching down behind some wooden boxes, she disturbed a rat that scuttled away. Lying low and well hidden, but convinced they would hear her fast heartbeat, she froze. Peering through a gap, she saw the Master emerge, followed by two of his cronies who were forcibly, walking a petite, young girl, no more than sixteen, through the cellars.

Fighting the urge to rear up and scream obscenities at them, she forced her body to lie still, but her limbs and head were full of pent-up tension and adrenalin and her foot inadvertently, kicked back, disturbing a box. The footsteps and voices stopped abruptly and closing her eyes tightly, she imagined their heads turning around in her direction.

Hearing one heavy set of footsteps approaching her, she knew she had to act quickly and leaping up, she began to run the length of the last cellar, towards the final door to the back kitchen. Pulling over a heavy shelf behind her, to block their way, she ran for her life, increasing the distance between herself and her assailants.

Yanking the door handle she pushed it open using her full body weight, falling straight into the arms of Helen. 'I'll find you,' Helen whispered, and Jasmine realised she was still not safe. Grabbed and pulled back through the cellar door into the darkness, to face the eerie light from the candle glow, as the Master held it under his smug and sneering, grotesque face. Stepping towards the wall, cornered and snared, she stared up with abhorrence, at her main captor.

'Refractory,' the Master said plainly, addressing his two men, who grabbed her none too gently and almost dragged her back through the cellar to the 'dungeon' or refractory punishment block. Ahead, the Master had hold of the much younger, very thin girl who was crying and visibly shaking. As if to rub salt into her wounds, he paused and licked his lips, blatantly showing Jasmine his intention and to make her see how powerless she was. He then opened a door to an adjoining room in the network of cellars, pushed the girl in and followed behind. He returned briefly, Jasmine could hear the girl pleading and sobbing, guessing he had just told her of his intentions, as he poked his head back through to address his men.

'Ensure she's 'lock'd up' for twenty-four hours down here on bread and water and then put her in the Bridle for two hours in the main hall, then I'll flog her publicly myself. I'll prepare the Pauper Offence Book later.'

Horrified at her harsh punishment, she wondered how she would get out of this one and doubted she would. At least Helen had seen what had occurred and promised to find her and would tell the others. As she was left alone and locked up, her survival instinct kicked in, she could cope with the solitary confinement and reduced food, but then the thought of the bridle and being flogged were inconceivable.

She had seen the 'scold's bridle', used in the Workhouse once. An instrument of corporal punishment used as a form of torture and public humiliation, which all the women feared. The woman would be additionally humiliated, by the act being carried out in public, the intention to send out a warning to others, to refrain from such behaviour and to control them. Beth had told Jasmine that some women had even been paraded through the town with it on. The device consisted of an iron muzzle in a hinged metal framework that enclosed the head. A bridle-bit or adjustable gag projected into the mouth and acted as a tongue compressor, with a very sharp edge. When wearing the device, it was impossible to either eat or speak. Any movement of the mouth could result in laceration or a severe piercing of the tongue and pallet.

Jasmine's punishment would be justified in claims that her speech and actions could be deemed as 'riotous and troublesome,' despite her true intention being to warn other young women, in a bid to keep them safe. The idea of the 'scold or brank,' as also known, was to 'curb a woman's tongue.' It was in the Workhouse Rules displayed in most communal rooms and read out before dinner at least twice a week.

After listening out for what seemed like hours for signs of hope and possible rescue in the darkness, only to hear the distant sobbing from the younger girl in the master's lair and rats scurrying past, Jasmine finally heard single footsteps and candle light beckoned. It was only one of the master's cronies though, the one known as Gilbert, who brought her stale bread and murky looking water along with two handwritten sheets. He lit another candle, not much bigger than a tea light with his own, and left her with it, telling her to read them both in order.

Punishments

1.'Following a spell in the refractory cell, it is ordered that Jasmine Ravenscroft, for riotous and other ill behaviour, by word and deed, did make insult or revile towards officers, be confined within a Bridle for two hours.'

2.'Jasmine Ravenscroft, a Pauper in the House having wilfully disobeyed many lawful orders of officers of the workhouse, ordered by the Corporation that she be deemed disorderly and publicly whipped in the Hall immediately before Dinner on Wednesday next.'

She thought of the sorcery she had witnessed with her friends Helen and Joseph and the almost comical rhyming line, 'Following a spell in the refractory cell,' and laughed aloud, although nervously. She would take this 'punishment,' and later claim revenge. Her friends would help her find a way to put an end to the Master's abuse and power over the inmates. She also needed to home in on her own magickal powers and escape it if she could.

Exhaustion finally overtook her will to remain awake and alert and she tossed and turned, dreaming not of her punishment and confinement, but of owls, her mother, 'The Show,' and both Joe's.

24

REPERCUSSIONS

Lies were told, in an announcement by the Master before supper that evening. Most inmates were aware of the disturbances in the house earlier that day and had seen the closed off doors and passageways, so it was easy to concoct a story. It was described as a 'plot against the Corporation,' by an ungrateful pauper who was also a so called 'helper,' whom they had captured in the act of trying to form a rebellion to 'bring down the house.'

The punishments were read aloud and they were all told to, 'Let it be a warning to anyone who behaves in this manner or joins such a revolt.' The Master then led in the prayer to say grace and granted permission to eat. After a deliberate delay of serving the evening meal, there was now little chatter or opinions expressed, as inmates hungrily tucked in to their meagre portions. One young woman whispered to another, 'There by the grace of God go I.' As always, the general mood of the inmates in these sombre times was relief, that any unwanted attention was on someone else rather than themselves.

Earlier that day, Marie had heard a fabricated story from the Mistress herself, then the truth from Helen, followed by lies from the Master's announcement. Willing if necessary to risk her own skin but not wanting to blow her cover, she knew she needed to help her friend Jasmine. Deciding she had to act sooner rather than later, she deluded herself into thinking she could aim to appeal to Gwen's more 'compassionate side.' The next morning, Marie looked for an opportunity. Mistress Gwen Parker was looking very ill lately. She had many complaints for a woman of thirty-two and had to rest frequently. Seeing her wince in pain, Marie had an idea. Going to her aid and offering her concerned words and a chair, she reached for the Laudanum from the mantle shelf. Helen had made a tincture of opium and wine and re-filled it for her only that morning.

The Mistress used Laudanum for the pain of gout and her 'female maladies,' also known as 'the vapours,' which comprised of hysteria, depression, fainting fits, and mood swings. Readily prescribed by her doctor and available over the counter in chemists, it was accessible and addictive. Laudanum was known as 'women's friends,' for troubles associated with menstruation and childbirth. Although the Mistress had never conceived a child it was often voiced by her as the 'bane of her life.' Laudanum would later be referred to as the 'aspirin of the nineteenth century.' As it was classed as a medication, it was not taxed as an alcoholic beverage, so cheaper than poppy oil, wine and gin and had the added potent effect.

When Helen had told Marie to bring her the flask, she had said she would replace the contents with a stronger preparation. Gwen was using increasingly more than even the doctor would prescribe as a painkiller, a sleeping pill and tranquilizer. It was a reddish-brown, bitter tasting drink, made of ten percent opium and ninety percent alcohol, and Helen always flavoured it with cinnamon. Today it would be 40/60 with an added ingredient. Marie handed Gwen the bottle and she readily agreed to take a 'nip,' which was more like a hearty swig. As it quickly reached her brain, it visibly sent a warm rush of mental repose and relaxation that seemed to seep through every vein as she smiled contentedly at Marie.

Gwen was a Laudanum addict, who enjoyed highs of euphoria, followed by deep lows of depression, along with slurred speech and restlessness. Her withdrawal symptoms included aches and cramps, nausea, vomiting and diarrhoea. But she was also prone to violent rages, paranoia and jealousy. She was barren and clearly had an unhealthy interest in the workhouse babies, particularly those under one year.

It was hard to know if she was fully aware of her husband's antics or turning a blind eye, but now euphoric, it was Marie's only chance to talk with her. Marie decided to come straight out with it, and pleaded with the Mistress to help her friend Jasmine. Using the current relaxed situation, she attempted to appeal to her as the caring, kindly woman that she was not, but thought she might be flattered by that presumption. What came out of Gwen's mouth was hard to take in as it did not fit with her face somehow, as she was smiling as the vile words spewed from her mouth. Marie was dumbstruck and could feel an icy chill run down her spine. She found herself slowly backing out of the room, wide eyed and aghast. Marie tried to take in and make sense of what this monster had just uttered, aware now of the danger of this evil, but weak loose tongued woman. As she spat out her distaste for all the young women or 'whores,' as she called them, detailing the Master's true intent, Marie felt very scared and unsafe too.

It all made sense now, there were many young women at risk and now she, Jasmine, Emily and unbeknown to her, the young girl in the cellar were top of the list. Reaching the door, she turned on her heels and ran, knowing nothing would ever be the same again as she heard the mistress's slurred, strangulated cries for her to, 'get back now,' before a loud thud, as she presumably fell forward hitting the floor. Marie hovered for a second, considering returning to help the Mistress before continuing to run.

Down in the kitchen, Helen knew about the girl Megan, who had been paraded through the cellar and had suspected for some time that the Mistress Gwen, was implicated in her husband's philandering and scheming, but she had only recently realised just how far it had gone. It was something that Marie had said about Gwen, that had made her question her involvement, and once she was sure, she had decided to deal with the problem herself, before anyone else was really hurt. After Emily's ordeal, and now Jasmine's capture Helen would never let them get away with it

She had protected herself with a simple herbal spell that made her, 'out of sight out of mind.' In fact, the Master and his cronies had not even remembered Jasmine had fallen into Helen's arms, when she ran through the kitchen door from the basement, where they had pulled her back through. It was as if Helen had not been there. She had quickly pieced together what was happening with the likes of young Emily and other girls and their babies. Satisfied that they were part of something bigger, a baby trafficking and money laundering scheme, she knew it was time for drastic action.

Joseph had immediately come on board and had dutifully collected the rat poison that they had never needed previously, with the three workhouse cats. Arsenic trioxide, was a white powder that looked quite like sugar or fine flour and was practically unnoticeable in food and drink, apparently tasteless but deadly in small amounts.

He had called in at a corner shop and asked for an ounce of arsenic 'to kill the rats,' for a few pence, with no questions asked. A would-be killer could obtain enough poison over the counter to wipe out half the neighbourhood. Nicknamed 'the inheritor's powder,' Arsenic later became harder to obtain, after being found to be used by potential beneficiaries of wills whom if caught, found themselves at the end of the hangman's rope. Arsenic poisoning was also pre-eminently a female crime.

The Mistress's Gwen's new Laudanum recipe prepared by Helen was:

3 cups of Wine

60 drops of Laudanum.

A pinch of cinnamon

* ¼ teaspoon of Arsenic *

Gwen had already recovered from a life-threatening overdose of a prescribed opium tincture, due to high morphine content in the preparation. The doctor had been unable to help but Helen had been summoned to prepare something. The Morphine's effect had led to profound respiratory depression and hypoxia. Helen's herbal medicine and instructions to the nurse had saved her life, preventing her from falling into a coma with respiratory arrest and death. After this episode, Helen had been entrusted to help the Mistress with her 'medication.'

Arsenic poisoning produced symptoms of vomiting and diarrhoea, which were also indicators of common diseases such as food poisoning, dysentery, and cholera. If you collapsed, became seriously ill, grew weaker with tingling hands and died after lingering in agony for days, it may still be undetected as deliberate arsenic poisoning. The Antidote was, 'Emetic of mustard and warm water, the white of eggs and castor oil. Keep body warm. Call Doctor.' A preparation that Helen had only made in case 'an innocent got hold of her lethal drink. Not that she would need to call a medical man, her skills were far greater than any local apothecary.

Joseph was with Eddie in the glasshouse in the garden, working out a plan. There was no turning back now privy to hearing even more dreadful details, including the predicament of Jasmine and the new girl captured. Immediate action needed to be taken, and with so many of the corporation suspected of being involved, going to the constable just yet was not an option.

At the same time, Marie found herself running blindly to the schoolroom where Emily was working with Nadia. Beckoning her breathlessly from the doorway, Emily who had been unable to concentrate all morning, ran over to Marie whose face had her imagining the worst. Blurting out her conclusion, no time for the whole story but summarising the terrible truth, Marie then cried, 'We need to get you out, they're going to take your baby and Jasmine's in danger after exposing them and their evil doings. They know I know everything and we're all done for, if we don't get away!' Emily pressed her hand against her swollen stomach, she looked across at the young, dependent children in the room and sat down abruptly.

'Please save Jasmine and yourself and go quickly, but it is my place to stay here with the children now,' Emily spoke calmly as if the realisation of what Marie had said was believed and accepted and there was a resignation of her own fate.

Nadia leapt up, urging Emily to save herself, she would be there for the children she said, but Emily was adamant. She had not told anyone, but had not felt the baby move for days and had stomach cramps and light bleeding and considered herself to be a burden to them. The mistress had visited her several times, offering a solution to her illegitimate 'bastard' baby. Just as they had when they took baby Lorraine. Now she knew this baby inside her was dead and Emily's plan was to ensure her own life was over very soon.

But Marie and Nadia would not have it, and calling Miss Gemma Corbett, who was the new schoolmistress in charge of the girls aged seven to fourteen, they made some excuse about Emily's baby coming imminently and practically lifted her up, half carrying her out of the room, heading for Beth on the Lunacy Ward.

As they approached the ward, Emily no longer protested as the pain reached fever pitch and she fell in and out of consciousness due to haemorrhaging and acute pain. Bursting through the door, they were surprised to find themselves looking straight into the frowning face of Elsie, not Beth. Sensing their shock Elsie appeared to smirk, but then quickly reassured them that Beth was safe and at her home. They had swapped shifts, as Beth had a family matter to sort out. Something stopped Marie telling Elsie what had happened; she had seen her face and heard her whispering with Mistress Gwen and wondered now if she was in on it all.

Focusing on Emily now, her face contorted with pain and legs buckling as she collapsed, all three women carried her over to a bed. Hearing loud bangs and raised voices on the downstairs floor, Elsie turned to Victoria her pauper helper, instructing her to watch the inmates and acting quickly to attend to Emily, she ushered the other two to go.

'I can't leave Emily!' Marie exclaimed, but even Nadia was insistent. Elsie was already administering some medicine to Emily, who was breathing more evenly, and appeared to be in full control of the situation. Nadia promised she would return briefly to the school room and come back to assist Elsie.

Unlocking the door to the back stairs, Elsie placed a small iron key in Marie's palm, closing her own hand over and made intense eye contact with her,

'This will let you out of the coal chute, when you crawl up, use this to unlock the top and push up the grid above you, and stay close to the house before you run for it!'

Marie felt more reassured, but looked apprehensively down the narrow stairway, remembering Jasmine's fate and still not sure if she was down there.

'Helen is going to help Jasmine,' said Elsie, as if reading her mind. 'Get as far away as possible.'

Feeling more confident, Marie picked up a small candle in a holder and descended cautiously down the draughty, dark staircase. Listening intently, she quickly realised she was not alone down there. Marie froze, shutting her eyes tightly, as she did as a child, believing it would conceal her and prayed that the footsteps would turn before passing the bottom of the stairs, for there was no hiding place. Not daring to move until she was sure the heavy footsteps and raised male voices had become faint, she cautiously ventured further down the steps. The Master and his cronies were down here.

As Elsie had indicated, the coal chute was within sight, and she recited in her head, the stages of escape to freedom. Approaching the entrance, Marie stood motionless, her gaze fixed in horror on the locked padlock on the opening. She tried the key Elsie had given to her, but could see it was much too big for the lock. There was no way out! Looking up the chute, she could see the other key hole that would fit the iron key but she could not get past the first lock.

Covered in coal dust with panic welling within, knowing the men were not far away in the network of cellar rooms and tunnels, she headed back up the stairs. Seeing the door slightly ajar and daylight beckoning, she hurried, but half way up she became aware of a woman stood at the entrance, with a vindictive snigger on her face.

'Elsie?' she whispered the question as loudly as she dared, seeing only the outline of her face in part shadow.

'Wrong way Marie,' she said chillingly. Still hoping she had made a mistake and Elsie was just afraid, she tried again.

'There is another lock Elsie, do you have that key?' The woman spat the next sentence out, her words so venomous, they nearly knocked Marie backwards.

'There is no way out for you child!' the door slammed shut, the waft extinguishing Marie's candle before the key was turned in the lock.

Sliding down on her haunches, her heart pounding in her chest, Marie began to hyperventilate, fear overpowering her as her mind started to piece everything together. Realisation that Emily was in Elsie's 'care,' which she now knew to be harmful, she jumped to her feet and was about to thump her fists on the door when she heard light footsteps below. Sensing that this was not the men, but unsure, she backed against the wall and listened intently, her heart beating loudly in her chest.

A woman stepped out from the shadows below and looked up at her, it was Helen! She looked ethereal, her hair usually fixed in a tight bun, hidden beneath a cap, hung loose, down to her waist and she wore a long robe that touched the floor. She beckoned Marie down, with a silent hand signal and a reassuring smile. Relieved, Marie started to run down, but Helen placed a finger on her lips to signal less noise. Once by her side, Helen seemed to know everything, 'We will return for Emily,' she whispered, and summoned Marie to follow her into the darkness.

Helen walked confidently through the cellar passageways, despite the darkness enveloping them and potential danger lurking around every corner. With Marie walking close behind, Helen occasionally paused to listen, placing a hand on Marie's arm to avoid all verbal communication. A little further on they heard a soft crying from behind a door. Trying the handle and finding it locked, Marie heard Helen quietly utter a few unfathomable words, and the lock turned despite there being no key.

Entering the room, they found the girl, who had been intercepted on arrival to the workhouse, crouching and shaking in the corner. Seeing the two females, she instinctively ran towards them, burying her tear-stained face in Marie's shoulder.

'What is your name?' Marie asked her gently.

'Megan,' she answered loudly.

Again, Helen hushed them to avoid detection, with no time to waste she beckoned them and led the way out, along the passageway towards a turning to another room. It had a slab for a bed and known as the 'Refractory.' Here, several deeper voices could be heard, and the higher but strong, protesting voice of a young woman. The Master had watched as one of his cronies Gilbert, had placed the scold's bridle on Jasmine's head, while the other George, tied her hands together behind her back.

Despite her instinct to scream and fight, Jasmine was afraid to even move, as the bitt was pushed into her mouth compressing her tongue and grazing the roof of her mouth, with sharp spikes on both sides. Warned it could cut her tongue and slice the roof of her mouth, she began to employ a meditation technique to calm herself.

She had heard about a poor woman wearing the scold's bridle, dragged through the streets, mercilessly, the brank shaking about on her head. Spitting out teeth, blood and vomit, her jaw broken. She had been urinated on, subjected to physical and verbal abuse, lewd comments, and sexual assault.

Standing back as if to admire their work, the Master demanded that Jasmine would soon be taken to the dining hall, where she would be paraded before supper, 'to be a lesson to all.' Helen had indicated for Marie and Megan, to stand back and shrouding herself in her cloak with the hood covering her hair, she began to chant in a whisper, casting a 'shadow spell,' before stepping forward to the open door.

'Stone of earth, stone of shade

Into thee this spell be made

That no eye may notice me

Whilst traveling to wander free

Spirits of the night

Lords of the shadows

Guide my path

Envelope me in thine cloak of darkness

And let this spell be done.'

In her trance like state, Jasmine could see her gaolers through the iron bars and taste her own salty, warm tears, falling silently down her cheeks. But beyond them, she could see a serene figure surrounded by a bright egg shaped, gold aura. The colour of enlightenment and divine protection. Yet her captors seemed oblivious to the figure in the light. Securing the device tightly, she was then yanked back, via a chain at the base. Keeping her head as straight as possible she smiled, undetected, at Helen. Her saviour was close by.

'Trot on,' she was ordered, like an animal, and so she did, head held high, through the shadowy cellars by candlelight, to the steps of the main house above. As she moved, she focused her thoughts and energy on Helen whom she knew was close behind, although hidden in the shadows, unseen to her gaolers.

She could now hear Helen utter a familiar chant for protection, to surround her with protective light.

'AD GURAY NAMEH, JUGAD GURAY NAMEH, SAT GURAY NAMEH, SIRI GURU DEVAY NAMEH'

Jasmine began to say the words in her own head fluently, and with surreal confidence, but not out loud for fear of being caught or injured in this archaic torture device.

The words, unheard by the Master and his cronies, swirled around her until she felt no pain, only healing light and warmth. It was as she stepped up the cellar steps that she felt the mouth piece fall away, disintegrating, and the iron framework locked to her head loosened but seemingly unobserved by her captors. The brank cage was still positioned over her head, but felt as though it could be lifted off like an unfastened bicycle helmet. The ties on her hands behind her back, also seemed to fall away, but something told her to not let on. Daring to glance sideways, the men appeared fixated on their route to the hall, oblivious even to her movements now.

Helen must have used a banishing spell to hex them, causing them to almost forget about her and hopefully, some protection magic to help ensure their attention did not come back.

Spotting the doorway leading to the hall and front door, Jasmine took her chance turning sharply, pushing it open with her shoulder at the same time as turning the handle. Behind her, she could see the master and his cronies continuing their walk to the noisy dining room, as if strangely unaware of her departure. Smiling to herself, as she realised the power of Helen's spell, Jasmine began to make haste towards the huge oak door. Forced to turn her head as flashing, swirling lights were detected from the corner of her eye, she saw the mirror and her chance to go home. Running back towards it, she was met with a staggering, bloated figure blocking her way, almost in silhouette, with the lights around the mirror, dazzling her.

She half recognized the woman, but could not initially place her and seeing how physically ill she appeared, Jasmine started to approach her to help. Bent over now, groaning, and clutching her abdomen, unbeknown to the woman, her poisoned blood had inflamed her bodily tissues and was causing all her organs to pack up.

Her head suddenly shot up, stopping Jasmine in her tracks seeing her face contorted and twisted. Gasping for breath as her throat, lungs and bronchial tissues were burning from the damage, she wheezed, and in a hoarse, raspy voice, with obvious difficulty even swallowing. She pointed her bony finger at Jasmine and spat out her accusing words.

'You ruined everything!' Her spittle yellow and frothy was dribbling down her chin but the saliva in her throat had dried up. Unbeknown to Jasmine she had ingested high doses of Arsenic and was about to go into shock, followed by cardiac arrest as the toxicity consumed her from inside.

Turning away, Jasmine realised it was the Mistress Gwen, who's voice sounded like pure evil and was now beyond help anyway. Opening the huge front door was impossible and she soon realised it was locked, the large key missing.

Hearing deep voices behind the second door leading to the main house, Jasmine remembered Joseph saying that the Shadow and Protection spells may only last for a short time. Discarding the unlocked bridle from her head and looking up in desperation, she saw the key lying flat on the top of the doorframe, too high for her to reach. Looking down, there were tall tables either side of the door with plants stood in pots. Pulling one out and tipping the plant off, she dragged the table over to the other door, which led to the hall, and pushed it under the handle.

As she retreated, a scrawny hand reached out and grabbed her ankle, making her fall forward, face to face with the mistress, who now had red foaming spittle flowing out of the corner of her mouth, her eyes wide and accusing. 'Emily's baby would have been mine if you hadn't started meddling!' she hissed.

Pulling back with all her might, her strength fuelled by fear and anger welling up inside, at what she was hearing. Jasmine leapt to her feet and stood over the mistress whose grip softened and the woman was still again. The lights around the mirror had disappeared. Jasmine ran over to it still, almost tripping over the Mistress's unmoving body and held the frame tightly on both sides.

Staring at her reflection, she barely recognised herself; scrawny, dishevelled and grubby with a combination of terror and anger in her eyes. Gravely aware her opportunity to go home through the portal had gone, she raced back to the front door, pulling out the second table and stepped up onto it. Reaching up on tip-toes the key was till out of reach, so she jumped, aware of how precarious the rickety table was and then it started to break. Losing her balance as the table legs buckled and collapsed, she was just able to knock the key down, where it clattered to the floor and she scrambled to get it. Hands shaking as she picked it up, she inserted it into the lock.

By now, the banging from the hall was getting louder, paupers demanding their food but also chanting a protest song, heard over the top of the bangs, 'No more pain, no more cruelty, no more hunger or hate.' As if the spell was broken and they had now noticed her disappearance, the door behind her, that she had attempted to jam shut, was being pounded and forced open. The table wouldn't hold for long though, cheap and ramshackle like the other one and she could hear the wood splitting. The lock was stiff, and it took both hands to turn the key, before the huge, heavy door finally opened and she was met with daylight and freedom ahead.

As she ran down the bank below the Workhouse to the river, she could feel the movement and hear faint groans beneath the grass and path under her feet of the long dead rising. She pictured skeletal bones from the Black Death of 1650, scattered and piled up, the unmarked graves that were plague pits and TB burials associated with the Pest House here.

She willed herself to stop focusing on it, she was scared, but this had to be stress induced, not real. She couldn't see anything; it was all in her head. Jasmine used the power of her mind as Beth had taught her, coupled with her determination to be free, to ignore it. 'IT'S NOT REAL!' her own voice shouted in her head, but it was another strange experience derived from her knowledge of local history.

Human bones were found at this spot in 1956, but it was also mixed up with her very real fears of being captured and the residue of her fragile delusions. She only hoped that after all she had been through, she could escape, go home and be mentally stable and feel safe again one day.

'I must get away,' she panted, tearfully out load as she ran for her life trying to drown out the horror, but with all the evil in the house she felt whatever it was outside, it was not after her.

As she reached the water's edge, bizarrely, Eddie was there, as if waiting for her and he promptly paid the ferry man Gordon, to take her across. 'We'll meet you by new St Chads, wait for as long as it takes,' he instructed her.

Crouching down in the boat, she could hear a lot of movement and noise around the Workhouse, but she could also see Eddie racing back up the grass incline, under the cover of bushes as much as possible. Once at the other side, the ferryman prompted her to 'go swiftly,' as if he knew everything too, and she took heel towards the church.

25

RAT KING

Feeling vulnerable, standing shakily outside St Chads Church, Jasmine tried the door but found it to be locked. She was starting to attract attention now, her dishevelled, soiled appearance combined with short, shallow breaths and deep sobs as panic welled up. Seeing the entrance to the graveyard again, she ran blindly through the gate. Almost running straight into a sign saying, 'KEEP OUT!' she stopped abruptly, to avoid collision. Turning on her heels to the left, she stumbled across another sign which announced the warning, 'CHOLERA INFECTED.' Shocked at this frightening information, she turned to find herself stood in front of the tombstone of Ebenezer Scrooge, only to see the engraved letters still spelled out her own name and death.

Finding it difficult to inhale, her chest so tight, she fought that familiar state of not being able to get enough air in and out of her lungs. In spite of her attempts to alter the ending by improving things here, her situation continued to go from bad to worse. She remembered Beth talking about the last Cholera epidemic and how easily it could happen again. Spades lay abandoned, the gravediggers had left a macabre and grisly scene. The overcrowded churchyard had completely changed again, from an early summer evening to an autumnal night, although it appeared bright in the moonlight. There were coffins piled up high in deep pits; the ones at the top could be seen poking out through the damp earth.

Why had these just appeared? She wondered if time had again moved forward to an era of death and despair, another epidemic of incurable disease enveloping the town. The demand for burial greater than the available resources; the stench from poorly interred decaying bodies, poisoning the air.

In a corner of the graveyard, there was a large area marked 'CHOLERA PIT,' holding what appeared to be hundreds of people interred, with a small sign wonkily written with the words,

'Common dead, Destitute and Workhouse Inmates.'

Pits held mass unmarked graves; bodies wrapped in cotton. She could smell the tar the bodies were doused in, a peculiar smell when burnt before internment. It reminded her of the 2001 foot-and-mouth pyres, burning carcasses of sheep and cattle. The smell of roasted meat, mixed with a coppery, metallic odour from the iron rich blood. A musky, sweet nauseating scent from their cerebrospinal fluids. Bodies set on fire and already decomposed, released methane by-products, giving the corpses their distinctive stench.

She could see decaying bloated bodies, now swollen with foul-smelling gases, a noxious stink. Some were buried in quicklime, to dissolve the bones and hasten the decay. The Lime reacted with the body fat turning them into a soapy substance. Caskets floated on the surface in one area. Holes drilled by sextons and undertakers to 'tap' the coffins, releasing the leaking 'miasma,' from rotting bodies, emitting the suffocating 'cadaverous vapours.' Beth's description read from a great book of the last epidemic, filled her mind and now her nostrils, making her heave.

'Corpses filled up the small churchyards, burial grounds and vaults. The stench emanating from the ground, a 'miasma,' or poisonous vapour containing suspended particles of decaying matter, with a foul aroma worse than a cesspool.'

Looking around she could now see the putrefying bodies had been disturbed and dismembered, as if to make room for newcomers. There were broken coffins, full of bones and moving congealed fluid, infested with rancid maggots. Areas had been cleared and coffins stacked, with a sign saying 'FIREWOOD.' Scattered by the gravestones, the disinterred bones, carelessly discarded.

She had read in her studies, around George 'Graveyard' Walker's theory on 'miasma,' rising from the graves and polluting the metropolis. It was from his 19th century theory of overcrowded, London graveyards, which he termed 'a menace to public health.' She knew that as the germ theory replaced and disproved Walker's ideas, sanitary reform led to the removal of the origin of many bad smells. The tearing down of slums, improving housing, sanitation, and general cleanliness led to a dramatic fall in disease. Removing bacteria and the effect of liquefying, decomposing bodies on local wells and water supply, the real cause of many diseases, improved things by the second part of the 1800's. The time had jumped in 50-year leaps so far. Shrewsbury's next cholera epidemic had been the Asiatic one in 1853, but if it was fifty years on would it now be 1884?

If this macabre scene before her was the future, then it would be soon that garden cemeteries were constructed to support the overfull 'boneyards.' She thought briefly of the London Road cemetery in Shrewsbury, where her mother Jackie, had sat and cried, not at her own mother's grave but at her maternal grandmother's. What had happened there? Her dad would walk her and her brother Joe around the neat rows of headstones to distract them, while her mother quietly wept as she tidied the area, adorning it with a simple spray of forget-me-nots.

Behind her, Jasmine turned as she heard the explosive force of a coffin breaking open, the swollen body sat upright, eyes white with spidery blood vessels opened, before the air sucked out the gas and the body banged back down into its internal tomb. Pulling out her handkerchief which she pressed to her mouth and nostrils, the foul stench and peculiar taste filled the night air. Unclassifiable 'body bugs,' sprang from the corpses and lurked in her hair and clothing.

Was this really happening? Wasn't this like a film from a text she had read on George Walker, in Dirty Old London - The Victorian Fight against Filth by Lee Jackson? Feeling nausea creep up to her throat, her head banging and her limbs heavy, she realised in horror, that the corpse that had sat up was familiar. It was the bloated remains of her brother Joe. She then vomited.

A rustle from behind made her turn quickly, a sudden burst of high-pitched squeaking and hissing filled the air, but nothing could prepare her for what she saw moving in the grass. An infestation of black squirming vermin, forming one giant swirling mass of rat that moved separately and as one, hunting together. She had seen a mummified one at a museum, made up of thirty-two dead rats, originally found stuck behind a fire place, but this one was alive. She remembered they called it a 'rat king,' created when a colony of rats become intertwined at their tails, entangled, and stuck together with excrement, blood, and dirt or sticky sap or gum. Formed when trapped in a confined area, they would face outwards prepared for danger, their tails entangled, forming knots permanently glued together. They were a bad omen associated with the plague and a breeding ground of disease, right here in her proximity.

Hearing the scream of an owl, the scurrying creatures stopped in their tracks, as if holding their breath and listening. They sensed their enemy, a perch and pounce predator big enough to take small rabbits. A bird of prey with a perfect connect between ear, eye and striking talon claws. The rat king's downfall was to attempt to run in panic, in different directions, disabled by their entwined tails.

With a sudden swoop and dart, talons fully open forming a spring trap of claws to slice in, the owl made a quick dispatch, a pure strike and kill. If the prey did not die from shock or puncturing of a vital organ, she would finish it off, with a nip from her hooked beak tearing into the flesh. The noiseless flyer hovered over and dived down to nip the tail close to a rat's rear end, so she could separate her kill and fly away with her wriggling, soon to be lifeless meal. The remaining rats squealing loudly, moved as one again, their only chance for cover in the shrubs. Jasmine watched in horror as they dragged two dead bodies, killed in the attack and still attached by tail, relieved they were moving away from her.

As soon as her fear lessened and she could move, Jasmine knew she needed to run from the churchyard to safety. She did so almost blindly, tripping amongst human bones and wooden coffin chippings, in the long-wet grass. Followed by the flapping of wings and hooting of an owl, she skimmed passed her own grave, now open, nearly falling in. Outside the gates, she could see blue sky and bright sunlight. Leaning forward to catch her breath, steadying herself on the gate, she turned her head to see what her hand was touching.

Soft and feathery but warm and wet, it was the blood of an owl, very recently nailed to the gate, an old practice designed to keep evil spirits at bay. Pulling her hand away in disgust she fought the urge to scream.

With the vaguely familiar skyline of the Quarry Park in front of her, her instinct to run through and cross the bridge to her Belle Vue home was overwhelming. Looking back down, she pleaded for the town to be back in its 21st Century form, but she was met by bleaker looking surroundings despite the sunny summer day, with no footbridge or home in Belle Vue.

With so many strange occurrences, Jasmine barely questioned the absurdity of situations like this, but turning to look beyond the gate, it was no longer dark and wild. Everything was back to normal but no sign of Joseph by the rendezvous point. She had escaped the Workhouse Master and his cronies, but hope of reaching her friends was diminishing and returning would put them all at risk if she was captured. She could never go back to the Spike now and with nowhere to go, she was still trapped in this century where she did not belong.

Doubting she belonged anywhere and starting to believe again that she was responsible for all bad things happening, the 'voices' woke up, using the opportunity to reinforce all of her negative thoughts and despondent feelings.

She could not let this happen, 'No!' she shouted firmly, too afraid to stand up to them previously, she now knew she had nothing to lose, only her illness returning. If it did, she would be vulnerable and fall into the wrong hands or be incarcerated somewhere and she would not have her guardian angels with her this time. She dismissed her own powers but knew now she had inherited her grandmother's healing and spiritual gifts, but had only ever channelled them in the presence of her friends. She had been shocked by her ability to partake in enchantments and witchcraft.

The power of simple assertiveness in dealing with the 'voices,' sent them away, although they promised they would be back. But despite this new insight and inner strength and confidence, Jasmine's vision went green and her hearing silent, until her legs gave way and everything went black.

The next thing she knew, there were strong hands raising her up under her shoulders and the aroma of ammonia, as a hanky waved in front of her face. Jasmine's eyes opened wide in panic, only to find the kind and concerned faces of Joseph and Eddie, trying to rouse her with smelling salts. They looked nervously around them, telling her they were in grave danger and needed to move quickly. Leaning against Joseph, but with Eddie supporting her on the right side, Jasmine was whisked through the busy streets, passing shops, houses and pubs. As they approached the Coach and Horses, Jasmine heard the clip-clop of horse's hooves behind them and the sudden crack of a whip, a loud shout and a shrill neighing, followed by a charge at breakneck speed.

Looking over their shoulders whilst swerving to the side, they could see the Master, white knuckled hands gripping the reins, veering the two horses and the cart towards them. The whites of his wild eyes and those of the startled horses, were almost upon them. In the split second before Joseph pushed her into Eddie and out of the path of the cart, she could see Joseph was not going to escape the collision. Instinctively, grabbing his arm, she held on tight as Eddie pulled her, ensuring that the three of them fell and rolled under the veranda of the shop front together. Knowing he would land on her small frame but had a chance of surviving this attack.

Falling in and out of consciousness after a forceful blow to the head at speed, Jasmine began to come around and viewed the carnage around her. The cart was on its side as were the two horses, one panicking, twitching as it tried to stand, the other motionless, its front leg bent upwards and snapped, the bone piercing the skin. It blinked at her through terrified eyes, a tear rolling down its cheek. Jasmine had always hated to see the suffering of animals and turned her face away, tearfully.

The Master was lay very still, the cart trapping his head and shoulders, but the long stream of blood running down the side of him gave a clue to his predicament. She could see both his two 'cronies,' had jumped free, but were brushing themselves down and shaking their heads as they looked at the barbaric scene before them in disbelief. Keen to be no part of this now, they ran away.

Jasmine's attention again turned to the upturned cart that belonged to The Workhouse, where she noticed a distinctive engraved illustration of an owl. Immediately taken back to the scene in her head of the owl vehicle that hit and killed her brother, a fluttering movement caught her eye. A noiseless flyer, took off from the side of the cart and briefly hovered above her. A huge owl, its wise eyes a soft brown and almost human-like, seemed to penetrate and pierce through Jasmine's own eyes as if they were windows to her soul. Jasmine could sense it was urging her to run.

'Quick, get away fast!' came a young voice and in front of her stood Lorraine, the little pick pocket she had helped at the green and apple market. Emily's daughter the 'little urchin,' as she had been called that day, quickly disappeared and Jasmine looked down at Eddie and Joseph who were now both stirring. Propping themselves up on their elbows. Joseph turned to Jasmine to check on her welfare, hugging her with relief at their lucky escape and thanked her, remembering how close he had come. He would have been under the wheels of the cart if not.

Thinking of little Lorraine's words of warning, Jasmine hastily urged them to get to their feet and they began to flee the scene. Lorraine was nowhere to be seen now. She wondered had she finally done what she was here to do. Made amends by saving Joseph, after failing to save her brother Joe. The owl connection was uncanny and yet appeared significant.

26

REUNION

Running blindly through the vaguely familiar streets, the timbered buildings were brown and cream, the norm, before the Victorian fashion of black and white took over. They stopped to catch their breath at a place of shelter from the main street, Eddie and Joseph vigilant as always. Looking around her, she found they were standing amongst a hodgepodge of yards and passageways, crowded within small dilapidated dwellings and large timber-framed buildings. She gazed in awe at the familiar outline of a sizeable pair of buildings, whose distinctive shape she knew well. The future town's Museum & Art Gallery, a large timber-framed building with an adjoining mansion, the town's first brick building. Rowley's House, and Rowley's Mansion built in the late 16th century. It would eventually go into dilapidation but be restored four centuries later, to its former glory, standing impressively in isolation, since the clearance in the 1930s of the slums, that were currently surrounding them.

Finding their bearings, Eddie, and Joseph, exchanged a few words, and hurriedly, ushered Jasmine down a 'shut,' where they stopped at a side door that was the entrance to a small dwelling. Led by Joseph, she stepped into a narrow-darkened hall. On a high perch in the corner stood a magnificent Snowy Owl with piercing lemon-yellow eyes, and three tail bands. He was close to pure frost white with the demeanour of a disdainful ice king.

'He's thirty-five years old and is the companion of a very good friend of yours,' said Joseph, observing her admiration. She was no longer afraid of owls; their presence had proved to be enlightening and they seemed to be showing her the way. Owls were something she had collected since her first cuddly pram owl, given to her by her grandmother at three weeks old. 'Can I?' she asked Joseph, and he nodded, and they both gently stroked the plumage of the great, untethered bird.

He then led her to the left into a back room, a warm kitchen where the most welcome sight befell her eyes. Beth was sitting in a rocking chair by an open kitchen stove, stroking a longhaired black cat who purred contentedly on her lap. Seeing them enter the cat stiffened, arching it's back as it leapt away from Beth, giving Jasmine the opportunity to run into her arms, tears flowing freely down both cheeks. With Beth holding her tightly, Jasmine began to calm down and finally found herself able to speak.

'What has been happening?' she half sobbed. Pulling up another chair, Beth beckoned Jasmine to sit down and placed a warm shawl around her shoulders. Joseph took the steaming kettle from the stove and began to prepare some tea, while Eddie kept an attentive watch on the doors and windows.

Handing Jasmine, a cup of strong, sweet tea and placing a reassuring arm around her, Joseph settled in close and looked towards Beth who nodded to him, indicating that the story could begin. Jasmine was fascinated at the exchange, she had come to think of Joseph and Helen as powerful sorcerers, but clearly Beth was in command and nodded again as Joseph spoke.

'Let me introduce you to our High Priestess.' Jasmine had to steady herself on the chair and was aware her mouth was agape. She had known Beth possessed powers, but her deliberate low profile had disguised her position among her friends. Beth smiled warmly and was instantly recognisable as her old self. Suddenly, Jasmine began to feel panic well up, 'Where are the others?' she cried, looking around her.

'Hush Jasmine, Helen will use all her powers to keep them safe, but bad things have been happening and not everything is within our control right now my child,' Beth stated confidently but could not hide the worry in her eyes.

Looking up at Joseph, Beth motioned for him to continue and he proceeded to update Beth. Jasmine listened carefully, learning more herself about the mysterious events that had unfolded and led to her own assisted escape. It seemed that her friends had known too much for the Master to keep his ghastly secrets and baby farming scam quiet for much longer. It was so lucrative they were prepared to eliminate anyone who got in their way, one by one and hide the evidence. But the Master, his wife and cronies had underestimated the power and determination of their enemies.

While he spoke, Jasmine was aware now that Eddie was not only keeping vigil by the door and windows, but was also unfolding a protection spell to surround them.

The best news to share with Beth, given the circumstances, was that the Master had undoubtedly met his end under the wheels of the cart, and the Mistress was presumably dead now where she fell in the hall. Joseph beamed, when he revealed that Jasmine had in fact saved his life when she pulled him towards her from the pathway of the coach, although he cussed her for risking being crushed by him. The horses' fate was a tragedy which saddened them all.

Jasmine heard that Helen had gone down into the cellars to find and release her, when she realised that Marie was also down there. All hell had let loose when the mistress, her brain addled by opioids and poison, had blurted out their ghastly secrets and shocking truths, making Marie panic and flee to warn Emily. Nadia from the schoolroom, was a good sort through and through, but Elsie was in on it all, as Beth had suspected not long after the Shrewsbury Show. Although she had covered for their absence and let Beth and Jasmine back in through the back door that night, information was being leaked and Beth had identified her as the only possible source.

Elsie had been 'gotten to,' with false promises from the Master of being given her own baby, as had the Mistress. She was feeding back everything she heard or knew to him. Beth had shared her findings with Helen, Joseph, and Eddie, but had decided Elsie was less dangerous under her watchful eye. 'Keep your enemies closer.' Beth told how she had deliberately misguided her, shrouding herself and the others in shadow spells to keep them safe, including the one that Helen used that made her 'out of sight, out of mind,' when needed.

The Master and his cronies had gone down to the cellars to collect Jasmine earlier than planned, to carry out the bridle scold punishment and then make her disappear for good. Therefore, Helen, Marie, Jasmine, and the young captured girl Megan, were all down there at the same time.

'Helen gave me the chance to break free and her spell unlocked the scold's bridle and stopped them noticing me escape, but I should have gone back to help,' Jasmine bemoaned.

'You had no idea of the state of play Jasmine,' Joseph reassured her.

'Your fate would have been dire; they intended to lacerate your tongue with the brank at the very least.' Eddie stated.

When the Mistress had begun to cause a scene and Marie had left hurriedly to find Emily, the Master had been alerted to his wife's plight, as she was by then screaming blue murder in between spewing up blood and he must have recognised she had been poisoned.

Jasmine had so many questions, 'Will Helen be able to help Emily?' Beth looked down sadly, her expression spoke volumes.

'You and Helen introduced me to magic Joseph, I felt honoured, but how did you know I would respond as I did?'

Joseph smiled and looked up at Beth who answered. 'You have the gift too Jasmine. There was always something about you that was special, an enigma. You knew things that were from another time and we believed your claim to be from the future. I have encouraged you to keep that part quiet, but now we can trace where you came from and why, therefore your work here is nearly done.'

Joseph added, 'Your wisdom, knowledge and intuition are unique and your compassion and skills mean you are one of us, even if in another form and from another time.'

Before she could reply, Eddie walked by again and said, 'you have a white aura too Jasmine,' which made her smile. It had completely surprised her to find Beth was a High Priestess, but she would never have guessed Eddie had abilities and practiced magic too.

Joseph put his cup down and drew his chair closer, taking her hands in his. She looked up shyly at him; he and Helen both had a powerful effect on her that she had never experienced before. She wondered if it was a love spell with Helen but she had felt it immediately, from the first time they had set eyes on each other and it had grown as they planted herbs in the garden together, to the harvesting of the crops, the preparation of the tinctures, to the introduction of her identity as a healer and white witch.

Joseph looked at her seriously, as he spoke, but with kind, gentle eyes. 'Jasmine,' he began, 'Your white aura is a pure state of light. It represents a new not yet designated energy with Spiritual, etheric and non-physical qualities. It is transcendent, with higher dimensions of purity and truth; angelic qualities.' Jasmine smiled in awe but Joseph frowned slightly and could not disguise his worry. Beth looked down as if in quiet contemplation also.

'There are white sparkles and flashes of white light around you; angels are nearby but this also indicates that you are with child or will be soon.' He knew of her relationship with Helen and how she kept herself safely away from the Master and his cronies, so what on earth did he mean?

Her mouth agape she slunk back into the chair, pulling her hands free. The white aura she had laughed aside had implications that were more significant. 'I'm not PREGNANT!' Jasmine cried. 'Nor have any intention of being, Emily's pregnant, what's going on?'

27

RETRIBUTION

Meanwhile, at the Workhouse, Helen had turned back towards Marie and Megan, who had stayed low and in the shadows of the cellars as directed, whilst she had ensured Jasmine's safe pathway. Her spells would keep Jasmine protected and give her the opportunity to lose her captors and she was confident she would do it. Marie was leaning over a crumpled Megan when she reached them again.

'She's so weak!' whispered Marie, who was becoming anxious.

'It's okay,' said Helen, placing her hands around Megan, without touching her, and the young woman rose to her feet as a healing Reiki energy flowed through her. Urging them to follow her quietly, Helen led the way back through the basement to the foot of the stairway leading to the Lunacy Ward. Marie looked worried again, remembering Elsie's last venomous words and wondered what they would face, if they managed to even enter the ward. She need not have worried about getting in, just as Helen had dissolved the locks on Megan's locked room and Jasmine's 'scold's bridle,' she whispered some enchantment and the door slowly opened.

Approaching cautiously, the terrible sight that befell their eyes was almost more than they could comprehend. Patients were restless and agitated, pacing the ward, the pauper helper, Victoria, unable to calm them. Victoria was trying to contain Joshua who was becoming increasingly disturbed. As one of Nadia's young charges in the schoolhouse as a boy, Joshua was a poor soul who could not be saved. After being rescued from a rat infested, sewage filled cellar, shared with nineteen other people, malnourished and diseased, he became a pauper child at the workhouse.

He had received good medical and nutritional care and had been nurtured by Nadia. However, his destiny was later to be sold off, as an orphaned child once aged fourteen, as pauper apprentice to a master from the textile industry. He worked long hours, in hot and humid spinning rooms, the air in the mills were thick with cotton fluff and he would crawl underneath dangerous machines to clean them, where he lost three fingers in two separate accidents. One day, after exhaustion overtook him, his master threatened to 'knock out his brains,' if he did not carry-on working. He had yanked him to his feet and pushed him down again to the floor, with so much force, he broke his femur, which never healed properly and caused him constant pain and a permanent limp. Returning to the Workhouse, he soon developed a severe mental illness, traumatised by his troubled life. The only time in recent years he had shown any interest or acknowledgment of other people was when Emily was nursed there.

Leaning over a motionless Emily, Elsie hovered with a sharp bloody, knife. A blood splattered Nadia could be heard pleading with her tearfully, using her hands in a bid to protect Emily. Despite the madness and obvious urgency of the situation, Helen beckoned to them to wait quietly, as she moved silently over, uttering quick, magical words to bind Elsie from doing harm, under her breath. A spell to reflect away harm and restrain Elsie metaphysically, preventing her from wielding her knife.

'By Air and Earth, By Water and Fire

So be you Bound, As I Desire

By Three and Nine, Your Power I Bind

By Moon and Sun, My Will be Done

Sky and Sea, Keep Harm from Me

Cord go Round, Power Be Bound

Light Revealed, Now be Sealed.'

The knife slipped suddenly from Elsie's grasp, clattering on to the hard floor. Turning to see what had happened, Elsie found herself making direct eye contact with Emily's friend, young Joshua, the pauper lunatic with extreme paranoia. He had reached down, grabbed the knife, and was pointing it at Elsie, with a shaky hand, his eyes wide with anger and hatred.

'Walk away Joshua, all is well now,' Helen spoke calmly but firmly and began again to whisper potent words.

'Sun, shine through my cloudy heart, let resentment fall apart.

Give me strength to let this go; forget the hatred that I hold.

Bring thy warmth and love to me, with harm to none,

So Mote It Be.

As the words were uttered Joshua blinked and stepped back. Victoria was soon right beside him, her arm gently under his elbow, as she gestured for him to hand her the knife which he did, after seeing a blood splattered Nadia nodding, as she steered him away.

'Be gone!' Helen hissed venomously to Elsie, who had a horrified look on her face, as if realisation of her own actions had just hit her.

'I was supposed to have this baby!' she wailed feebly. As she turned and fled, Nadia and Helen reached over Emily's lifeless body.

Nadia was distraught, 'She was going to cut out the baby!'

Helen was tranquil and still. 'They have both departed this life.' She spoke sadly.

Marie's body folded, her hand pressed over her mouth unable to stifle the low sob from within and Megan slumped slowly down the wall to the floor.

The blood was from Nadia's hands as she had repeatedly put herself between Elsie and Emily. Fortunately, the cuts were superficial, and the knife had not touched Emily, or her unborn child as intended, but they were both gone from this world none the less. Dropsy and Typhoid Fever had taken her, and as Emily had already known, the baby had died in her womb several days earlier.

Back in Beth's cottage, Jasmine was struggling to cope with her sanity again. This new distress triggered the 'voices,' who returned to Jasmine's head with a vengeance.

'You will be pregnant soon and there's nothing you can do!' hissed a loud, female voice.

Jasmine wanted to push them away and shout back, but she could sense there were others waiting in the background, whispering about her in a derogatory way.

'She's had it coming for some time, always interfering.'

'She made things worse for that poor girl and she didn't save Emily.'

'She didn't save Joe either, he's dead because of her!'

Tortured by their accusations and the guilt she carried, which overwhelmed her, she could no longer focus on anything but her internal anguish. Oblivious to everything else and forced to listen, with no way to escape from her own head, she thought they would get worse if she argued. Head in hands, locked in her own world, she rocked in the chair, helpless to defend herself in the face of her florid psychosis, which to her was real.

This time Joseph, seeing her torment rose to his feet and went to embrace her but Beth stopped him, signalling to him to wait with her hand. She began to talk gently to Jasmine, not magic, just calm, gentle, familiar, reassuring words, that began to penetrate Jasmine's brain. Seeping in, Beth's words empowered Jasmine use all her strength to overpower the persecutory delusions and auditory hallucinations, drowning them out, replacing hate and blame with love and strength. With the confidence to stand up to them again, Jasmine spoke firmly,

'Go away.' This initially alarmed Joseph, but Beth smiled and nodded, knowing the words were not meant for them but for the unseen stimuli. At last able to embrace her, Jasmine and Joseph stood close together, and her mental torment began to ebb away, the voices quieter and less potent.

Over at the Workhouse, there was little else to be done.

'We need to leave now,' Helen said firmly, taking control of the helpless situation. Marie helped Megan up from the floor.

'I have to go back to the children,' Nadia wept, not taking her eyes off Emily's waxen like face.

'We'll go back that way with you, and if it's safe, lock yourself in with them, we will get help.'

They left the Luna Ward silently, Victoria, the pauper assistant was terrified, and it was decided she should go with them, so they locked the door on the ward. With Elsie gone and nothing more they could do for Emily and her unborn child; they remained in danger and Helen knew they needed to convene at Beth's house. Helen had calmed the ward, with words that appeared to discharge the tension from the air, evoking positive energy and all was tranquil and still. Joshua was sat in the corner of the room, as if he had totally forgotten the incident he had just witnessed. Nadia covered Emily's still warm body with a sheet, whilst making the sign of the cross and dabbing her own silent tears.

Meanwhile, Jasmine sat back down close to Beth. There were so many unanswered questions for Jasmine as well as new insights and it now felt the right time to tell her friends more about herself. But where did she begin? They knew she had mental health problems or 'madness,' which she struggled with just like her grandmother Ellen-Grace. They had introduced her to magic and healing which she had taken to very quickly and naturally, as if it were innate, having obvious, unknown abilities.

Beth had admitted to finding her a mystery and both she and Joseph had explained it through her unchanneled gift, but Jasmine felt the need to tell them everything. She has never mentioned her brother Joe and how she felt her purpose here was to save Joseph and find the mirror to return home.

Back at the Workhouse, leaving Nadia safely locked in with her young charges, Helen signalled for the women to follow her quietly. Listening at the top of the stairs for movement or sounds below, they ran quickly down and across the corridor to the doorway to the hall and the main front door. The area at the foot of the stairs in the hall where Gwen had lay dead was clear now, with only smears of congealed blood, mucous and poisoned bodily fluids remaining.

Before they left through the open door, Helen took the gilded mirror from the wall and tucked it under her arm carefully. Keeping them to the edge of the slope, partly concealed by bushes, they hurried down to Gordon the ferryman, who helped them all aboard and moving his fixed rope line, took them safely to the other side.

28

REALISATION

Jasmine was still certain the answers to her destiny were becoming more apparent, as she was starting to piece together the story and understand her part in it all, which would eventually explain the reason for her being here. Looking between Beth and Joseph for answers, they signalled to each other and Beth began.

They had discovered a baby trafficking operation, targeting desperate and vulnerable young women, abandoned by husbands or faithless lovers.

'A baby born, a lost situation, nothing for her and her child but the river or the workhouse,' Beth said sadly. If a young woman was targeted or 'selected,' and made it to the workhouse, they were approached by those involved initially in a gentle manner, shown kindness, sympathy and made to feel like none of this was their fault. Offers of help gradually changed to sewing the seeds of doubt, making the women feel guilty, ashamed and unworthy and if this did not work, then ultimatums and threats were issued.

Informed this could 'all be put right,' if the women were to hand over their babies with the promise that the infants would be given an affluent, educated life, that they themselves would never be able to offer, they relented, fearing they had no choice. The young women themselves were dangled an imaginary carrot, in that they could be employed as a 'lady in waiting,' in one of the town's grand mansions. Some of those young and unmarried women, who did not comply, were told that their baby had died during, or soon after the birth. Denied the chance to see the body of the infant or attend the burial, several women had later gone to the Police, insisting their baby had been alive, even hearing the infant cry whilst being taken away, without ever even holding their child. They were of course not believed, especially when those involved gave accounts of them as, 'mad or grief-stricken, or fallen, deceitful women.

Babies were sold to comfortably off, well to do, nicely dressed, childless couples, who were, 'without encumbrance.' They would pay handsomely for entire surrender of a healthy baby, to 'a good, comfortable home,' and were informed that the child's mother was dead or dying or 'insane,' and that the babies would otherwise be 'cruelly abandoned,' or put into the Workhouse.

As soon as the happy couple left with their much-wanted baby, and the banknotes were re-counted and stashed away, the letter would be drawn up, to be sent off in three months' time. Once bonding had occurred and the baby had become attached and irreplaceable to his or her new parents, they would receive a note demanding more money. This was said to compensate for either the father, who had supposedly returned to collect the child, or the 'dying or lunatic mother,' who had completely recovered. If it did not work, they would be relentlessly bribed and threatened.

In reality, the babies' fathers were rarely on the scene and the workhouse mothers would of course be long gone, subjected to a life of drudgery as a servant by their new mistress or sometimes abuse, from the master or other servants from her new place of work. As a lowly maid, any further pregnancies that followed, fathered through sexual exploitation, led to the workhouse taking that baby off her hands too. Agreeing reluctantly with no real choice, so she could remain in her work position and not be thrown out, the infant was taken away and sold on to another desperate, gullible, wealthy couple.

In Emily's case, it was the other way around, Beth and Helen had initially found her a maid's position in a home with a good reputation and had thought she was protected, but it was the brother of the gentleman of the house, who had had his evil way with her and then tossed her aside. Emily was initially treated well by the mistress of the house in her confinement, but became mentally unwell and started threatening to tell her story. To protect the brother, his barren wife appeared and took the baby, but Beth knew the truth by now and had seen the hatred and jealousy in her eyes.

She cast an 'immaculate conception' spell, which led to the brother's wife getting pregnant shortly after, and then worked magic to ensure Emily's baby, named 'Lewella,' by the couple, was safely abandoned too. Left wrapped warmly in a basket by the Workhouse, watched out for by the women, until she could be quickly rehomed from the clutches of the institution, with cousins in the town and renamed Lorraine.

However, as with anyone who abuses their position of trust for financial gain, the master and his associates became greedy and there were not enough 'accidental pregnancies,' to keep them accustomed to the lifestyle they were now used to.

The Master came up with a plan, executed with the help of his trusted cronies Gilbert and George and one of the governors Geoff. He had links with two prominent parish councillors with no scruples and a very dodgy accountant. A red dot was placed on the list, where new paupers about to be admitted, were of a young age, female, possibly fertile and entering alone. Sometimes, when numbers were low and they were desperate, red dots were put by the names of young unmarried mothers or prostitutes, considered the lowest of the low after vagrants.

Marie had overheard and seen things, working with the Mistress Gwen in the office. With the Mistress becoming more confused from the effects of Syphilis and Opium misuse, she had started to let things slip. Incriminating paper work was left lying around before Gwen got around to throwing it on to the fire, and Marie witnessed things that she initially dismissed as inconceivable. This had led to Marie talking to Helen about her suspicions, regarding the intended use and fate of the new young female inmates. Under the cover of magic, Beth advised Helen to seek evidence covertly, and hidden paperwork was also found, giving details of the whole baby trafficking scheme.

Marie herself had been one of the first young women deliberately separated from her mother on arrival and steered away, but Jasmine had intercepted them, pretending she was a long-lost cousin and insisting she would escort Marie herself, to the female dorm. Knowing their real intentions, after listening to Emily's traumatic tale, Jasmine had saved Marie and warned her to watch the Master and to keep away. Ironically, the Mistress had taken Marie on as an assistant, as she was 'educated,' prior to succumbing to the workhouse. She had felt safe in this role at first, believing the mistress did not know and had been let be, but although valuable to them as she was literate, the Mistress and Master were really watching her and keeping her there as a young, fresh reserve.

Mistress Gwen's jealousy and insecurity had fortunately for her, toppled the whole baby trafficking arrangement, despite the prize of her own baby promised and dangling within reach, if she had only bided her time. It turned out she had her sights set on Emily's baby, after all, the baby's father was her own husband. He had other ideas though, to sell the baby to Elsie who promised her life savings, but Jasmine was too close for comfort. This led to the Mistress plotting to have Jasmine killed and then blurting out her sick intentions to Marie. She was losing her inhibitions, on the higher opium doses, eventually mixed with minute doses of rat poison by Helen at Beth's command.

Nadia had seen the signs, the mistress's frequent visits to the nursery, where her only interest was in the pregnant Emily, whose simple trust in human nature, clouded her judgement. Emily had never, ever spoken of her first baby Lorraine, her trauma so embedded, the events were suppressed and seemingly inaccessible to her. There was no one better to care for the young children than Emily, but she was fooled, as many were, by the real intent of Gwen and Elsie, the latter, who had misled them all until recently. Nadia had brought the Petit Albert book with her to the house, and was a Parisian cunning woman, or 'devins-guérisseur,' herself.

Aware of the white witchcraft in the house, she was secretly friends with Beth, Helen and Joseph, and also used her magic to combat malevolent Witchcraft or evil doings. Nadia had worked hard to keep Emily and the little ones safe in collaboration with Beth. Each day she worked elaborate, ceremonial magic and protection spells, keeping them away from the hands of harm and the destructive self-interests of others.

Once it became clear who was in on the Master's plot, Elsie had also been kept from doing too much harm under Beth's spellbound watch, but somehow it had all gone wrong. They were still waiting on the fate of Emily, which was now in Elsie's hands. Would Helen and Marie reach her on time? When Eddie went back for Joseph all havoc was wreaked and a state of pandemonium unleashed. The priority had been to get Jasmine out, and for Beth to leave first thing, which she did that day, with the incriminating letters that would bring the whole house down, once in the hands of the right authorities. Recent developments indicated that Jasmine and Emily were most at risk and that the mistress was in on the whole thing. Beth leaned over and lifted a basket full of paperwork on to knee. The evidence was all there but so many had suffered and the outcome remained unknown.

29

ROSA-GRACE

Beth finally told Jasmine her own sad story next. She had given up her chance of love and marriage at the tender age of nineteen, as her own mother became ill with 'madness,' and Beth became the carer for her every need, as well as supporting her younger sister Emily and cousins Helen and Joseph. Realising she also had her mother's abilities to heal, work magic, create herbal remedies, provide charms and offer fortune telling services, she was able to earn a fee for her work. Making just enough money for food and rent, she managed to stop her and her family becoming destitute.

By word of mouth, callers to the house came with their ailments and afflictions. Beth had to be careful though, as she had acquired her gift through heredity, her mother's magic had been a mixed bag of folk medicine and occultism. She herself learned she could work with supernatural powers to increase the potency of her charms and spells. As one of a line of cunning folk, she used anti-witch measures, curing malevolent sorcery, and creating charms that would repel or break the spells of other witches blamed for bewitchment. As her mother had become more disinhibited and outspoken in her 'madness,' she became a target for accusations of witchcraft, particularly if she treated someone who subsequently died.

Beth knew this very well as her own grandmother Anna, was condemned and executed as a witch, after trying to help a woman who passed away in childbirth. Despite being a common occurrence of the times, it led to bitter lies and accusations by the woman's husband and family. Although cunning folk were considered useful, the opposite of witches who were seen to do harm, they were only protected and left alone in the absence of complaints and accusations.

Beth told how she had met siblings Helen and Joseph as young children, when both of their grandmother's were publicly hanged for witchcraft at the same time as two other accused women. Their father, who had already lost their mother in childbirth, had drank himself into an early grave, deep in sorrow, neglecting the young children. Beth's mother stepped in, eventually taking Helen and Joseph into her care, where it quickly became apparent, they too had the gift, and effortlessly helped prepare simple herbal remedies and charms from a young age. There was thought to be an illegitimate family connection between their grandmothers, so they were probably distant blood cousins and the hereditary magic passed down.

When the children's true gift became apparent and they started to become known for their ability to successfully find the exact location of missing animals, they inadvertently uncovered a lucrative dog fighting operation, where pets had been stolen as 'bait,' to test a dog's fighting instinct; and were often mauled or killed in the process. Their detection of this illegal scheme led to death threats as it was a lucrative business. Then one prominent, underworld citizen, was tipped off that the 'cunning folk,' were the grandchildren of Agnes Murphey, a convicted 'Witch.

Fearing for their safety, Beth's mother moved them all to the outskirts of the town boundary in Frankwell, where they all continued with their work, clandestine and much lower key. It was in 1824 that the first animal welfare charity, 'The Society for the Prevention of Cruelty to Animals' or the 'SPCA' was set up. It considered the welfare of animals at markets, horses at knacker's yards, pit ponies in coal mines and those animals used for entertainment. It confronted the practice of dog fighting and bear and bull-baiting. It all went on underground of course, as with anything banned or made illegal.

In a bid to keep them from the dreadful conditions offered in child labour on factory floors, coal mines and down chimneys, they continued as semi-professional practitioners of magic, and gradually moved back into the town. As Beth's mother Sybil became senile and bedridden, the four of them took turns to care for her and after her death, they began to pursue jobs in nursing, gardening, and cooking, which resulted in them ending up working at The Workhouse together.

It was agreed that Helen and Joseph would pretend to be man and wife to avoid further detection as the grandchildren of Agnes, who was of course, an innocent healer. Agnes's sister was Grace Medlicott, the wonderful old lady Jasmine had met twice who also protected and helped the young family throughout. When Emily was found a prestigious local town house to be maid, it was some time before the realisation of her fate at the hands of the master's brother and that nothing would ever be the same again for her.

Beth kept their home, rented to cousins and was recruited in training, funded by monies collected for the promotion of trained nurses in Workhouse Infirmaries and Sick Asylums. A five-year contract was signed with the Fund, requiring each probationer to receive board, lodging, washing and uniform. They would be under the authority of the Matron. When she first started, patients with undressed sores were lying in filth and the wards were in wretched conditions. The small size of some of the wards and their ventilation and unsanitary condition, beggared belief. The infirmary had been a freezing cold and draughty room, the only furniture, crowded iron beds with thin straw mattresses.

Florence Nightingale, a prominent figure and campaigner on conditions in workhouses, had advised on the training of nurses to improve the welfare of patients. Quite apart from humanity, the sick would recover more rapidly if properly nursed and treatment would therefore be more economical. It was reported during reforms that before there were trained nurses and supervised pauper helps the attendants were, 'imbecile and wholly incompetent women still largely utilised in the sick-wards of workhouses.'

Carer's were often of the lowest moral character, vicious and drunken, and utterly ignorant of what they were required to do. There were many tales of the sad acts of cruelty and suffering inflicted by them, despite tending the most pitiable of all sufferers, the 'incurables, friendless and destitute.' Mental cases were unkindly described as 'imbeciles, idiots or lunatics,' yet many were suffering from epilepsy or some treatable complaint and no doubt, their surroundings led many to a state of institutionalised chronic depression and melancholy.

A mixture of magic, folk medicine, and occultism aided part of the changes made by Beth on the wards, with the help of Helen and Joe. Folk magic, passed along in oral tradition, but grown into the practice and learning of full white witchcraft. At times, dark magic was used for bad intentions, but only to alter the energy and stop the evil acts of adversaries, once the truth started to unfold. The books of magic were wrapped in cloths and hidden safely.

Emily's destiny was starting to change again. After the brother of the Master of the private house raped and impregnated her, she was quickly discarded, accused of promiscuity, and lying and ended up in the town prison and then the Workhouse. But unlike her sister and childhood friends; as an inmate. Her story got worse, despite Beth, Helen, and Joe's attempts to protect and free her. When Emily was thrown into gaol, they had used their magic to release her and to ensure her safe passage back to the Workhouse with three others, Jasmine lucky enough to be one of those women.

But Emily was vulnerable and easy prey and quickly taken, this time by the Master, as a commodity for their undercover baby selling business. She was subjected to further abuse of the worse kind and left broken and pregnant with child again. In their plot to stop the Master and his wife, Beth said they began to use darker, more occult practices.

'You came along Jasmine and fitted in with all of us straight away.'

'Why didn't tell me about your connection with Emily though Beth?

'Maybe for a similar reason that you didn't tell me everything about yourself Jasmine,' Beth smiled, 'It was too risky for all of us at first and then everything quickly came to a head.'

'But since I have been here, there have been several fifty-year time jumps!'

They all turned to look at her, but it wasn't so much disbelief as realisation.

'The Mirror does funny things Jasmine, it has brought you here more than once and taken you on a strange journey, as it did with your ancestors from times that have passed.' Looking at Joseph who nodded reassuringly, she wondered how they seemed to know everything. She had not mentioned her connection with the mirror. She had told them she was from the future and they had worked out her grandmother had been here with Helen and her mother had come to take her back but never discussed how before.

Jasmine now understood her grandmother's fascination with the mirror, a family heirloom, and one that her mother was afraid of, but Jasmine was drawn to. Taking a deep breath, it was now or never, it was likely they would believe her and if not, maybe she was delusional, or it was not meant to be that she would ever leave. She would begin with what she knew of the mirror.

Before she could speak, footsteps outside made them all look up quickly towards the door. Eddie was holding up a wooden club, but stood down when Beth indicated all was well. He opened the door, trusting her completely and four adult females and the 'little urchin,' Lorraine, almost fell in.

Helen, Marie and Victoria the other pauper help, entered the narrow hallway. Jasmine's heart flipped seeing Helen and everyone safe, but her eyes desperately scanned the group for Emily. Helen introduced Megan, whom Jasmine recognised as the girl lured into the refractory cellar. Emily's child, young Lorraine, looked lost and afraid for the first time. She had come in and out of Jasmine's life since arriving here, from the Shrewsbury Show to the hungry apple thief at the market, to appearing after the collision today, warning of danger and urging them to run.

Lorraine's eyes darted across the room, until she found her Aunt Beth, and she ran between the adults into the safety of her arms. There was one person missing though, and as Jasmine looked around at their faces, she knew it was not good. Marie took the others into the front room, prising Lorraine gently away from her aunt, where Eddie stayed with them. Helen began, telling Beth, Joseph and Jasmine, the sad story of Emily and her baby's demise. Jasmine fell to her knees, her head in hands, utterly distraught at her ultimate failure to save her friend. Beth was numb, unable to speak for long moments, but had indicated before, that the prognosis was not good and out of their control.

'I have everything prepared, we will make sure all responsible who remain, are brought to justice in this life and beyond in the spirit world.' Helen spoke serenely.

Joseph was clearly battling anger and guilt at not saving his childhood friend and cousin. He blinked back tears and made fists in the air and chanted something inaudible to Jasmine.

'No! Its not worth repercussions, justice will be done without this!' Helen interjected, but a dark mist entered and Joseph's familiar, his animal spirit guide, emerged to do his bidding. In the guise and shape of a large, mottled brown, Tawny Owl, the spirit landed on Joseph's outstretched arm, with the odour of crumbling, musty, rotten, ash timber, clinging to his wings.

'Go, through the vapours, darkness and mysteries of the journey to the land of the dead and wretched souls,' He was heard to say, and the owl, who looked gruffly benevolent, appeared to answer, 'As you wish,' before vanishing through the dissolving mist.

Then unexpectedly, Beth addressed Jasmine who was already speechless, with an instruction that seemed to break the spell.

'Jasmine, you must leave soon, Helen will accompany you, and she has hidden the Mirror at St. Chads churchyard. It is your only way of getting back. Joseph will return it to me and it will come to you again one day.'

Looking at Helen who nodded reassuringly, she now understood the connection and knew this was her one opportunity to both leave and live. Jasmine gulped down an audible sob and felt like her heart was breaking and her chest was tightening. Beth stood, indicating her departure needed to be imminent, but giving one more partial explanation.

'The mirror was my mother's Jasmine, and hers before that. In fact, it has been in the family for many generations as a family heirloom. Although I kept this house on, I took the mirror to the Workhouse with me when I had a room there, but its potency at times disturbed even me. I always wondered if it sent my mother mad, as she talked to it many times. Emily was drawn to it also. When the Mistress took a liking to it and offered me money to put it in the main hall I accepted. I did not know the future but knew if I ever left, I would take it with me. Mother spoke of the mirror having bright lights, swirling colours, and that it led to another world but although I knew it was magickal, I thought it was her senility. You talk in your sleep Jasmine, and the night after the show, I woke to hear you uttering something similar, as had your ancestor before you.'

Jasmine just nodded, there was no need for any more explanations, as it was all falling into place. She knew it was her grandmother's biggest secret. Helen reached over, helping her to her feet, a deep sadness in her eyes. She had already lost Ellen-Grace and was now losing Jasmine-Grace, 'Ellie's' granddaughter in this bizarre time warp. She and Jasmine had never fully become lovers, but their deep affection and magnetism was strong.

It was all starting to come back to her now, like a lightning bolt. The white aura. Memories suppressed, unsurfaced like a cloak dramatically lifted. Jasmine knew she was not pregnant, but her brother Joe's girlfriend had been. She was called Emma and was devastated at losing Joe. Emma's own mother was a drug addict, who wanted the baby to be adopted and had even talked of selling it to a childless couple in the guise of a planned surrogate child. Jacquie, Jasmine's mother had intervened and offered Emma a home with her baby, but Jasmine's worsening illness had prevented it, so she had been staying at her mother's sister Julie's house. What was the baby's name? She remembered now it was a girl, but she couldn't recall what she was called.

Everything was so much clearer, she needed to go now and rid herself of some of the guilt from not picking up Joe that night. The owls that represented the hit and run vehicle had followed her here, but their connection was much deeper. She had to make amends for Emma and her baby, she could not save Emily and her baby here, but she had saved Joseph. She was pretty sure her parent's marriage was over, but she could be there for them both, take her medication and get well.

Maybe, even return to university? Follow in the pathway of her mother and ancestors and train in Mental Health Nursing maybe, if only she could remain well. But wasn't it every other generation who nursed and the next struck by mental illness? And despite her care work here, history was her greatest love and she had now experienced it first hand through a strange intangible time loop. She must pursue her dream of becoming an historian.

Her experiences here were as if her history books that she had poured over day and night, had come to life, although the accuracy was not perfect. She was not as symptomatic with her mentally health here either. This, and the connection with her brother and his girlfriend was not all though, she knew now this was the same mirror that somehow survived to be passed down the generations. She wasn't sure her mother had the gift, but her grandmother definitely had, and although her mother had never liked the mirror, her grandmother had obsessed over it and passed it down to her. Maybe Ellie had wanted Jasmine to travel here to meet Helen Joseph and Beth too. If only she could have saved Emily.

'I realise I must go.' she said sadly, hugging Beth, whom she was now sure was her great grandmother five times removed. Looking across at the closed door to the front room, she asked them to say goodbye to the others for her. It was too painful, and she needed to hurry. Taking Helen's arm, they turned to Beth who blessed them both and shrouded them with a protection spell.

She paused to turn to her friends, with one more poignant question she had to ask, 'What will happen to you all and the Workhouse?'

'We will move to the new Shropshire and Wenlock Borough Lunatic Asylum, Jasmine,' she said calmly and with optimism.

'The 'Big House,' Shelton Hospital,' Jasmine smiled knowingly. 'One day The Workhouse will be sold on and become the new Shrewsbury school.'

They all looked surprised at this, but not at the fact that she knew, only of its future salubrious status. Joseph squeezed her, 'Justice will prevail, the corruption, embezzlement and cruelty is over, and Emily and her daughter inside her, will live on in our hearts and receive a dignified burial.'

'Her daughter?' Jasmine asked wondering how they knew.

'Rosa Grace, named after a flower like you,' Helen replied smiling bravely. The sadness was palpable, hovering like dank fog in the air. One precious life destroyed prematurely, the other never lived at all.

Jasmine clutched the table remembering.

'Rosie is the name of my dead brother Joe's child, to his girlfriend Emma,' she suddenly remembered.

'Perhaps Rosa-Grace has been reborn in another time and will indeed have a good, long life one day,' Beth said, as if they had just said something 'normal.'

'I'll make sure she does,' said Jasmine, she was sure her niece's middle names, were Grace Emma too, after her mother's name and the matriarchal family name for girls. Jasmine smiled more confidently, knowing she was going home this time, her job here done.

But her expression changed when she looked at Helen who was bravely trying to smother and fight back her shaking sobs. Comforting her instantly, she was interrupted by the urgency in Joseph's voice as he persuaded them to go quickly to ensure Jasmine's safety. The parlour door suddenly opened a crack and Lorraine peered through.

'Look after them for me,' she said in her singsong voice before closing the door again, making them all gasp in wonder at how much extrasensory perception Lorraine had inherited herself.

Taking Helen's arm the pair left the house covertly, but safe under a powerful protection spell cast by Beth, their white and magenta auras swirling around them but seen by none. Before they turned the corner Helen pulled Jasmine into her arms and held her tightly for a few precious moments in time and neither could stop the flow of tears at the prospect of what they were about to lose.

'I need to give you this now,' Helen stated in as stronger voice as she could muster, when she pulled back to face Jasmine. 'It's an identical copy of my Almanac that I made for you. It has all the knowledge you will need to keep safe in your future world. I hope you sometimes think of me when you turn the pages.' Pressing the gift against her lips she then pushed the paper book securely into her apron pocket, and embraced Helen closely once more. ‘I will treasure this gift Helen and never forget you for as long as I live.’

The two would-be lovers reluctantly resumed their journey with heavy hearts that seemed to slow their every step as grief dragged them down.

30

SOPHEA

The mirror was exactly where Jasmine knew it would be, next to the grave where she had seen her own name, now thankfully just an empty plot with no name. The swirling lights and colours emanated around it. She had begged Helen to remain at the gate, their parting was painful as the feelings they had for each other were mutual. Jasmine had been true to herself for the first time whilst here and now embraced her sexuality, which she guessed played a big part in her finally accepting herself. It would be easier to have a same sex relationship in her century, if she had stayed with Helen they would have had to live like cousins or 'companions,' their love hidden behind closed doors.

But her heart ached for what she was leaving behind and the thought of never seeing her first love ever again. Jasmine turned one more time to wave goodbye. Helen appeared to wave back, but she realised Helen was releasing something that was silently and serenely heading towards her.

Native Americans thought that owls were a messenger of death but also, a guide to the other side. They flew the spirit to the other world, as known to be able to see through vapours, darkness, and the mysteries of the journey to the land of the dead souls. In China, owl figures were placed in graves to escort the dead to the afterlife.

Appearing to float across the graveyard, like a ghost caught in the car headlights, her front plumage, dazzlingly phosphorescent, like blazing snow. The bird hovered and turned her heart shaped face towards Jasmine and clearly summoned her with a wing to follow, she flew through the mirror. Reluctant and torn by her own feelings for Helen, she hesitated; but was suddenly afraid the portal might close, so knew she must step through into the unknown.

In the future, Jasmine would visit St Chads 'boneyard,' and go to the Ebenezer Scrooge head stone, with the faded writing on the opposite end. It would still be illegible, but she would know who it belonged to and place forget-me-nots and roses there for Emily and her stillborn child Rosa Grace. Maybe if she looked around, she would find Lorraine's grave too? She hoped that 'the little urchin,' her ancestral cousin five times removed, would live a much longer and happier life than her mother Emily and unborn sister Rosa Grace had. Unbeknown to Beth, she too would have at least one daughter who would carry the generations of strong women through to Jasmine's own grandmother, mother, and herself. She hoped Lorraine would always be part of Beth, Helen, and Joseph's life.

It occurred to her Beth's future 'beau,' might be Gordon the Ferryman. He had always been kind to her and the others, and she recalled glimpsing a secret smile and intimate giggle shared between him and Beth, on more than one occasion. If only the mirror could be used more proactively and the pattern of 'madness' in every other generation could be broken. She wished Helen and her brother Joseph love and happiness. She would miss so many people here, Victoria, who had saved her on arrival, Marie who had risked so much to save other young women, Nadia who was a white witch and 'mother earth,' to the orphan infants, and not least the dear patients on the Luna Ward whom she had come to feel deep affection towards. She thought how close she had come to severe reprimand and possible death and of those who had lost their lives and liberty, especially Emily.

She had met the amazing Grace Medlicott, another ancestor and powerful healer, and someone who had recognised her and addressed her as from the future. She had sewn the little owl thimble in the lining of her skirt to ensure she didn't lose it. But her heart felt broken at losing Helen and leaving her behind, Helen had already lost one love, Jasmine's own grandmother.

She had discovered she and other maternal family members had also travelled through the mirror and she was not the first, or going 'crazy,' as she had thought. But she had endured and survived serious mental health problems for a time, seeing first-hand the treatment of those much earlier sufferers, before medication and better treatment had come into effect.

Beth had taught her so much though and had a different attitude to many carer's of this Victorian era, intent on using botanical methods that reduced suffering and treating her patients with dignity and respect. Jasmine had at least brought with her, the knowledge of some simple, possible life saving practices, like improved hygiene which was yet to be properly recognised in these times as the cause of much disease.

Beth and Emily were seemingly her direct descendants from many generations back, but if Mrs Medlicott was the aunt of Helen and Joseph, then she was distantly related to them also. She would complete the family tree once home, aware there were many more stories to still discover.

It was time to go back to her mother, reassure her, sit down and really talk. The revived memories of her own mother crying over her great grandmother's grave were something she felt was significant and would ask her mother about, but her own grandmother's story intrigued her more. She knew now she could never bring Joe back, but she could support his girlfriend Emma and her blood niece Rosie Grace and pick up her own life.

Her brother Joe could rest in peace in her own mind now, a tragedy that was not the solitary fault of her alone. She had been saved by Joseph and saved him in turn and surely done some good in this bleak era. Her regret was due to another resurfaced memory Jasmine had blocked out, to stem her unbearable feelings of guilt. It seemed Helen wasn't quite the first. The reason she had forgotten to pick up her brother was because she had been talking for two hours on the phone to a young woman, she had met called Carly. For the first time, she had allowed herself to embrace her sexuality and be true to herself. She had never felt so happy and excited that evening at the mutual connection she had made and the anticipation of where it might lead.

After Joe's death, she had declined all phone calls and refused to see Carly, even when her mum had told her she was at the front door desperate to see her. She had repressed not only her sexuality again, but allowed her personality to disintegrate, denying herself any peace or happiness. Jasmine had gradually become locked in her own mind, inviting only persecutory voices in as her just deserts. After Carly, Helen had been proof that she could never ignore who she really and she was now determined to be true to herself, allowing future happiness in.

Turning towards the mirror in the stillness of the graveyard she smiled, her purpose here was over and this had to be her final destination in this century, before homeward bound. The force of the mirror pulled her through effortlessly as she followed the wings of the great bird into the swirling, coloured lights.

The End

EPILOGUE

Opening her eyes took some time; they were slightly sticky and her vision was cloudy. It was the way she imagined her grandmother's eyesight, when she had once described her view of life through cataracts. Jasmine was sat in a high back chair; in a room she did not recognise that looked like a small sitting room with a bed. There was a modern looking walking frame just out of reach, but there was no sign of the elderly person it belonged to.

Placing her hands on her knees she looked down at the thin arms and gnarled fingers on her lap. She pulled her own arms away quickly and winced, a second before comprehending that these unrecognizable, aged limbs were her own. Looking around the room in mild panic, her watery eyes fixed on an oval gilt mirror, framed by tiny engraved owls. She heard voices coming closer and two young women, about the age she thought she was, entered the room wearing a carer's uniform and chatting about their boyfriends.

'Please,' she interjected, causing them to stop and glare at her as if she had rudely interrupted them. She watched them turn away, ignoring her and resuming their private conversation loudly, whilst showing each other recordings on some device they held, that projected images and videos on the walls.

So, this was what it had come to... Jasmine touched the deep creases on her face, her hands felt cold and arthritic. The carer's disappeared into the ensuite bathroom, their voices echoing in the tiled space, their cosy, girlie chat continuing in the same vein. Jasmine was sure of one thing; she was not staying here. If this was her future and this type of 'caring' was still going on, she needed to get back to 2006 and make her life's work around care reforms, especially as she had helped change things for the better over two hundred years ago!

Her attention was briefly caught by the many framed pictures on the shelf opposite. Her eyes were weak, but she noticed some spectacles hanging down, attached to a chain around her neck. Putting them on, she craned her neck to view the people in the photos. One was her childhood family photo taken years before Joe died. She smiled remembering happy times before their life was torn apart.

There was another of Jasmine and her mother with Joe's girlfriend Emma, holding a baby girl, who must be Rosie Grace. She knew now she did return home! The next was a photo of her and her father, but he was old and infirm and she in her forties, looking the image of her own mother at that age. Where was her mother? She stopped herself from going down that line of thinking, it could mean anything. Next along, was a photo of herself around age thirty, linking arms with a woman of a similar age, both laughing happily at the camera with a young girl of about four, swinging between them holding their hands.

The flowery background was The Dingle in The Quarry in town. Home of the Shrewsbury Flower Show and Kingsland Shows that went back over hundreds of years. The magnificent building now Shrewsbury School, once The House of Industry, i.e. Workhouse or 'Spike,' its commanding presence the backdrop in the image, captured in yet another time.

Other photos that followed, showed her with the female whom she now believed must be her future partner, posing at various stages of their lives with the same female child. The girl in the framed photographs grew from baby in arms, to toddler, teenager and finally a young woman, as tall as Jasmine and the other female, her arms around both of them. She wondered if it was their adopted daughter but then gasped as she realised, she looked just like herself at that age. The same crooked nose and smiling eyes and even her mouth was so like Jasmine's. Could she have given birth to their child?

There was a framed wedding photograph dated 2014, which surprised her as it was her and the same woman, with two young bridesmaids, some years apart. Marriage between same sex couples was not legal at the time she found herself at the Workhouse. She wondered if the girl with Rosie Grace was their daughter. She couldn't remember this part and realised with a mixture of excitement and trepidation that she needed to get back to 2006 and begin to live her life to the full.

The past was still fresh in her mind, the unique herb garden scent of Helen lingered in her nostrils and she could still taste their final lingering kiss on her lips. She thought of the precious 'Almanac' book of shadows that Helen had made for her and wondered if that had withstood the test of time.

Looking around through her unfamiliar spectacles, she caught sight of a book case where she could see history books, both fact and fiction and felt relieved her interest had only got stronger. In between the hard books she spied a familiar small paper book, which appeared to be laminated and she knew she had always treasured Helen's gift.

Coming back to the unknown present and missing decades, she wondered what would happen if she just kept poking up in different time zones, with chunks of missing parts of her life that she had skipped? Was she demented now and that's why she could not remember the woman and child in the photos? The last item on the shelf was an urn, presumably holding ashes, but whose? She deliberately looked away and told herself firmly that must not think of this and focus instead on her exit and return to her younger life. Feeling a weakness in her knees Jasmine pushed down through her hands on the armrests to help herself stand up. Her upper body strength was good. Taking a second to straighten her legs, grimacing at the stiff achiness she experienced, she realised she could now reach over to the frame and used it to safely edge forward. She could not, and would not stay here and willing the mirror to respond, it answered her and she smiled to herself, no longer afraid. It was dusk outside, and the silhouette of a large owl sat on a branch in an ash tree opposite the window. Despite her poor eyesight she could see it clearly. Somehow, she understood the owl was her 'familiar,' and named Sophea, meaning Wisdom.

'You've taken me too far forward.' she laughed half to herself, ignored by her carer's, but knowing somehow, it was the same great bird Helen had released as her guide. Then, entering whatever energy field accompanied the whirling colours and lights, she felt the familiar tug as it pulled her through to her new destiny.

About the Author

Email: katemclanachan.author@gmail.com

Introducing my debut novel set in Shrewsbury, the place I consider my hometown, in an era I am fascinated by. As a mental health nurse who trained 33 years ago at Shelton Hospital I have always been intrigued by the history of asylums and early 'treatments,' but found myself going back further to the pre-asylum days of the Workhouse.

Living on the rural Welsh border now with my husband of 20 years and our two adult sons, I am also surrounded by my cats, dogs and chickens and love walking the hills and nearby woods.

Still loving my job as a nurse therapist with patients with eating disorders, but my dream is to retire in two years and move to the coast. I hope to buy a fisherman's cottage overlooking the sea and write in a cosy window seat, inspired by the views and my imagination.

I plan to write a trilogy in this series, as my main character Jasmine, has much more to encounter before you have heard the last of her. Working full-time and being a mum, has meant this book has taken 5 years to complete, but there is always a story running through my head, itching to get out onto the page. My love of the genre of historical fiction with mystery, horror and fantasy thrown in, will hopefully be my main occupation soon. So watch this space.

Introducing my debut novel set in Shrewsbury, the place I consider my hometown, in an era I am fascinated by. As a mental health nurse who trained 33 years ago at Shelton Hospital I have always been intrigued by the history of asylums and early 'treatments,' but found myself going back further to the pre-asylum days of the Workhouse.

The Workhouse loomed impressively over the town, a majestic but formidable building that would become the prestigious Shrewsbury School.

An institution and Asylum for destitute paupers, lunatics and vagrants, it's past secrets and atrocities locked away behind closed doors.

'Voices' whispered to her the gory details of her brother's death, inserting pictures in her head, naming her as the one to blame.

The Court condemned the hit and run driver, but the trial had never ended for her. There was a jury of malevolent, faceless persecutors who lived in her head, attacking her mind with accusations, ridicule and abuse.

Trying to put a face to them, she only saw birds with sharp talons and curved beaks, their large eyes penetrating her, which was why she now stood motionless.

The owls were pinning her to the spot. But they were also powerfully pulling her through a portal in time that opened to another era through an antique mirror.

Printed in Great Britain
by Amazon

18521634R00159